Praise for Kelly Jamieson's
Hot Ride

"This book runs full throttle from beginning to end... *Hot Ride* is an exciting book that will have you on the edge of your seat and leave you breathless. The love scenes are sexy and plentiful, the action exciting and chilling, the outcome satisfying and amazing."

~ *Guilty Pleasures Book Reviews*

"*Hot Ride* was a non-stop, heart pounding action-packed adventure, with some seriously through the roof sex scenes thrown in that will make you swoon and drool."

~ *Sizzling Hot Book Reviews*

Look for these titles by *Kelly Jamieson*

Now Available:

Love Me
Friends with Benefits
Love Me More
2 Hot to 2 Handle
Lost and Found
One Wicked Night
Rule of Three
Sweet Deal

San Amaro Singles
With Strings Attached
How to Love
Slammed

Promise Harbor
Jilted

Print Collections
Love 2 Love U

off. If only she could convince these suits of that. Working on the Quintano Cartel case had become her mission, but nobody else knew why it was so important to her. That was very private.

Her body felt like a buzzing ball of anticipation. She shifted her gaze from Darren, still standing, to his superior beside him, to case agent Josh Witter who was running Operation Black Abyss, holding each man's gaze steadily.

"Give...me...a shot," she said quietly, seriously.

The only sound in the room was the faint wush of the air-conditioning fan as the men all looked at each other. Sera's heart bumped in her chest.

Darren sat down. Laid his palms flat on the table. Tapped his fingers. He looked at Ward. Ward looked at Sera. She nodded. And waited.

Darren turned to Josh. "What do you think, Witter? You'll be running the surveillance."

Sera was afraid to breathe as she fixed her gaze on Josh Witter, her chest tight.

"It's risky."

"Yep."

"She can't wear a wire."

"Can you keep her safe?"

Sera resisted the impulse to roll her eyes at their talking about her instead of *to* her, yet again.

"No guarantees."

She didn't *care*. She'd keep herself safe.

Darren grimaced. "Okay. One night. See how it goes."

A sweet rush of elation shot through her like a Harley at full throttle, almost propelling her out of her chair, making her want to pump her fist in the air. But she pressed her lips together and sat back, hands clasped in her lap. It was hard, but she had to show them what she was made of. "Thank you," she said in a carefully neutral voice.

"Tomorrow night," Josh said. "We go to Clover City. Here's the plan."

It was like driving into a tunnel with no headlights. Blindfolded. She knew there could be other undercover agents in there, but didn't know who. She had to think they were all gang members, had to treat them as if they were, had to convince them she could be one of them.

Despite her protests to the agents in charge, snuggling up with outlaw motorcycle gang members wasn't all that appealing to her. But she could do it. She could do whatever she had to, to make this work.

They'd given her an alias, gotten her some basic pieces of ID, and if things worked out, they'd do the full backstop, create a whole new history for Sara Lambert.

She followed Beck into The Patch, the Death Angels' favorite hangout in Clover City, about a hundred miles north of L.A. Beck was a snitch—otherwise known as a confidential informant for the ATF—a full patch member of the DA's Clover City chapter, who was cooperating with Operation Black Abyss to avoid being prosecuted for extortion charges against him. He was willing to take her to The Patch, introduce her around.

The bar wasn't exactly classy, but she'd been in worse. Far worse, in fact. AC/DC blasted them in the face with *Highway to Hell* as they walked in the door, along with the stale odor of beer and cigarettes. Despite the smoking ban in effect in the state of California, the air inside still carried the lingering stench of tobacco smoke embedded into old wood. Sera's eyes adjusted to the dim lighting.

The heels of her boots thunked as she walked across hardwood flooring scuffed smooth and pale with age. People filled every booth along the wall and occupied every small table. At the end of the room, a man and woman played pool on an ancient pool table, the clack of pool balls barely audible over the driving music and cacophony of voices yelling and laughing. Customers lined the bar, leaning against it, drinks in hand. Mostly men. A few women.

She followed Beck to the bar, and he lifted a hand in greeting when his name was called out.

"Hey, Beck!"

"Beck, buddy, where ya been?"

She leaned casually on the bar as Beck shouted to the bartenders, "Two Buds!" then accepted the cold, wet bottle. No glass was offered and that was fine with her. She lifted the bottle to her lips.

Beck introduced her to the men they stood next to. "This here's Chomp and Zocco."

"Hi, guys." She hit them with her highest-wattage smile. "Nice to meetcha." They tipped their bottle at her and smiled back. She couldn't mistake the male interest in their leers.

Beck and the men began talking about an upcoming rally in El Mirage in Nevada. She pretended an interest but her eyes scanned the bar, head nodding in time to the whining guitar and guttural lyrics of Metallica's *Death Magnet*. Most of the patrons of the bar wore their colors, making no secret of the fact that this was a Death Angels hangout. Men with long hair, beards and arms sleeved with tattoos mingled with cleaner-cut guys, some with neatly trimmed goatees and short hair. Most of them were big—was that a requirement?— although in some cases size had more to do with fat than muscle.

She cocked a hip, took a big swallow of the cold beer, bubbles biting at her nose and throat, and took in her surroundings, moving her gaze to the others seated at the bar. From where she stood at the end, no stools left to sit on, she could see the face of every man seated there. Every man except one, who'd swiveled on his stool to watch the pool game. His leather jacket obscured his shape other than wide, wide shoulders, giving an impression of massive strength. A piece of red cord held his dark hair tied at his nape.

Then he turned around and she saw his face. Hoo. Now that was a good-looking biker. A well-shaped mouth, a square chin and high cheekbones could have been pretty boy, but thick, straight brows drawn down into a near-scowl above deep-set eyes gave him a badass, don't-fuck-with-me attitude.

He turned his head and his eyes met hers. She blinked in surprise at the physical reaction she felt to his gaze, a clenching low down inside her, a flare of heat. Interest sparked in his eyes. A corner of his mouth kicked up and one brow lifted.

Well, why not? If she was going to get in with these guys, might as well do it with the best-looking one. Those suits in L.A. had accused her of being too feminine. Didn't they know the advantage that gave her? So she flashed him her smile and gave him a slow wink.

He smiled back, and along with the badass attitude, he became even more...appealing. She held his gaze long enough to let her own interest show before turning back to Beck, lifting her bottle to her mouth.

"Gotta talk to A.J.," Zocco said. "Come on, Beck." Zocco rose off his stool to tower over her. God, he must be six-foot-five. She was five-seven, but he was a monster.

"Yeah. A.J. Come on, Sara." Beck gestured and with a shrug, she followed him down the bar, toward the man she'd eye-locked with a few minutes ago. Beck and Zocco stopped and addressed the guy next to him.

"A.J. Man, you got those parts I asked you about the other day?"

A.J. shook his head. "Talk to Tommy, here. You want Harley parts—he's the man."

Tommy. His name was Tommy.

Zocco, A.J. and Tommy began an in-depth conversation about drag bars and pipes and forks. She felt the weight of Tommy's gaze, even though he was talking to the others. When he'd assured Zocco he'd get the parts the biker was looking for, he turned to her. "Hi."

"Hi."

He looked her up and down. So, painted on black jeans, black boots and a low-cut red T-shirt weren't her usual attire, but she knew she looked good.

"I'm Tommy."

"Sara."

"Friend of Beck's?"

She hitched a shoulder. "Sort of. He knows my cousin. I'm in town visiting her."

"Oh yeah? Where you from?"

"L.A."

"What're you doing here?"

She deepened one corner of her mouth into a wry smile. "Just lost my job, so thought I'd come for a visit."

They studied each other and warmth slipped over her, starting at her chest and working its way up to her face. Good god, was she blushing? She never blushed! His size, his blatant masculinity and radiating sexuality caused every nerve ending in her body to prickle. His shameless male appraisal should have pissed her off, made her feel objectified, but instead her nipples tingled and tightened beneath her thin T-shirt, and her pussy clenched.

This close she could see his clean-shaven face was actually shadowed with dark stubble, adding to the dangerous appeal. An earring glinted in one ear, gold like his eyes.

A.J. again included Tommy in the conversation with the other men, talking about their motorcycles. "What kind of Harley do you have?" she asked Tommy.

"Road King."

"Nice."

"It's old, but it rides sweet."

"I like the Road King. Kinda retro looking." He lifted a brow and she held his gaze, fingers lightly holding the beer bottle by the narrow neck, even though she quivered inside. "My brothers all have Harleys."

One corner of his mouth kicked up and the interest deepened. And the warmth inside her intensified in equal measure, heat spreading from her core to her fingertips and even her earlobes.

They talked about his bike, then he introduced her to a few more people around them including a couple of women. Jessie was Chomp's girlfriend, and Carly was married to Vince Danez, the club president. Jessie had a vacant look, like she was all kinds of out of it, but Carly seemed reasonably coherent.

"I like your necklace," Sera told Carly. "Where did you get it?"

"I made it?" she replied, fingers fluttering over the stones at her neck. Her voice rose as if she was asking a question.

"No! How'd you do that?"

"It's really nothing," Carly mumbled, but Sera persisted gently, genuinely impressed by the pretty jewelry, and they edged away from the crowd of men.

"Do you sell your pieces?"

"Uh...not really. Some of my friends have offered to buy things but I just..." She shrugged. "It's not good enough to sell?"

"I think it is."

She and Carly moved over to an empty table and sat down. Jessie joined them and then two more women did as well, and Carly introduced her.

Then Vince and Tommy sat down with them too, Vince sliding his arm possessively around Carly. She leaned into him. "Get me another beer, babe," he ordered her. Without a word, she stood and went to the bar for him.

Sera had to bite her lip. She studied Vince. His leather jacket stretched across broad shoulders and a tank-like chest, and he held his nearly empty beer bottle with large, very hairy hands. He kept his beard neatly trimmed, and was actually a good-looking guy, his long hair pulled back similar to Tommy's, but the way he ordered Carly to serve him gave an impression of control...dominance...and cruelty.

In an effort not to show how she felt about that, Sera looked at Tommy and smiled. He leaned back in his chair, big and broad, muscled thighs spread, beer clasped between two hands.

"Tommy, you coming to El Mirage next weekend?" Vince asked.

Again, the big rally being held at El Mirage. This was an annual event for the DAs.

"I dunno." Tommy tilted his head, and it was such a sexy move that liquid heat settled low and hot inside her, so intense she shifted in her chair.

"You can ride out with us."

"Hey. Thanks, man. Sounds good."

"Where's Manny? He can come too."

"Great. He's over there." Tommy jerked his head. "Playing pool."

Hot Ride

Tommy turned his gaze back to Sera. "How about you, angel? You going to El Mirage?"

She shook her head. "No."

She waited for an invitation that didn't come. But that was okay. Couldn't get too far ahead of herself. If she was going to do this, she'd have to take her time, get to know them slowly. Patience.

"What the hell's taking her so long?" Vince growled, rising to his feet. He stomped toward the bar where Carly stood. Sera flashed a glance her way, hoping Carly wasn't in trouble, then turned her gaze back to Tommy. They sat alone at the small table now.

He leaned forward, elbows on the table, and she noticed the beer he held was almost empty. "Do you want another beer?" she asked.

He lifted a brow. "You gonna get it for me?"

"If you want. Sure." She resisted the urge to grind her back molars together.

She waited. A big shoulder lifted, then those delicious, warm golden eyes turned back to her and studied her, another long, sexually appraising look that should have made her cringe but instead made her melt.

"Nah, that's okay."

"Hey, Tommy." Another man approached the table, also big, his head shaved totally bald, earrings glinting in both ears. It was a look that worked for him, his face handsome enough and his head well-shaped enough to carry it off. Wow. "I want some food. Let's blow this joint."

"Let's stay here a while," Tommy said, without looking up at the man, still holding her gaze, and her smile deepened. "Nice scenery here."

She pursed her lips, but still smiled, then turned her gaze to the man standing beside the table. He frowned at her.

"This is my buddy, Manny." Tommy waved a hand. "Manny, Sara."

"I wanna go get a burger or something," Manny said.

"Eat here."

15

Manny heaved a long sigh then turned away.

She and Tommy looked at each other, alone again. Heat shimmered between them, and her body clenched and trembled inside. She wasn't used to having reactions like this. She almost thought it was fear...or nerves...except she knew it wasn't. It was lust. Excitement. She wanted to close her eyes, turn away, give herself a smack to refocus herself, but of course she couldn't.

Instead she held his gaze, letting her head move to the beat of the music as she waited for his next response. Black Sabbath's *Heaven and Hell* picked up the tempo, nearing the end of the song, drums pulsing, guitar yowling, and her body moved almost involuntarily to the rhythm, a subtle shift of hips and shoulders.

He took all that in. She felt his eyes on her, knew exactly when he looked at her hard nipples, tingling mercilessly beneath her bra and shirt. They tightened even more, and she clenched her inner muscles between her legs. She couldn't back down.

"What's a nice girl like you doing in a place like this?"

She rolled her eyes. "There's an original line."

A slow smile tugged his lips. "Yeah. Okay, it's not a line. I really want to know...what's a nice girl like you doing in a place like this?"

"Okay, two things wrong with that question." She held up a finger. "One. What makes you think I'm a nice girl? And two..." She added another finger. "What's so bad about this place?"

He reached over and captured the fingers she held up in his big hand. Big, but gentle. "This place is rough, honey." His deep voice held a hint of warning.

She grinned and rested her elbows on the table, leaned closer to him, letting him hold her hand. "Maybe I like it rough."

His topaz eyes darkened. She gave a soft laugh. "Don't worry, Tommy. I can take care of myself. And..." She looked around, hitched a shoulder. "This place isn't so bad."

His rapacious smile tugged at something inside her. Her body, over which she always had firm, determined control, betrayed her. Something about him just caught at her, pulled her to him.

Hot Ride

She so did not need this right now. But she had to go with it.

He released her hand and she moved to the music, still looking at him, still smiling. "I like bikes. I like beer. I like to party. This place is great."

"D'you like bikers?"

The question hung suspended between them.

"Yeah," she said, holding his gaze meaningfully. "I like bikers."

He tipped the bottle to his mouth. His lips on the rim were sensuous, and his throat working as he swallowed the last of the beer made her want to press her lips there.

Then Vince and Carly returned to the table, and she sat back to listen and watch Tommy through a haze of repressed lust. She had to get a grip on herself here. This was important and she could not screw it up by getting all hot for a sexy biker. God.

Someone came and dragged Tommy off to play a game of pool and she resisted the urge to watch him, turning her attention back to Carly and Vince and the others who joined them, talking, laughing, drinking.

She didn't want to rush it, but as it neared midnight, she figured she'd been reasonably successful and wanted to do one more thing to prove she was capable of this undercover gig.

"Who's holding here?" she murmured to Carly in a low undertone. "I need to score."

"Meth? Coke?"

"Angel sugar."

Carly nodded, unfazed by the request. She looked around then tipped her chin. "Zocco. Come on."

She took Sera over to Zocco and said a word in his ear. He looked up at Sera. Studied her. Her skin crawled and her insides quivered. If he didn't believe she was for real, didn't buy her act, didn't trust her enough to sell drugs to her, she was going to find out now.

She realized she was holding her breath, and let it out slowly and carefully. She tossed her hair behind her shoulder and tipped her head to the side with a hint of impatience.

She held his gaze, his dark eyes narrow and mean looking. Then he nodded, stood up, and Carly said, "Go with him."

Sera knew the danger. She watched Zocco lumber away from her. Her feet moved. She had to do this. She wasn't afraid. She could look after herself.

She followed Zocco's wide shape down the dark narrow hall. The driving beat of Judas Priest's *Angel of Retribution* faded to a distant thump of bass behind them and she followed him into a small empty room, chairs and tables pushed up against the wall.

They were alone.

Her stomach tightened and she relaxed her hands and shoved them into the front pockets of her jeans, trying to look casual. A trickle of sweat traced a shivery trail down the groove of her spine.

He faced her and said nothing. Shit. This was it. Maybe she'd gone too far. Pushed too hard. Had she blown her one and only chance?

Zocco's eyes narrowed. "What d'you want?" he asked.

Her throat tightened. What did she want? Didn't he know what she wanted?

He waited, his arms folded across his chest, and his brows dipped above his nose.

"I…uh…"

Zocco looked at something behind her and she half-turned. Tommy stood in the doorway watching them, scowling.

Chapter Two

"He's okay." Zocco nodded toward him. "Tommy, you want some?"

"Nah." He tried to keep the disgust and disappointment from showing on his face. She was so sweet— lean, wholesome, pretty—and here she was buying goddamn drugs. Shit. He should've known. She was hanging around The Patch, she sure wasn't a cheerleader from the suburbs.

She also wasn't that bright, disappearing into a back room with a hulking biker she didn't even know. Which was why he'd followed her. Jesus.

What the hell was he so disappointed about anyway? He knew better than anyone not to get involved with someone he met there. She was nothing to him, just a pretty face who'd shown up and added a little sizzle to his evening, which hadn't exactly been going well. He hadn't had that sizzle for a while. A helluva long while, in fact.

He stepped aside to let her leave the room, having made her deal. He watched her tight, little ass in the snug jeans as she walked down the hall ahead of him. Hot, little body—she had a lean, athletic grace that appealed to him, with strong shoulders and narrow hips. Her long, dark hair shone with a healthy luster, and those unusual light blue eyes, like blue zircons, had snared him.

He wanted to ask Beck who the hell she was, because Beck was a shit-for-brains crack head and there was no possible way she was his girlfriend. Ah hell. It. Did. Not. Matter.

He ordered another beer at the bar, only his second of the night, although others probably thought he'd drunk much more. One more and he'd be outta there too. Tomorrow he had to get to see his mom.

His gut clenched at the thought. She was going downhill quick now that the breast cancer had spread to her lymph nodes and bones. The home she was in did a great job of looking after her, so he knew she was well cared for, but he still felt guilty about how little time he had to spend with her. Business was seriously impacting his personal life. Not that he had much of a personal life.

She probably only had weeks to live. And here he was hanging out, shooting the shit and drinking beer. Hell.

His goal that evening had been to talk to Monkey about a machine gun he supposedly had. He wanted to buy that gun from him. Really bad. But when he'd tried to question Monkey about it, all he'd gotten were faintly suspicious looks and a change of subject.

Damn. The DAs were starting to trust him, and Manny and Axel. But they weren't one of them. The Coyotes were a different gang and there were still walls up, barriers preventing them from getting too close.

He watched Monkey, the man he'd wanted to cozy up to that night, as he stood up unsteadily. Then Monkey walked up to Sara at the bar, threw his beefy arm around her narrow shoulders and leaned in lasciviously. Fuck.

He stood and moved toward her. As he neared her, he heard a grunt, and Sara say, "Thanks but no thanks, buddy."

Monkey doubled over in pain.

Ah shit. What'd she do to him? She was going to get herself killed.

Monkey gasped for air then straightened. "Uh..."

Here it came. He waited for every other DA to rush in to Monkey's defense, for all hell to break loose. But nothing happened. He looked around. Hell, nobody'd even noticed that she'd just hurt the man. Fucking weird. He kept going.

"Problem here?" he muttered into Monkey's ear, helping him to stand straight.

Monkey snorted, gasped again. "Tommy. Dude. I'm fine." Clearly he wasn't, but male pride prevented him from revealing a girl had spanked him.

The DAs didn't like women who had a mind of their own. They wanted women they could dominate, control, demo their macho masculine strength with. She was smarter than he'd thought by doing

Hot Ride

something—*what?*—so subtle to get her "hands off" message across without humiliating him in front of his gang.

He glanced at Sara, saw her smirk. What the fuck?

Monkey straightened, tossed his long hair back. "Bro, you don't wanna mess with her." He staggered away.

He met Sara's eyes. She gazed back at him innocently, blue eyes sparkling, and he blinked. He narrowed his own eyes at her then looked around, still waiting for war to break out. These guys did not respect women.

She slid off her stool, tapped her empty beer bottle down on the table and patted her purse. "Gotta go," she said. "Nice meeting you, Tommy. Maybe I'll see you again sometime."

Speechless, he watched her leave, with a hug for Carly and Jessie, and a bump of fists with Vince. He sank onto the stool she'd vacated.

She'd come with Beck, but he watched her say something into Beck's ear, then with waves and goodbyes she walked out of The Patch alone.

"What the hell?" Manny murmured beside him, also watching Sara leave. "What was that with Monkey?"

"Hell if I know." He couldn't take his eyes off her cute ass as she strode out of The Patch on those long legs.

"Pretty hot stuff. Can't believe you turned her down."

He huffed out a short laugh. "There wasn't an invitation."

"Ah. Too bad."

He shook his head. "Ain't gonna happen."

"Yeah, I know." Manny disappeared again.

He reached into the pocket of his jeans and pulled out a roll of antacids, popped two into his mouth and chewed.

"Hey, Tommy." Jessie came up and stood beside his bar stool, pressed her tits against his biceps. "How's it going?"

Oh man. She was stoned, again. He sighed. She'd been coming on to him every time they were alone together for the last couple of weeks. Now here she was doing it in public. Where the hell was Chomp?

"Good. How you doin'?" He moved away from her, but her body followed. She leaned against him and he was afraid if he moved again she'd fall down.

"I'm okay. You know, Tommy, you're really hot."

Fuck. He glanced around to see who was noticing. If he got caught with another dude's wife, he was a dead man. He tried to slide off the stool, but as he'd feared, Jessie'd had her weight against him and she stumbled and almost fell.

"Whoops!" She gave a little laugh and grabbed for him, getting a fist of T-shirt. He reached for her too and to his dismay got a handful of boob. She was generously stacked, that was for sure, but her stomach was almost as big as her boobs and he wasn't even a bit turned on by the free groping. In fact, he was scared shitless.

Because Chomp appeared just then with a menacing scowl on his face. "What the hell you doing with my woman?" he growled, staring at the two of them glued together.

He held up both hands, leaving Jessie to wobble precariously on her own. She fell against her husband with another laugh. "Nothing, man. Chomp. I didn't do nothin'. She just lost her balance."

"I did, baby," Jessie said with a hiccup. She giggled. "I damn near fell down. Tommy's such a hottie."

He wanted to close his eyes. Son of a bitch.

"You think he's hot, huh?" Chomp's mean little eyes narrowed even more, his thin lips disappearing behind his beard. "Fuck that. You know, Tommy, there are rules around here. Number one rule—you never touch another Angel's woman."

"I know that, man, I know. I swear I would never do that."

Chomp's eyes glittered. He was either stoned or drunk. Or both. Fuck, fuck, fuck.

When Chomp reached for the knife in his boot, Tommy knew he was screwed. His fists clenched and adrenaline coursed through his body in a rush of heat and light.

Then Vince stepped between them and grabbed Chomp's arm. "Tommy didn't do nothin', Chomp." He shoved Chomp back, away from him. "I was watching. Nothing happened. Go home."

Chomp glared at Vince, then, without a word, he turned and helped his stumbling wife out of the bar.

Vince shook his head. "You gotta watch it, buddy. She's not the first old lady I've heard talk about you like that. You're gonna get yourself in deep shit. Why don't you wanna go out with my cousin? I told you she's single and she's cute. I'll fix you up."

He looked at Vince. "Thanks, man." He unclenched his fists, forced a smile, and shoved a hand into his hair. "Yeah. Maybe I should do that." Vince had come to his rescue and he probably owed the rough, tough biker his life. He could've hugged the guy.

Vince was right about one thing—he needed a girlfriend, like, yesterday. He tipped his bottle and drained the last of the beer.

The next afternoon at the ATF offices in downtown L.A., Ryan Thomas sat at a long boardroom table, tracing the grooves of ancient pen marks and cigarette burns with the tip of his index finger as he waited for the others to arrive. His paperwork was behind and his SAC was riding his ass for it, but they'd called this meeting and he could only hope it was good.

He'd lost Axel last week because of bureaucratic crap. The Special Agent in Charge, Darren Forsythe, had sent an e-mail to Axel's SAC in Pittsburgh, the field office they'd "borrowed" him from, asking for Axel to stay longer on the case. They were making good progress but it was going to take longer than they'd first anticipated. But he'd worded the e-mail in his usual blunt, jerk-off style and had pissed off everyone in Pittsburgh so much they'd said no to his request. Axel was gone.

On top of that, Jackrabbit, their confidential informant, the one who was their link to the real Coyotes gang in Mexico, had been acting weird. He'd agreed to work with the ATF as an informant, and had been very helpful to them, but they suspected he was back doing drugs. He was unreliable, unpredictable and therefore unsafe. Likely off the case.

Ryan leaned back in his chair, linked his hands behind his head and looked up at the square white ceiling tiles.

It was down to him and Manny now. They couldn't do it alone. And things were getting hot for Ryan because of his unwillingness to do any chick who moved. For some reason, the DAs didn't believe a guy like him wasn't willing to do anyone with tits, because Christ only knew, chicks were willing to do him. They needed a female agent, but so far they'd had no luck with that.

Ryan wasn't oblivious to the way he looked and the effect he had on women. He just didn't give a shit. He liked women. He liked sex. More than liked it. And it had been a helluva long time since he'd had any. But women involved with a case were bad news and he didn't have time for a normal relationship. Hell, his record-short marriage had proved that.

He lowered his arms, reached for the coffee cup on the table in front of him and peered into it, as if it may have been magically refilled while he sat there pondering his life's problems.

So women were good for fucking, and that was about it. But never women involved in a case when he was working undercover. That was just asking for trouble. That was just asking for a knife at his throat. A bullet in his chest. Forget it.

Last night he'd been tempted, more than he'd ever been. But once again—mistake. Do not get involved.

He'd learned that lesson the hard way.

The door to the meeting room opened and Josh Witter strode in. "Hey, Ryan. How ya doing?"

"Great."

He and Josh had been working together for three months on this case, but had known each other a lot longer. As case manager, Josh ran the operation. He did the behind the scenes work, ran the surveillance, got all the backstopping in place. This wasn't the first time they'd worked together, but this was their biggest case so far.

"What's going on?" Ryan asked.

"We may have another agent for your team."

Ryan brows lifted. "Great. But, Josh, you know I really need a female agent. Last night—"

"I know. Just hold on."

Others started walking in, Manny and the ATF Special Agent in Charge, Darren Forsythe. Ryan greeted Darren coolly. A by-the-book paper-pusher nearing retirement, he and Ryan did not always see eye to eye on how this op should run. Darren was always worried about rules, procedures and money. Ryan couldn't give a shit about rules, procedure and money. He had a job to do.

Darren was followed by a man Ryan didn't recognize, then by the Group Special Agent in Charge. Ryan nodded and greeted him, waited for an introduction, almost not noticing the woman who followed them in.

Ryan glanced at her. His head jerked back so hard to look at her again he damn near gave himself whiplash. Holy shit. Sara.

Chapter Three

At least he thought it was Sara. She looked different without the heavy makeup. She didn't need all the black crap around the eyes to make them noticeable; the light, crystal-blue irises still grabbed his attention and held it hostage, and with paler, shiny lips she looked younger and softer.

She took a seat at the table, all the while holding his gaze. Ryan practically had to pick his jaw up off the scarred oak surface. He turned a questioning glance to Manny, who'd also recognized her, a broad grin splitting his face. Ryan frowned. What the hell was so funny?

Ryan directed his gaze next to Josh, who smiled back calmly.

"Let's get started," Darren said. "Ryan, Manny, this is Ward Tanner and Sera Manning from the DEA. Sera and Ward—Ryan Thomas and Manny Garrido. I believe you all met last night."

What the fuck? DEA?

Ryan and Manny traded a look and nodded.

"We know you need a female agent on this op. Sera's been working on a case trying to implicate the Death Angels in a prominent drug ring. She's done a lot of work and we think she's connected the drug lab cooking angel sugar to Dominick Casas."

Ryan blinked. Angel sugar was the new version of "angel dust", or PCP, being sold up and down the west coast, particularly to high school and college students. Young girls seemed particularly susceptible to the lure of the new drug. A number of deaths were attributed to either overdosing on the new drug or to doing stupid things while under the influence of it. Ryan's brows tugged together.

"Dominick Casas is president of the Oakland chapter," he muttered. "He and Vince are buddies."

"That's right. And we think he's cooking the sugar."

"You need a female agent, and the DEA needs inside the DAs to complete their investigation. Sera Manning might be the perfect fit."

"Might be?" Ryan cranked his gaze over to Darren.

Darren nodded. "Her lack of undercover experience is a concern."

"How much undercover experience does she have?" Ryan demanded.

Sera leaned forward and slapped a hand down on the table, a frown edging her brow. "I'm right here!" she snapped. "If you have questions, ask me."

Ryan blinked and turned his gaze back to her. "Uh. Okay. How much undercover experience do you have?"

"None," she began. "But—"

"Then it's a no-go." Ryan folded his arms across his chest and leaned back. The ancient chair screeched in protest.

"Wait a minute—" Sera began.

Ward Tanner held up a hand and shot her a look. "Hold on, everyone, let us finish."

Josh took over, addressing Ryan and Manny. "Last night was a test. A trial run to see if she could handle it. Beck took her in there and let her loose to see if she could do it. And so let us ask you guys—since you were there—how'd she do?"

Ryan scowled, didn't look at Manny who was probably still smirking. He couldn't believe this little paper-pusher had walked into The Patch last night looking like a biker chick and had pulled it off. And had fooled him. Completely.

Although he had noticed an unusual classiness and...he didn't know the right word. Sweetness? But fuck him, he hadn't even dreamed she wasn't what she said she was.

"What'd you do with the drugs you bought?" he demanded of her.

She gave him a slow smile. "I already handed it in and recorded it."

She'd made a fucking drug buy. Ryan shook his head in disgust, but he knew most of his disgust was with himself for being taken in.

"What'd you do to Monkey?" he asked next.

"Just a little martial arts move."

"You have martial arts training?"

"Fourth degree black belt."

"Well, if you think that's going to protect you against the guns and knives those guys carry, you're fooling yourself."

She lifted a brow. "I've done my firearms training, just like you."

They stared at each other and heat grew until Ryan's every nerve ending sizzled. A sharp jab in his side made him glance at Manny, who, sure enough, still wore a goofy smile.

"She's good," Manny said. "She handled herself well. She had all of us fooled. I think Carly and she really hit it off, and they trusted her enough to sell her drugs."

Ryan pressed his lips together as he nodded his reluctant agreement.

"And," Manny continued, "there's some kind of chemistry between the two of you that will make a relationship between you completely credible."

Fuck him, what was Manny talking about? Chemistry? Was he trying to imply Ryan was horny and hot for her? Because he wasn't. "I'm not..." he began—but then he didn't know where to go with that and snapped his mouth closed. He met Sera's eyes again and amusement sparkled there.

"It's out of the question to put someone in an operation this dangerous without any undercover experience," Ryan said instead. "It would be like putting a kitten into a cage full of tigers."

"I'm hardly a kitten," Sera said.

"Oh yeah, honey, compared to them—you are."

Ryan became aware the others were watching their exchanges with interest. He glared at Josh. "You shouldn't have done that. It was dangerous sending in another agent without me and Manny knowing. Fucking harebrained."

Josh shook his head, unoffended by Ryan's words. "We wanted to see how you'd react to her. It had to be that way, Ryan. You know that."

Yeah, he did, dammit.

This whole thing annoyed him to the point of making his blood boil. He wanted to bolt out of his chair and walk out. A four-alarm fire burned in his gut. He shook his head, reached into his jeans pocket for the roll of antacids he lately carried with him everywhere, unwrapped a couple and popped them into his mouth.

"This has 'big fucking disaster' tattooed all over it. She'll jeopardize the entire op. We've made it this far—we've accomplished so much. We can't screw up now. She makes one mistake, we're all dead."

He stared at her with hard eyes when he said that so she'd understand what she was getting herself into. This wasn't a game. This was literally life and death. These guys were killers, without hesitation or remorse if they needed to be, and any cop who was caught among them would be snuffed instantly. Her mouth tightened and her eyes narrowed.

"I know the risks," she said, her voice low and steady. "And I know I can do it."

"We've talked about the pros and cons already, Ryan," Darren said. "I feel the same as you do—it's risky. But you need a female agent, and she needs an in. It's win-win for both agencies."

"You're the one who said you need a female agent," Josh reminded him, and with a stone in his gut, Ryan remembered last night.

"We do," Manny confirmed, also leaning forward, elbows on the table. Ryan glared at him, willing him to shut up, but no, he had to shoot his mouth off. "Last night one of the wives made a drunken pass at Ryan. It's been brewing for a while. Her husband was drunk, stoned, whatever, and probably would've killed Ryan if I hadn't been there with another DA to stick up for Ryan. To reassure him Ryan hadn't done anything. But next time...we won't be able to convince Chomp." Manny shot Ryan a glance. Ryan sat there rock-still and fumed. "Next time he will kill you, man, whether you've done anything or not. You gotta get a woman of your own. Then Jessie and the others will leave you alone. And they're wondering why you never hook up with anyone."

"What about you?" Ryan demanded. "Why don't they wonder

about you?"

"I have hooked up with women." Manny shrugged. "But I'm not the one their wives are all over. You are."

Ryan shook his head. Once again, he knew Manny was right, but he was so pissed off at how this all came down, he hated to admit it.

"Fine," he said shortly. "I need a female agent to play a girlfriend role. But surely to god we can find someone with some experience?"

"Not someone who looks the part, who has such extensive knowledge about the DAs and who's available right now."

"Also," Manny added. "If Sara...Sera?"

"Sera," she affirmed with a small smile. "Like Vera."

"If Sera can get in with the women, there are things she might find out that we can't."

Ryan sat there, staring at everyone, then down at the scarred table top. He rubbed his lips together, nodded his head slowly. "Looks like I don't have much say in this."

"I think after last night the decision is made," Josh agreed. "You and Manny both confirmed she pulled it off, and the drug buy pretty much sealed the deal."

"Fine." Ryan met Sera's eyes and relief and joy shone there, although she appeared to try to repress the smile tugging her pretty lips. "I just hope you understand what you're getting into."

She nodded, her obvious delight pulling at something deep inside him.

"We need to get to work," Josh said. "You can brief her on everything she needs to know. We created a new identity for her for last night, got her some basics, but we need to do the full backstop, make sure she's airtight in case they check her out."

The DAs were known to investigate anyone who associated with them, and had dug deep into his and Manny's backgrounds to ensure they were who they said they were when they'd started hanging around with them. The ATF was experienced at rock-solid backstopping. Manny and Ryan had new identities complete with social security numbers, credit histories, even high school transcripts, and they'd created a fake arrest record for Manny with some misdemeanor arrests for assault and drug violations, and one for him with arrests for possession.

"We're thinking at first you show up with her a few times, like you two are dating. Within the next week or two, we'll move her into the house to live with you."

Jesus Christ. Ryan couldn't look at her. Fine. Whatever. It was business. He nodded.

"She has some ideas how she wants to play this," Josh continued. "So we'll let the three of you work on that."

Ryan nodded again, spreading his hands flat on the table. The suits got up and left, and Ryan knew Josh would be working hard on the behind the scenes stuff.

When the door closed behind them, he looked at Sera again.

"You sure about this?"

Ryan's lack of confidence in her abilities was just as annoying as their superiors' had been two days ago when she'd tried to convince them she could do it. Now she'd proven herself. She'd done it, but for some reason he was being a jerk. Like he was pissed off at her, or something. She wasn't brainless. She knew what she was getting into.

"I'm sure." She met his gaze levelly across the table.

"Look Sera or Sara or whatever your name is." Ryan sighed, ran a hand over his pulled-back hair. "You may know a lot about the DAs but you have no idea what you're getting into here. In their world, having a chick on your arm or your bike—a fender bunny—is just one more accessory. Women are treated like shit. In fact..." he paused. "A lot of them are abused. Physically. Emotionally. Most of them have a lot of problems. Low self-esteem. Drug and alcohol abuse. You really think you can play that role and pull it off?"

"No."

His eyebrows rose.

"I can't play that role. I'm not even going to try to play an abused uh...fender bunny. I can't do that, I know that. But I think I can be convincing in the role I will play. If you work with me." She held his gaze.

He stared back at her. "How do you plan to play it?"

"I'm going to work for you. Helping with your parts delivery business. I need a job." She smiled. "Since I just lost my job at the bank for suspected embezzlement."

Ryan's mouth twitched. "An embezzler. Huh."

"That would work," Manny said. "It would explain both of you being out of town at the same time."

She nodded. "So, tell me how you guys accomplished this amazing feat of getting in with the DAs."

Ryan glanced at Manny. "The Coyotes are a small OMG down in Mexico. We've got a guy—Jackrabbit—who's a full patch Coyote and we set up a fictitious Coyotes chapter in Clover City. Manny and I have been hanging out there for a few months, getting to know people, establishing ourselves. Then we showed up with Beck at an Angel rally wearing our colors, managed to convince them we didn't want to hone in on their territory."

She listened, amazed. It sounded simple, but she knew only too well what a difficult task they'd set themselves and how astonishing it was that they'd been so successful.

"We were trafficking guns down to Mexico," Ryan continued. "They're selling narcotics. We assured them we weren't trying to take away their dope business. They bought the story and gave us the okay to traffic guns in their territory. We started hanging out with them and just last week they told us it was okay to sell some drugs in their territory too. Told us it was okay to fly our colors. If things continue the way they have been, we can get inside information like no one ever has."

"Have you met Dominick Casas?"

"Yes. He and Vince are friends, they party together when Dominick's in Clover City. We were there a couple times."

"Do they talk about him? What he does?"

Manny and Ryan exchanged glances. "No. We haven't heard much about him. He'll likely be in El Mirage next weekend."

"I'll be coming with you, then."

"No." Ryan's face tightened and he shook his head. "You won't be. That's too soon. We need time to bring you in."

"That's almost ten days away."

"That's not enough time. You can't rush things."

Patience had never been one of her strengths. She knew it and she intended to work on it. Some day. "Ten days seems like ample time."

"No."

Their gazes collided and the long, thick silence was broken by Manny's chuckle. Ryan frowned at him.

"Let's see how it goes," she suggested. A damn compromise. Another one of her not-so-strong suits.

He studied her. "I'm the leader of this team," he said. "What I say goes. You listen to me and you do what I say if you're going to work with us."

Her blood heated and she felt it pulsing in her head. "We're a team."

"Every team has a leader. And in this case it's me." His mouth firmed into a hard, straight line, his square jaw tight.

"Look. I know in the past, female UCA roles have been limited to playing the girlfriend," she said. "But get with the times. I have my own goals for this operation, so that isn't going to work for me. I need to get in there and gather my own intelligence."

They faced each other down again and she vibrated with the need to convince him she was up to this.

He slowly shook his head from side to side, but said, "Fine. Gather your intel. But once again, you're a rookie and I'm the leader of this team. That's the way it works."

Manny inclined his head in agreement. Even he deferred to Ryan.

She clamped her lips together and nodded reluctantly. She hated being told what to do, but it was the reality of being a rookie, the reality of working in a hierarchical government organization.

"The reason we were so successful was because we didn't push," Ryan continued, his voice low and tight. "I took my time, showed them the things they needed to see—confidence, loyalty, courage—and I let them come to me. That's how we did it. We cannot push this. I can't emphasize that enough." His eyes flashed.

"I get it."

"The rally would be a good time," Manny said. "The whole idea of going there is to show off bikes and girlfriends. And the top dogs will be there for us to pay our respects to. We can talk to Casas."

Ryan scowled. She looked back and forth between them. She was getting an impression of each of them—Manny level-headed and rational, Ryan a temperamental, egotistical hothead who did things his way or no way.

"What about you?" She lifted her chin and caught Ryan's eye challengingly. "Are you going to be able to pull this off? Because clearly you hate my guts."

Manny made a choked, snorting noise, but she didn't even look at him. Ryan's scowl deepened.

"I can do it," he snapped. "And I don't hate your guts. I just think you're too inexperienced for this and I don't have time to babysit. We're in this deep and I want this operation to succeed."

"Babysit!" Her mouth dropped open and she closed it with a pop. "I do not need babysitting!"

"Whatever." He sliced a hand through the air. "You know what I mean. I don't have time to look after you to make sure you're safe. It's going to endanger all of us."

"I don't need to be looked after," she said through clenched teeth. "I can look after myself. I've been doing it for a long time." She leaned forward across the table and he did the same. They met nose to nose. Sparks flashed and heat shimmered between them, just like last night. Every muscle in her body tightened, including the little inner muscles of her pussy, which contracted with hot, wet arousal.

Oh crap. Never mind being afraid of the DAs. She could handle anything they threw at her. But Ryan...was a different story. She was going to be his girlfriend, living with him in the same house for god knew how many months, while this intense sexual awareness sparked between them. Now *that* was enough to scare the hell out of her.

Chapter Four

Ryan and Manny spent the rest of the day documenting everything they'd done the night before in great detail. Goddamn paperwork—timesheets, activity reports, investigative reports. Ryan hated it. He liked being out in the field, undercover, using his wits, flying by the seat of his pants. Not sitting in this airless office with ancient metal desks, worn linoleum and flickering fluorescent lighting that gave him a headache.

"Finished reviewing those tape transcripts yet?" Darren Forsythe stopped at his desk.

"Almost." Forsyth's eyes were way too small for his face, which was round and pale because he sat inside at a desk all day. His body was round and pale too, in a wrinkled white shirt, ugly tie loose around his neck, sleeves rolled back on scrawny forearms, gut overflowing his belt.

"You know, after that screw up with the Gonzales case, you're lucky you're not pushing paper all day, every day."

Ryan lifted his eyes to the SAC's. "You have to keep throwing that in my face?" he muttered. "I know I screwed up. I learned my lesson."

"Let's hope you did. Because I saw the way you were looking at that hot little DEA agent this morning. You'd better not let your dick run this case like the Gonzales case."

That was too much. Ryan slammed a hand down on the papers, stood up and stuck his nose in front of Forsyth's face. "I did not let my dick run that case. I wasn't screwing that girl. I just cared about her. Like...like a little sister. She was a good kid, got hooked up with a scum pusher boyfriend."

"Sure." Forsyth didn't back down. "A little sister, my ass."

"It's the truth." He glared at Forsyth. Ryan knew what the talk had been after that case had all gone to shit, but he'd maintained he'd never gotten involved with Lucie Gonzales. Not like that. "In your dirty mind, maybe, but it never happened."

"Whatever. Just take a lesson from that."

"I have! That's why we need a female agent on this case. God!" Ryan took a step back, rubbed the back of his neck under his hair. "If I was sleeping with every chick I met on this case, we wouldn't have the problems we do. We wouldn't need someone to pose as my girlfriend. For Chrissakes, half those bikers think I'm gay."

Forsythe's laugh was a dry bark. "Now that's funny."

"Yeah, I'm laughing so hard my side hurts." Ryan scowled at his superior, longing to drive his fist into his nose. How long until he retired? Everyone knew he was just putting in time. Why didn't he just go, for Chrissake, and let someone do the job who actually gave a shit. Ryan didn't know how he'd gotten so lucky to be assigned to his unit after that last case. Maybe someone saw it as punishment. The only thing saving him from punching out his supervisor's lights was working with Josh. He had a ton of respect and admiration for Josh and the work he'd done, and he wanted to do good for Josh.

And he wanted to do good for himself. To prove he wasn't a total screw-up. To show everyone he was a damn good agent. And to take down those sons of bitches who were killing people every day with the drugs they bought, cooked and sold. Just like they'd killed Lucie Gonzales.

He had to get over this bitterness that kept rising up inside him. He'd screwed up. He deserved whatever he got. If this was it, he was lucky. He needed to get his head on straight and make the best of this. Show them what he could really do.

Forsyth picked up a report and scanned it. "Typos," he said, tossing it down on the desk. "Redo it."

Ryan's jaw clenched. "Okay." But before he went back to the computer keyboard, he popped two more antacids into his mouth and crunched the minty tablets to a chalky powder.

Partners had to trust each other. Sometimes with their lives. The problem was, trust wasn't something that came easily to Ryan. It was something that had to be earned. But he and Sera didn't have time for that. No time to get to know each other. They were in this together now and they had to make the best of it.

"Tell us what you know about this drug he's cooking."

He, Manny and Sera sat in a coffee shop on Figueroa in downtown L.A. Sera sat beside Manny, across from him, a domed plastic cup full of iced mocha between her long, slender fingers. She wore no polish on short, rounded nails, and no rings adorned her fingers.

"Angel sugar. Back in the Sixties, it was angel dust. Phencyclidine. It was pretty popular for a while, but it has wicked side effects—delusions, hallucinations, paranoia, impaired speech. People even become violent or suicidal."

"Combining it with pot and smoking it helps with the side effects," Manny said.

Ryan looked at him, one eyebrow lifted. Sera rolled in her lips.

"What?" Manny said. "I'm just saying."

"The side effects can still be bad," Sera continued, lips twitching. "So a couple of years ago, this new stuff showed up on the market. They've combined it with a chemical called HCC3, which eliminates the bad and enhances the good—the strength, power, invulnerability, and the numbing effect on the mind."

Ryan made a snort of disgust and she looked at him. He rolled his eyes. "Why do people do that shit?"

She tipped her head to one side and looked at him. "Don't you know? You're a federal agent, working in this business for...how long? And you don't know why people do drugs? How hopeless and empty their lives can be?" She leaned forward, and her fingers tightened on the plastic cup to the point he thought she might crush it. "How afraid they can be? How powerless they feel? How drugs seem like the only thing that gives them any escape from the hell their life is?"

He stared at her tight jaw and flashing eyes, then scrubbed a hand over his face. "Yeah. I know that. I just think people should be strong enough to not need it."

"If only everyone was that strong," she muttered, dropping her gaze and giving her cup a little shake, rattling the ice cubes. He sensed something more behind that comment than she was saying.

"Anyway," she continued just as he opened his mouth to admonish her. "It also has an anorexic effect."

"It kills appetite."

"Yup." She smiled. "And guess what lots of teenage girls angst about?'

"Their weight."

"You got it." She shook her head and gave both men a wry smile. "The effects seem to be something girls that age are looking for, so dealers are targeting them. So many girls are dying from this stuff. We believe the sugar is being produced by one main lab. And we think we've narrowed its location down to Oakland."

"Where Casas is president of the Oakland Death Angels chapter."

"Yes." She lifted her eyes to meet his again.

"Angel sugar is rivaling meth as the fastest growing drug problem in California, Oregon and Washington. There are only a couple of chemists in the U.S. capable of cooking that kind of stuff. The Death Angels have been selling it for a while, but lately there's been a huge increase in the amounts available. It seems to indicate a bigger lab, and I suspect who's behind it. I think they're supplying the lab, the equipment and the precursor chemicals and, of course, taking a chunk of the profits."

"Interesting. So who's behind it?"

"It's a drug cartel out of Mexico."

"Okay. That's who you've been investigating?"

She hesitated. Once again, Ryan's nerves jumped. He was a patient man, but this whole trust thing and being thrust into this situation so quickly with someone he didn't know was testing his self-control, and she was keeping secrets. He slammed a hand down on the table. Sera jumped, her eyes wide. Ryan leaned across the small table.

"Ever since we sat down here I've had the feeling you're holding back on us," he snarled. "We can't work together unless we trust each other. Our lives are on the line every fucking minute we're in that world. If I can't trust you, I'm not putting my life in your hands and this whole deal is off. You have to tell us everything, Sera."

"Easy, man." Manny spoke in a low tone, and Ryan noticed other people in the coffee shop giving them the eye. He sucked in oxygen and leaned back in his seat. Sera stared at him, huge eyes blue and shadowed.

"You're not telling us everything," he repeated. "I can feel it in my gut."

She nibbled her bottom lip, cast a sideways glance at Manny with her big eyes, and the picture she made was so sexy it dragged the breath Ryan had just inhaled right back out of him. He had to close his eyes against the sight.

His heart thudded slow and deep, and he heard the blood pound in his ears to the same rhythm. This was not going to work. Not if their so-called partner was lying to them. And not if he still wanted to jump her sexy bones.

Yes, she was holding something back, but it was something she shared with no one. Some things were just too risky to put out there. But she had to convince him that she was being honest with him. And she was. She hadn't lied about anything.

"What exactly do you think I'm holding back?" Sera asked carefully. Her fingers turned the slick plastic cup between them.

"I don't know," Ryan growled, and the menacing look in his eyes intimidated and unnerved her. She had to get a grip. She was going to be in far scarier situations than sitting in a coffee shop with two ATF agents grilling her.

See, that was the thing—she was way more afraid of Ryan than she was of any outlaw biker gang member, and that included Dominick Casas. But Ryan, on the other hand—her usual defenses didn't seem to be working against the overwhelming lust he inspired in her.

She had no time for lust. God, what a distraction at a time like this! Even in the past when she'd had relationships with guys—and she'd had a few, although never anything serious—she managed to keep them apart from her work. And her heart. Not that that was in play here, either. This was business and she had to keep Ryan at a distance. But damn, he made her feel stuff that scared the crap out of her.

"We're not idiots, Sera."

"I know that!" She stared him down. "Jesus, Ryan. I know you're not. All I said was, you probably know as much as I do. How does that make me holding back? Do you want to compare notes on Casas? 'Cause we can do that, right down to the nitty-gritty details like what kind of beer he drinks and how many times cops have been called to his home for domestic disturbances. I know you know all that."

His brows lowered, mouth tight, he nodded. "Yeah. But what else is there?"

"Just his link to Quintano."

"Quintano?" Ryan flicked a glance at Manny.

"That's the drug cartel."

"I've heard of it."

She nodded. "I don't have a lot of evidence linking Casas with Quintano, but I'm pretty sure it's there."

Ryan nodded. "Okay. So you think this organization set Casas up to increase the production of sugar? This group has the expertise to know how to do this?"

"For sure they do, and I don't think Casas does. He's not a chemist. Creating this new drug was no doubt complicated. It's...evil. Diabolical stuff. If we could find the lab, it'd decimate the Oakland DAs."

"And Quintano?"

"It won't destroy them. They're too big for that. But it would definitely hurt them. And severing the link between the cartel and an OMG would be huge."

Ryan nodded, stroking his chin. "Okay." He eyed her.

She looked at him fiercely, leaned forward. "I want to do that. I *have* to do that."

After a long pause, he said, "Okay. Let's do this." He reached into his pocket for a roll of...what were those? Antacids? Then he glanced at his watch on his other wrist.

"I'm off," he said, rising abruptly.

"The hospital?" Manny asked, and with a short nod Ryan strode out of the coffee shop.

Sera opened her door, her packing for her trip to Clover City interrupted. Oh lord. "Oh, hi, Leo." She swallowed a sigh. Her neighbor kept dropping by on all kinds of pretexts, and much as she wanted to send him and his friendly overtures away, she didn't have the heart when he was so clearly lonely.

Eyes as blue as her own gazed back at her. "Hi, Sera. How are you?" A smile creased his face.

"I'm fine." She paused. "Do you uh...need something?"

She studied his faded but clean shirt, and alert eyes looked back at her from a clean-shaven face. His still-thick gray hair bristled over his head.

"Can I come in?"

She gripped the edge of the door. "I'm kind of busy..."

His face fell. "Oh. Okay..."

"No, it's all right. Come in." She stepped back with a sigh. Leo had no family other than a daughter who lived just outside L.A.—Sera hadn't really paid attention to where—whom Leo rarely saw. Through their conversations it had become obvious that his daughter was a very busy woman and it hurt him that she had so little time for him, although he never criticized her. But Sera'd formed her own opinion of a self-absorbed workaholic who had no time for her father.

She was hardly one to judge, given that she was pretty absorbed in her own career, but the difference was she *had* no family, and there'd been times when she'd wanted to pick up the phone and call Leo's daughter and tell her she should consider herself lucky to *have* a father. But that wasn't her business.

She wasn't exactly looking for relationships with people. She was busy too. But when she'd discovered Leo loved apple pie, she'd somehow found herself baking pies in anticipation of his visits. Just to be nice. Because he missed his own daughter.

He walked in, close enough for her to smell a fresh scent like pine or spruce or cedar, close enough for her to see silvery whiskers on his lean cheeks, just starting to need a shave. "How's your job going?"

She closed the door, her back to him, and paused before she turned to face him.

"Good."

He knew she worked for the DEA but she'd only told him she worked at a desk job.

"Still working in the office?"

"Yeah." She wasn't about to reveal her latest news, much as she was excited to share it with someone. She had no one in her life to share things like that with, and that's how she wanted it. People just let you down.

"I worry about you."

She chuckled. "There's nothing to worry about. And besides, you barely know me."

He smiled. "Yeah, I know. But you're almost the same age as my daughter, so you know…" He hitched a shoulder. "You need someone to look after you."

"I don't need looking after," she answered lightly. "I can look after myself. I've been looking after myself for a long time."

And yet, even as she said the words, she kind of wished he was her father, the father she'd lost so long ago. Because sometimes she felt a need to lay her cheek on a strong chest, to have strong arms around her, to be looked after instead of always looking after herself.

She'd cried for her daddy. He hadn't been a model father, that's for sure. He'd drunk and gambled their lives away, but when he'd left, her mother's life had spiraled even deeper into hell. Sera had cried and hoped and wished her father would come back for her. But he never had.

She certainly wasn't going to get emotionally involved with a total stranger, some kind of father figure. That would just be crazy.

"I'm going away for a while," she told him. "On business."

"Oh. For how long?"

"I don't know. It could be a while."

"I can look after your apartment for you."

She shook her head. "I don't need anyone to look after my apartment."

Well, that probably wasn't entirely true. If she ended up being gone longer than a few days, someone would have to keep her mail and newspapers from clogging up and overflowing her mailbox.

She'd worry about that when it happened. She hated relying on anyone else, so she'd make do on her own as long as she could.

Chapter Five

"Nervous?"

Sera shot Ryan a disgusted look. "No."

They stood beside Ryan's Harley in the parking lot of the Palms Motel in Clover City, on their way to The Patch for a night of drinking, partying and hopefully recording incriminating conversations. The sun had just set. Palm trees were silhouetted black against the deepening blue of the sky and the streetlights gleamed on the monstrous chromed-up machine next to them. Sera wiped her hands down her thighs.

He laughed. "If you're not, you're nuts."

"Thanks very much." Sera jammed her helmet onto her head and eyed the spoked wheels, the huge engine, the large, chromed mufflers tunneling underneath black leather saddlebags.

"Got your recorders?"

"Yes." She'd received a crash course on how to use the surveillance equipment. Josh Witter insisted she had two, just in case. One tiny device was inside her cell phone; the other looked like an extra battery and was in the pocket of her jeans.

Ryan started the engine—a whine, a bang and then a rattling, bumpy idle. Sera closed her eyes briefly.

Ryan swung himself onto the bike then looked at her. She pressed her lips together. He arched a brow. "Sera?"

She gave a jerky nod then climbed on behind him, wrapping her arms around his waist. God. He was big and muscular and warm, and as she pressed against him she could even smell the scent of the shampoo he used on his hair, clean and tangy.

Okay, she was a little nervous. The machine underneath them rumbled with power and speed. With a roar of the motor, Ryan pulled out of the parking lot onto Juniper Road. Glancing over her shoulder at the rapidly retreating motel, Sera saw the surveillance car driven by Josh pull out to follow them. It was reassuring to know that wherever they went, at least two other agents were sitting outside keeping an eye on things. But that only went so far, as she well knew.

The tranny shifted into second with a clank and a lurch, making her heart lurch too. Her arms tightened around Ryan. Good god in heaven. The choppy roar of the engine and the wind in her ears drowned out any other sounds as she clutched Ryan's body and hung on.

She could not let on that she was nervous about riding on the Harley. The lack of control she felt hanging on to nothing but a black leather jacket while so exposed and vulnerable and flying down the street sent spears of panic through her.

On top of that, she was pressuring herself, like she always did. She really wanted to do a good job of this. She *had* to do a good job. She knew she could look after herself, but Ryan's warnings about putting all their lives on the line had stuck with her, and she worried she could do something to screw up and get a whole lot of other people killed.

No. It wouldn't happen. She had to think positively.

When they walked into The Patch, Led Zeppelin's *Houses of the Holy* pounded over the speakers. Ryan took Sera's hand and led the way. She stuck close to him, not because she needed to, but because it looked good.

Several men greeted Ryan—or rather, Tommy, as she needed to think of him—with loud calls and raised beers. He led Sera to the bar and put his arm around her waist as they stood there and waited to be served. She tipped her head and smiled up at him and he smiled back.

Jesus. She hadn't seen many smiles from him since the night they'd met in this exact place. She'd forgotten how sinfully melting-hot that smile could be. Thick, liquid wanting slid through her and down between her legs. She forgot to breathe.

He nuzzled her ear. "Okay?" he whispered.

Get a grip, get a grip. "Okay."

She dragged air into her lungs and smiled at the bartender who slid two bottles of beer across the bar to them. Ryan tossed him a twenty-dollar bill and let him keep the change.

"Throwing money around," she murmured.

"Makes them think I'm rolling in it," he answered back, gaze fastened on her so that anyone looking at him would have thought he'd just said, "Let's go back to my place and fuck each other stupid." Hot eyes and a sexy smile seduced her. "They know I have to get that much cash from selling guns or dope."

"Ah." She nodded, quivering inside. Suddenly doubt filled her. Doubt at her ability to withstand Ryan looking at her like he wanted to do her right there on the bar, smiling seductively, touching her with warm hands. But hey there—she didn't have to withstand it. They were a couple, and if they wanted to convince people of that, she might as well just give herself over to it. As long as she kept her wits about her when it came to other people, she could bask in the glow of Ryan's calescent attention.

She gave him her own sultriest smile then and watched his pupils expand. She tipped the bottle to her mouth and swallowed, icy cold beer tracing a path from mouth over her tongue and down her esophagus. Maybe she wasn't the only one affected. Interesting.

"Hey, Tommy." Vince approached them and gave Ryan a slap on the shoulder. "What's up, man?"

"Not much. Hey, you remember Sara?"

Vince eyed her and Sera smiled. "Hi, Vince."

"Hey, Sara." His eyes moved between them and he smiled then winked at Ryan. "Good work, man." He tilted his chin toward the back of the bar. "Carly's back there, she'll be happy to see you again."

Sera wondered if that was her clue to send her off, but Ryan pulled her against him and wrapped his arm around her. "You can go talk to her in a few minutes," he said.

Vince grinned. "Uh-huh."

"Hey, thanks again for saving my ass the other night," Ryan said to Vince. "I owe you big time for that. Chomp would've killed me."

Vince rolled his eyes. "He was fuckin' hammered. Nice guy, but turns into a mean drunk. Good thing you've got your own babe tonight."

"He here?"

"Not yet." Vince slugged back some beer. "Probably later. So I guess you don't want to meet my cousin Maria, huh?"

Sera frowned and gave Ryan an evil look. He grinned, squeezed her waist. "Nah. Thanks anyway."

"You coming to El Mirage this weekend?" Vince was looking at her. She looked inquiringly at Ryan.

"I don't know," she said flirtatiously. "Am I, Tommy?"

He scowled. "Don't push me, babe. I said we'll see." He looked at Vince and shrugged.

"Bring her," Vince urged. "It'll be fun."

"Maybe."

Sera pouted, but sipped her beer.

"Let's go talk to A.J.," Ryan said and pulled her along. Vince followed them down the length of the bar to a table in the back near the pool table, where A.J. sat with a group of guys.

They took up so much space, all of them big, in black leather. And there was Manny, just as big, bald headed and mean looking. Sera ignored him.

As they pulled chairs up to the table, the men all gave Sera a good looking over. She ignored them too, as she took her seat. Ryan sat close to her and leaned in. "You have just been eye-fucked, sweetheart," he murmured. "How was it?"

She couldn't help it. She laughed. "I've had better." She tossed her hair back.

"You got nice tits, honey!" one of the guys called to her across the table.

Sera sent a look his way that she hoped was sufficiently badass and said, "Thanks. So do you. Only, yours are bigger."

The guy looked down at his chest and she saw Ryan roll his lips in to keep from laughing, because it was true. The guy's beer belly was only marginally bigger than his man boobs. Everyone at the table hooted with laughter.

"She put you in your place, asshole," Vince said with a snicker. "I like this girl."

She and Ryan shared a grin and she thought she saw a flicker of admiration on his face.

She mostly sat and listened as Ryan talked to the guys, sipping her beer. She waved at Carly at the next table when they made eye contact. After a while she said to Ryan, "I'm going to talk to Carly." She paused a beat then added, "Okay?"

"Okay."

She pushed back her chair and strolled over to where Carly sat.

"Did you come with Tommy?" Carly leaned over, eyes wide and eager.

"Yeah."

"He's so damn hot." Carly sighed then glanced around. "Oops. Gotta watch what I say around Vince. He'd be pissed if he heard me say that."

"He didn't hear," Sera assured her.

"Is this the first time you've been out with him?"

"Second. We went out last night. I gave him my number the other night."

"I thought you two looked like you were interested!"

Sera smiled smugly. "Yeah. I like him."

"Cool. So maybe next weekend you'll come to El Mirage?"

"Is that all anyone ever talks about around here?" Sera pouted. "Tommy's not sure if he wants me to go, but the more I hear about it, the more I want to."

She snickered evilly inside. She'd force his hand and give him no choice in the matter. Ha!

"It's so much fun! We just party all weekend, lots of booze and dope and smack? You'd love it. People come from all over for this trip?"

Carly ended every sentence as if it was a question, which made

Sera want to roll her eyes with irritation. "Big party, huh?" she said.

They talked on, Sera wondering how she steered the conversation in the direction she needed it to go. Ryan had told her they were interested in any details about some motorcycles that had been stolen from a bar a week or so ago. Apparently some DAs had been drinking there, and when they came out they saw four chromed-up Harleys that they decided to take. The DAs weren't known for stealing bikes, but this seemed to be their doing, and Ryan, being in the parts business, wondered when the broken-down bike parts were going to make it to the market. But much as Sera liked bikes, she had a hard time getting the conversation to go that way.

Instead she got an earful about Zocco's drug business and how he had this fantastic new drug that helped you lose weight.

"Not that you need to," Carly said, looking enviously at Sera's slim body.

"I'd like to lose a few pounds," Sera lied. God, she'd be a stick if she did, but Carly accepted that statement. "Where does he get it from?"

"He gets it from a guy in Oakland." Carly put her finger to her chin. "He's a DA too."

Too easy.

"Really." Sera nodded. "I'd like to try it."

"Let's go find him."

Ryan could almost tell time by how drunk and stoned everyone was. He could handle quite a few beers himself, being a big guy, but he'd gotten really good at making it look like he drank more than he really did.

Everyone got louder and sloppier and clumsier, beers spilling, tempers flaring. A fight broke out up front, but was quickly split up by the bouncer. Ryan met up with Sera again, stood in front of her, pelvis to pelvis, looking down at her. She was probably a bit over average height for a woman, and her posture and strength made her appear taller, but he had a good six inches on her, and four-inch heels brought the top of her head only up to his eye level. He curved his hands around her hips, pulled her body into his. "How's it going?"

"Good."

She pressed herself against him, sliding her palms up his chest. Damn, that felt good. She tipped her head back and shook her long hair down her back. He wanted to tangle his hands in that hair. Hell, why not?

He wrapped the silky strands around his hands and tugged. Her pupils exploded, darkening her eyes, and her lips parted as she gazed up at him. The scent of her hair drifted to him, fruity like strawberries or something faintly tropical, startlingly fresh in the stale air of the bar.

"We can talk more later," he murmured. She nodded, eyes fastened on his. He lowered his head, inhaled that sweet scent. Their faces almost touched and he watched her eyes study him, eyelids heavy. Then she took a step back.

Which was just as well. He had to maintain his awareness of what was going on around them. Their eyes met and held as he communicated a wordless message to her. *I want you. Now.* She licked her bottom lip. Jesus. His cock thickened, heat sliding up from his groin all the way to his face, and all the way down to his toes. He swallowed through a tight throat.

Her throat moved too, and then her gaze tore away from his and she dragged trembling fingers across her mouth. She was just as affected as he was.

Shit. He had to get a grip, here. This was just an act. He was not really attracted to her. No fucking way. He pushed down the heat and aching need ruthlessly, but tried to keep the expression on his face the same—hot, interested, aroused. It was all an act.

She stared back at him, and those long lashes framed her eyes like starbursts. She was so confident, so in control, so composed, but at that moment, he could almost believe he had her befuddled with sexual longing and heated arousal. But she was just acting too. And doing a helluva job at it.

He had a job to do, and he was going to do it. And he was going to do it right this time. No emotional involvement. He could take advantage of the sexual heat simmering between them and use it, and that would be it.

It was just a job.

His gaze lowered to her mouth. Her lush, pillowy bottom lip parted slightly from the bow of her upper lip, the corners tilted up a bit even when she wasn't smiling, giving her an appealing, sexy look. He lowered his face closer, watched her eyelashes drift down, her lips quiver. He felt her sigh of breath against his own mouth, and his lips parted, brushed over hers. The sweet fruity scent of her surrounded him and he felt the warmth that shimmered off her body.

"I'm going to kiss you now," he whispered, not sure why he felt he had to give her the warning. It just seemed the thing to do. Given that this was work.

Chapter Six

When his mouth covered hers, gently, slowly opening over hers, Sera slid her hands down his arms to his biceps and held on. Her stomach muscles quivered beneath his thumbs and her mouth opened for him and moved against his, warm and wet and delicious. He drew back, his tongue sliding across her bottom lip. Their eyes met. And held.

Pale blue zircons sparkled back at him. "Wow," she said.

"Mmm." And he dipped in for another kiss, this time pulling her up against his body. Her slim, strong shape molded into him, soft breasts pressed into his chest. Heat sizzled over him.

"Nice," he finally murmured against her lips. "Very nice." He brushed his mouth over hers once, twice, then took a step back.

She nodded, looking bemused. He wanted to shove her up against a wall, yank her clothes down and fuck her hard, and the intensity of his desire for her shocked him.

He swallowed hard, fought for a grip on his emotions. This was crazy. A kiss, just for show, so everyone would know she was his. He hadn't planned to get himself heated up to the point of volcanic explosion. His cock throbbed painfully behind the zipper of his jeans and heat cascaded through his body in scorching waves.

Loud cheering and hooting drew him back, drenched his arousal with cold reality. He blinked then grinned. "We're putting on quite a show."

"Mmm. We sure are." She laid her palm on his cheek, brushed her mouth across his one more time, then turned to the bar. "Two more beers over here!"

He had to give her credit. She'd thrown herself into that in a very convincing manner, yet seemed to have maintained her wits. He, on the other hand, was breathing hard, throbbing behind the fly of his jeans. Physiological reaction. He couldn't help it. And hell, it just made the situation that much more believable.

He took the beer, tossed another bill onto the bar and turned back to the room, arm wrapped around Sera. She snuggled in against him. Hell, this was a lot more fun than the other nights he'd been here!

They meandered over to Vince and Carly and were talking to them when voices behind him rose and he heard some shouts. They all turned to see what was going on.

Jesus Christ. It was Zocco, high on god knew what yet again, and he'd pulled a knife on some guy Ryan didn't recognize. "I want my fuckin' money!"

Drug deal gone bad.

"I told you I'd kill you if you didn't pay up tonight!" Zocco raised his hand to the guy's throat.

Ah hell. A string of curses ran through Ryan's head. He couldn't let Zocco kill someone. He had to stop him, but how? If he interfered, he was interfering with biker law. This was how they settled disputes. He started forward, but Sera put a hand on his forearm. He paused, looked down at her. She gave him an intense look but he couldn't understand what she was trying to tell him. Was she trying to stop him? But she had to know that as federal agents they couldn't stand by and let someone be killed. Even if it meant the end of the whole operation.

He shook her hand off and started forward again, but he was too damn late. Zocco's blade had sliced the guy's neck and blood spurted. Female screams and the bang of chairs hitting the floor filled his ears, everyone else trying to get away. Ryan grabbed Zocco's arm and wrestled with him. "Stop, Zocco! Are you crazy? All these witnesses, you're gonna end up in the slammer for sure. Stop!"

Zocco was so drunk it wasn't that hard to disarm him and the knife dropped to the floor. So did the man he'd just attacked, clutching his neck, gasping, blood seeping between his fingers. Sera rushed to the guy and knelt at his side. Ryan wanted to yell at her—*no, stop! Be careful!* Human blood. Jesus, she had no protection, what the hell did

Hot Ride

she think she was going to do?

Zocco was fighting with him maniacally, and Ryan struggled to hold him back. "Look, Zocco, he's still alive, it'll be okay, just settle down."

Ryan desperately fought Zocco so he could turn around to make sure Sera was okay. *Fuck, a little help here!* Where was everyone else? They were just going to let Zocco do the guy in.

Finally Ryan landed a punch to Zocco's jaw that dazed him, and he slammed Zocco down into a bar chair. "Stay there!" he snarled, and he turned back to Sera. She'd grabbed a bar towel and had pressed it to the guy's throat, staunching the blood.

"Sara..."

"It's okay." She looked up at him, smiled reassuringly. "He's going to be okay, it's not as bad as it looked." She turned back to the man. "You still gotta go to the hospital, though. You might need stitches."

"Shit," he muttered. "Hurts like a son of a bitch."

"It's not as bad as it looked," she assured him, taking his arm to help him sit. "Here you hold the towel. Press hard. Think you can stand up?"

Ryan moved around to take his other arm, and together they helped him up. "Get the hell out of here," Ryan muttered to him. "If you're okay, get out, now."

The guy didn't need to be urged twice and he disappeared through the crowd and out the door.

Ryan stared at Sera as she brushed her hands together. "Well, aren't you just little Miss Florence Nightingale."

Ryan followed Sera into her room at the Palms Motel and shoved the door shut behind him. She turned to face him.

"You took a big risk back there tonight," he said, folding his arms across his chest.

"What are you talking about?" She stared him down, although she looked a tad pale. Actually, very pale. "The guy had a little cut, I

55

grabbed a towel, stopped the bleeding."

"You can't expose yourself to bodily fluids like that," he bit out.

"I didn't touch any blood. I used the towel. And since we're yelling at each other," she continued, hands on hips, "what the hell was with all the manhandling back there?"

"Manhandling?" His mouth dropped open. "*Manhandling?* We were supposed to be acting hot for each other. That's what that was all about. And besides..." He tilted his chin. "It seemed as if you liked it, babe."

"Don't call me babe," she snapped. "And I didn't like it. I was acting. I had no choice. Next time, tone it down a bit."

They faced each other. Ryan's hands clenched into fists at his side and he fought to control his breathing. There was no fucking way she had faked the way her pupils dilated, the way her nipples had gotten hard. He watched her breasts now, watched them rise and fall quickly as she stood there, every muscle in her hot, little body as tight as his. Blood surged in his veins and heat cascaded over his body. Jesus Christ. She was going to drive him insane. He was going to kill her.

"There was blood," he said, not sure why he'd gone back to that topic. "You had no protection. Are you crazy?"

"What was I supposed to do? Let the guy bleed out? Ask for gloves? I don't have any open cuts or sores on my hands. I'm fine."

"You'll be filling out forms and reports for the next week," he continued savagely.

"I don't care." She looked bewildered. "I'll do it tomorrow. Whatever."

They stood there, eyes locked, breathing heavily. Tone it down. Yeah. Sure. He wanted to turn her over his knee and tone her down with a few smacks to her cute little ass.

"Are you worried about me?" she taunted.

"Hell no." He clenched his jaw, forced the words out between tight teeth. "You want to risk your life, go ahead. Just don't risk mine."

"How was I doing that, exactly? You were the one stepping into the middle of a fight like some big hero."

"We can't let people kill each other," he said, jaw tight. "Even if they are criminals. Was I supposed to stand there and watch a guy get murdered?"

"He probably wasn't going to get killed."

Ryan could only shake his head. "Yes. He was." Incredulity sharpened his tone. "Those guys don't mess around. Zocco was high on something and pissed as hell. That guy owed him money. He had nothing to lose."

"Except going to prison."

"You think he was thinking of that? That's what I was trying to tell him. He wasn't exactly in a rational frame of mind."

She blew out a breath. "Okay. Fine. You saved the day." She massaged her forehead with her fingertips, a frown creasing the skin between her brows.

Jesus, she was even paler now. Concern tugged on his eyebrows. "Are you okay?"

"Of course I'm okay," she snapped. "I have a little headache, that's all."

"You look pale. You're probably running on adrenaline after that."

"I'm fine." She squeezed the words out between clenched teeth. "Are we done? I'm tired and I need some Tylenol."

"Yeah. We're done."

He yanked open the motel door and would have slammed it behind him except it was on some spring mechanism and it just bounced open again. Shit. He stomped over to his Harley and, with a rattling roar of the engine, he headed back to the house he and Manny were renting.

This was not going to work. He'd thought things had gone okay, and then she'd pulled that stunt at the end of the night. She was going to drive him crazy.

Ryan showed up on his Harley right on time Saturday morning and parked outside the door of Sera's room at the Palms Motel. She closed the door behind her, made sure it was locked, and walked toward him. He sat astride the Harley looking intensely masculine and badass sexy, the motor rumbling between his spread thighs in his leather pants. He wore his helmet, his hair pulled back as usual, and he pulled off his sunglasses to look at her, his thick, straight brows lowered over deep-set eyes.

She'd seen him a few times over the last ten days, back in L.A. where, as Ryan had predicted, she had done mountains of paperwork. The results of the drug analysis had come back from the DEA laboratory and showed the sugar sample Sera had bought from Zocco was the same sugar flooding the west coast, originating from the same place, the same laboratory.

Then she and Ryan had attended a party at Vince and Carly's home in an upscale suburb of Clover City, a sprawling Spanish-style bungalow with a swimming pool out back. Nice lifestyle. Although Vince worked as a sales manager at a car dealership, his drug dealing no doubt also provided funds for the lavish home and parties he liked to throw.

She and Ryan had both settled down since that night at The Patch. The adrenaline rush of that night—the tension of the roles they were playing, the forced sexuality, and then that fight they'd gotten mixed up in—must have gotten their motors revving into overdrive.

Now Ryan sat there on his Harley, looking at her, and his fiery intense gaze made her tummy quiver and somersault.

She had to make this work. But why did he have to be so damn difficult to get along with? Why so perceptive? No wonder he made such a good undercover agent— talk about good gut instincts. No wonder he also drove his handlers crazy.

"Ready?" The one word held a multitude of questions and she knew it.

"Yeah." She tried to infuse as much confidence into her voice as she could. The potential for violence on this run was huge. Put hundreds of gang members together with copious amounts of drugs and alcohol, along with guns, knives and other weapons, and it was just asking for carnage.

Hot Ride

Not to mention hours on a murdercycle. Her favorite mode of transportation. Right. She gritted her teeth as she climbed on behind Ryan, chills tracing over her skin beneath her leathers.

After hours of sitting on that hog, Sera was profoundly grateful to finally roll into El Mirage and then into the parking lot of the Red Fox Inn. She resisted the urge to slide off the bike and kiss the hot pavement. Josh and another agent had been behind them the whole time, in a nondescript government sedan, and she glanced around. Where would they park? Where were they staying?

She took in the rows and rows of choppers and all the bikers milling around outside the front doors of the inn, in their black leathers and DA's colors. She swallowed hard. This was bigger than a night at The Patch with a few DAs or even a party at Vince's house. This was DA chapters from all over California, Nevada and Arizona.

And Dominick Casas was there somewhere. She was finally going to meet him face-to-face. Her stomach tightened painfully at the thought, which she'd been pushing to the back of her mind.

She took a deep breath as she dismounted, removed her helmet and shook her hair out. The breeze caught it, like cool fingers stroking through her hair and over her sweaty scalp, and it flew around her head. She sighed with pleasure. When she lifted her head, Ryan was staring at her with hot eyes. Oh sweet Jesus. Not already.

He turned, pulled off his own helmet and walked toward the hotel. DAs greeted him and shook hands as he walked, and Sera trailed after him, thighs shaking with reaction to the arousal she'd read in Ryan's gaze. God! It was just an act!

They checked in and found their room, and Ryan stood there, still looking dark and moody.

"What is your problem?" Sera demanded, hands on hips. "Are you still pissed off at me?"

He shook his head, rubbed the back of his neck. "No."

"Then why are you acting all grouchy? Jesus, you're putting me in a bad mood too."

He paused, pursed his lips. His beautiful, lickable lips. She blinked, but maintained her aggressive posture.

"I don't want to be here this weekend," he finally said.

"Why not?" Was he still worried about her ability to carry this off? If so, he could just—

"It's my mom."

Again, a blink. "Your...mom."

"Yeah. She's not doing so well right now. Hell. She's dying. She has cancer." His voice roughened.

"Oh." Her breath sighed out of her. "I'm sorry, Ryan. I didn't know that."

He nodded, scrubbing a hand over his eyes. "Yeah. I went to see her yesterday and they told me she might not make it through the weekend. She's been going downhill for months now. But...I had to come on this trip. We aren't going to get another chance like this."

Her heart went squishy in her chest. For the first time, Sera saw him as a man with a life apart from his ATF career. A man with a mother he apparently cared about, a man who was torn between his job and his family. What other sacrifices had he made for this job?

She crossed the room to him, stood before him and without thinking anymore about it, she reached her arms around his neck and pulled herself up against him in a hug.

It was meant to offer comfort. Friendship. Sympathy. She didn't know if he felt any of those things, as he hesitated, but he set his hands on her waist, then slid his arms around her and hugged her back.

She pressed her face into the side of his neck, inhaled the crisp, fresh scent of him, the warm maleness of his skin.

"She might die while I'm away."

"She won't," Sera murmured against his neck. "She'll hang on. She'll want to see you again."

She had no way of knowing if her promises were valid, but she wanted them to be, wanted things to work out for him. She could only imagine how guilty and sad he would be if his mother died before he could get back to be with her.

Heat built between them as the hug lingered on, body pressing to body, breathing in tandem, hearts thudding together. There was no one else in the room. This was not part of their act.

Then a rap at the door startled them apart. The door wasn't closed all the way and A.J. and Vince pushed their way in. "Come on, you two lovebirds, you got all night for that," Vince said with a leer. "We're all going down to the bar."

With a glance at Ryan, unable to stop herself from contemplating the night to come sharing this hotel room with him after that toasty embrace, Sera pressed a hand to her stomach and followed the men down the long, carpeted hallway to the elevators.

The DAs had taken over the patio, music blasting, the distinct smell of marijuana scenting the air, drinks being poured with abandon. A barbecue at the side of the patio smoked with meat grilling; Sera thought it smelled like burgers. She surveyed plastic tables and chairs shaded with colorful umbrellas, looking for any familiar faces.

"Wanna talk to you, Tommy." Vince came up beside Ryan and clapped a hand on his shoulder. "We got some business to discuss this weekend."

"Oh yeah? Sure."

Vince turned to Sera. "You wanna go visit Carly, hon?"

She took the hint and with a brief look at Ryan, she smiled. "Sure, sounds fun." But she really wanted to stay and hear what *business* Vince had to discuss.

She found Carly sitting at a table with Jessie and some other women, all of them well on their way to being trashed. But they were laughing and having a good time while their men talked business in the far corner of the patio beneath a wilting palm tree. Sera tried to keep a discreet eye on Ryan as she talked to them.

"Did you like that sugar?" Carly asked her, not even bothering to lower her voice. Sera supposed it was unlikely any law enforcement—other than herself—was going to be sitting near them on the patio currently occupied completely by gang members. She was glad she'd switched on both her recording devices on the way down from the room.

"Oh yeah. It was great. And I didn't feel like eating at all."

"I know! I've lost ten pounds since I started using that stuff. Vince's all happy." She looked down at herself. "I wanna lose about ten more. I just can't lose these hips."

Carly was petite on top, but had a definite curvy, pear shape. Sera wondered who she wanted to lose weight for—herself? Or Vince?

"I love it too!" Jessie interjected. She patted her ample abdomen. "I've lost fifteen pounds."

"Can you get me more?" Sera asked.

"Sure! We just gotta talk to Zocco. In fact, I think his big supplier is here this weekend."

"Really? Who's that? We should talk to him. You know, I could definitely sell some of that to my friends in L.A."

Carly seemed unfazed by the suggestion. "You'd have to talk to them about that. It'd probably be okay as long as they get their cut."

"So who is the supplier?" Sera had to ask again, because Carly hadn't answered that, but she hated having to push.

Carly was either not so bright or loaded enough that she didn't think much of Sera's interest. "It's Dominick. The president of the Oakland chapter? He's a friend of Vince's."

"Oh. Is he over there with the guys?" Sera nodded her head to where Ryan was deep in conversation with Vince, A.J. and Zocco.

Carly looked too. She frowned. "No. I don't see him. I'm sure he's here, though. Don't worry. We'll talk to them later about it. Meanwhile—here, have a joint."

Sera froze in her seat, her beer halfway to her mouth. She could not smoke a joint. It was strictly prohibited for a federal agent to do drugs. She and Ryan had talked briefly about the possibility that this could happen, but now faced with it, she realized she had no idea what to do.

Chapter Seven

Ryan reined in the exultation rising inside him. Vince wanted him to do some deliveries for him next week, along with his Harley parts—cocaine and heroin. Yes! This was a huge break. This meant they trusted him enough to bring him into their criminal activities. He'd already bought enough dope from some of them to put them in prison for many years, but actually getting in on the organized crime was huge. They were getting so close to being able to nail these guys under RICO—the Racketeer Influenced and Corrupt Organizations Act.

He glanced at Sera across the patio, his first thought excitement at sharing the news with her. To his horror he watched her light up a joint.

His gut tightened into a rock. Jesus Christ. It was all he could do to keep himself from bounding across the patio, over tables and chairs, to yank the reefer out of her mouth. She held it expertly between thumb and forefinger. Clearly she'd done this before.

Anger raged through him, hot and sharp. Could they not have one night out without her getting into trouble?

He had to pay attention to Vince and A.J., though. This was huge. He turned back to them, but energy pulsed inside him, made it hard to sit still.

"Come on, I'll buy you a beer," Vince said, obviously intending to celebrate their deal. He led the way to the bar. Ryan watched Sera, talking and laughing with the other women. He scowled, but accepted the beer from the bartender. Vince held his bottle up, and Ryan clinked his own against it, grinned at the other man and then drank.

"Sara's gonna be working for me," he told Vince. "She got fired from her job at the bank, and she's been looking for something else."

"I heard that. Did she actually rip the bank off?"

Ryan shot Vince a look. "I dunno, man. I didn't ask her if she actually did it. She was never charged by the cops."

Vince laughed. "Banks have too much money, anyway. If she did it, good on her."

"Yeah." Ryan laughed too. "Anyway, we're getting along pretty well, so she's gonna help with some deliveries, and with office stuff. I hate that paperwork shit."

"Yeah. Goddamn government."

"Yeah." Inwardly, Ryan grimaced. This wasn't the first time they'd had bizarre conversations like this.

"Hey, Vince." A.J. appeared. "You know that prospect—Sam something."

Vince frowned. "Sam Cogan?"

"Yeah. Him. Someone thinks they saw him here."

"What the fuck?" Vince stood up and looked around. "Where?"

Who the hell was Sam Cogan? Ryan watched Vince's face darken into a mean, ugly look. Man, at times like this he was glad Vince was his friend.

"Not here in the bar. But at the hotel. Why the hell would that asshole be stupid enough to come here this weekend?"

He had to ask. "Who's Sam Cogan?"

Vince shot him a glare. "He was a prospect. Then he refused to uh...do something we needed done. We kicked him out."

"After we beat the shit out of him," A.J. added.

Ryan's stomach turned over. "What did you want him to do?"

Vince looked at him. And Ryan knew it was bad. They'd just invited him into their dope business, but if Vince hesitated to tell him this, knowing he wasn't one of them, it had to be bad. "Just business," he finally said. "I'm gonna look for him. Come on, A.J."

Shit. More trouble. That was all they needed. Ryan just hoped when they found the guy they just kicked him out and didn't kill him.

Left alone at the bar, he wandered over to the table where Sera sat.

"Hey," he said, dropping into a chair next to her. "How's it going?"

She smiled at him, and the haze of marijuana smoke surrounding the table was almost enough to make him high. Shit. He'd forgotten about that.

He looked for the joint but it was nowhere to be seen. Done. She'd fucking smoked a joint while she was working. She was going to get them both canned.

He scowled at her. "You been smokin', hon?"

"Um...yeah." She glanced at Carly.

"You know I hate it when you stink like that shit."

"I...I forgot."

"Don't fucking do it again, okay?" He made his voice low, menacing. She nodded, looking almost afraid.

"Yeah, sure, baby, I won't."

Carly looked worried, like she'd gotten Sera into trouble. "It was just one smoke, Tommy. No big?"

He nodded, still scowling, stroked his thumb over Sera's bare shoulder. She'd taken off her leather jacket and wore a black ribbed tank top with the black jeans she'd changed into. For the first time he noticed the new tat on her upper arm. He stroked over it, examined the image. Jesus Christ. It looked like St. Michael. She was a walking death wish.

He gritted his teeth and said nothing. Later. They had lots to talk about later.

A.J. and Vince returned then, too quickly to have murdered someone, so he took that as a good sign. They said nothing about the former prospect.

"Wet T-shirt contest going on out there," Vince said with a grin. He looked at Sera, eyes tracing over her tits in the snug tank top. "You should enter."

She turned to Ryan, and the eagerness in her eyes almost undid him. "Can I?"

He stared at her, speechless. She was truly going to give him a heart attack.

"No!"

"Oh, Tommy. Come on."

He almost choked. "No, babe." He hardened his voice. "No one sees your tits but me. Got it?"

She pouted. "Okay. Fine." She folded her arms across those contest-worthy tits. And hell yeah—he wanted to see them.

"Come on." Vince urged them outside where the contest was taking place by the pool. Ryan shot Sera a fulminating glance and led the way outside, beer still grasped tightly in one hand, Sera's small hand crushed in his other.

By the pool, girls had gathered where an emcee was encouraging votes by applause. Ryan took in the sight and the female attributes on display, glanced down at Sera by his side, who was grinning. "So you wanted to enter?" He slid his arm around her waist.

Her crystal blue eyes looked up at him. He could have drowned in those eyes, just like the sparkling blue pool to their left.

"Yeah," she said, tossing her hair back. "I could've won."

His breath caught in his throat and he felt like he was choking on a chicken bone. She grinned. Christ. Every time she did something like that it knocked him back on his ass. Amusement tangled with arousal and the urge to drag her up to their room almost overpowered him. He needed to take that mouth, taste it, he had to have her...

His cock hardened and lengthened in his jeans. Jesus, this was so bad. He was working, for Chrissake. He could not afford to be distracted by horny hormones. This had *never* happened to him.

"What were you and Vince talking about?" she whispered back, nuzzling his ear. His skin buzzed with the sensation of her breath feathering over him.

"Tell you later." He let his hand slide down from her waist to cup her ass and squeezed. She squeaked and jumped. They exchanged a hot look with so many different levels of communication, Ryan didn't even know what to think. The chemistry between them was all too real, whether either of them wanted to admit it or not, and while they could use it to their advantage, they also had to be damn careful things didn't get carried away. Like Sera. Over his shoulder. His hand on her ass, carrying her up to their room.

Fuck. Ryan swiped a hand across his sweaty brow. "Let's move to the shade," he suggested, nodding toward a table shaded by a big umbrella with a beer logo splashed across it. The four of them pulled up cheap, plastic chairs and sat down to watch the show, surrounded by hooting and appreciative applause as the contest got wilder and wetter and barer.

Ryan shot glances several times at Sera, wondering how she was taking this, but she seemed relaxed, exchanging comments with Carly that he couldn't hear.

"Where's Manny?" she asked Ryan at one point.

He'd wondered that himself. Manny shouldn't have been far behind him, but he hadn't seen him. Worry nudged him in the gut. "I don't know." He shrugged, trying to sound casual. "Thought he'd be here by now."

Sera and Ryan separated for periods of time, each of them recording whatever incriminating conversations they could, while the party got wilder, louder and lewder. The girls who'd shown skin to win in the wet T-shirt contest elected to keep their shirts off, partying topless, and some of the bikers were not only enjoying the show but were pulling the girls onto their laps and burying their faces between bare tits. Then two of the girls climbed up onto a table and danced. At the hoots of encouragement, they began an impromptu striptease, right down to nothing.

Ryan was finally ready to call it a night. It had been a long day of fresh air, hot, desert sunshine and a lot of beer, not to mention sex, drugs and rock and roll.

He steered Sera out of the bar with an arm around her waist, the feel of her slim, muscled body against his sending a reviving jolt through him. So much for fatigue. But they had to talk. Inside the room, Ryan closed and locked the door. They both switched off their recording devices, then he turned to her. "You wanna tell me what the fuck you were doing down there?"

She stood there, staring back at him. "What are you talking about?"

Her blue eyes shone like gems, her long lashes starbursts around them. She rubbed her bare upper arms.

"And what the hell is that tat?" he snarled, moving closer and grabbing one arm. He twisted it to reveal the image of St. Michael. "Why would you get that inked on your arm for the whole world to see, for Chrissake? You're an undercover agent! You might as well have 'cop' tattooed across your forehead!"

She yanked her arm away from him and her strength momentarily surprised him. "First of all, it's not a real tat. It's one of those new semi-permanent ones. Cost a freakin' fortune, but it'll wear off in a couple of months."

He scowled.

"Second, I know it's St. Michael, but nobody else is going to recognize it as the patron saint of cops."

"You don't think?" He frowned at her. "You better have a good story ready if anyone asks."

"I just liked the way it looks. That's all."

He rolled his eyes. "Riiiiight. Okay. So back to the joint you smoked earlier."

"I didn't smoke that joint! Are you insane?" Her voice rose. "Do you really think I'm that stupid?"

He took a mental step back.

"I don't think you're stupid," he said carefully. "I just think you're inexperienced and you might not know—"

"Oh, for the sweet love of god!" She raised both her hands to her hair, threaded through the strands and yanked. She closed her eyes and swallowed a scream. "I'm sick of you saying that!"

"Sssh." He tipped his head to indicate that the walls were likely thin between rooms.

She ground her teeth. "I know I'm inexperienced but give me some credit here!" She kept her voice low. "I'm not an idiot. I know I can't do drugs. I totally faked smoking it. Nobody noticed."

The tension vibrating in her body, the flush of anger in her cheeks and the spark in her eyes had the unintentional effect of turning him on. Hard. Fast.

His body roared to life like the engine of his Harley, full throttle. His jeans became uncomfortably tight and he turned away from her before she noticed. He stood at the dresser, clenched his jaw as he stared at the dark wood, hotel pamphlets stacked in a holder on one corner.

"You're not my boss, you know," she continued. "We're partners."

"You have no experience."

"We're still partners. I may be inexperienced, but we're equals and you don't get to mack on me for nothing. We can't work together if you think that little of me," she said, sounding calmer. "Seriously, Ryan."

"You can't bail now."

Silence. He wanted to turn and look at her, to try to read the expression on her face, in her eyes. But his hard-on pulsed uncomfortably. Then he heard her move, felt her warmth and she grabbed hold of his arm and yanked him around to face her.

"Look at me when I'm talking to you, at least," she ground out. She was so close to him, if she shifted an inch forward she was going to know how happy he was to see her. He kept his eyes on her face, hoping hers would stay there too. "Don't you want to know what I got tonight?"

He stared at her mouth, the way it moved when she formed the words, the sexy lift of the corners, the touch of her tongue on her bottom lip. He felt as if he were drowning, a roaring in his ears, a helpless, sinking feeling.

He realized she was waiting for him to say something and he had no idea what she'd just asked him. Oh man. He was over his head, sinking fast. Her eyes darkened then, her lips parted invitingly and her breath quickened.

"Fuck," he muttered, fisting a handful of her hair and yanking her against him. She gasped, and he knew his erection pressed into her softness. "Let's just get this over with."

He held her head in place by her hair and lowered his mouth to hers, covering hers in a scorching, mind-numbing kiss.

Shock and arousal curled her toes. Need and lust slammed into her.

This was a monumentally bad idea, but the sweetness of Ryan's mouth on hers, the pleasure-pain of his hand pulling her hair, weakened her legs, weakened her resolve. It was true—resistance was futile.

She opened her mouth and kissed him back. His tongue licked over her mouth and she moaned. He tasted yeasty-sweet like beer, his tongue hot and wet and invading. She clung to his wide shoulders as he bent her backward, kissing her with driving, eating kisses.

Electricity sizzled down her body. He thrust a big thigh between hers and she arched her pelvis into him, needing that pressure there, right there...oh sweet, sweet baby Jesus. She pressed her aching breasts to his hard chest, grabbed hold of his ponytail and yanked on his hair like he was on hers.

"Fuck," he gasped, nipping her bottom lip then kissing her again. She found the elastic that held his hair, tugged it off so his hair fell loose, and slid her hands into it. Silky and cool, the strands tangled around her fingers.

They ground against each other, mouths, chests, groins. She was almost riding his thigh, higher, harder, desperate, aching with a sharp need. "Oh god," she gasped, letting her head fall back as he tugged harder at her hair, pulling her head back, exposing her throat to his hot mouth. He kissed, sucked, licked his way down to her collarbone exposed by the low, round neck of her tank top. One hand disentangled from her hair and covered a breast, squeezing, and she cried out in pleasure. Flames licked at her body as lust flared like an inferno inside her.

"Tell me it's just an act," he muttered against her throat, his words vibrating against her skin.

She moaned again, unable to deny the very real hunger that mounted inside her, pushing her harder against him, rolling her pelvis against his hard thigh.

"It's not an act," she whispered. "It's not. But..."

"I know. God, I know." The husky low tone of his voice stroked over like a touch, igniting more flames, singeing every nerve ending.

"We shouldn't..."

"I know." His hand slid under the tank top to cup her breast over her bra and she swelled into his palm, achy, needy. She wrenched away from him, yanked the top over her head and stood there in her black lace bra, chest heaving.

He pulled the lacy cups of her bra down to reveal her nipples, and the cool air and his hot gaze on them puckered them into tight, tingling points. She wanted his mouth there and whimpered, closing her eyes. Then she felt it—warm, wet, sucking as he took her in, first one tight nipple then the other, sending flames shooting through her from nipple to between her legs as hot, liquid want flowed in her pussy in a desperate ache.

She was so close to coming, grinding herself against him, seeking that pinnacle of ecstasy, almost there...and a pounding on the door echoed the rhythm of her heartbeat in her ears. At first she ignored it, arching her back so he could take her breasts again, but he muttered, "Shit."

And he stepped away from her. Blinking, she found her balance as he released the hold he had on her. She raised a shaky hand to shove the tangled mop of her hair back off her face. She stared at him wordlessly, mind a blank. What...?

"Whoever it is, I'll kill them," Ryan muttered, raking his own hair back. Long and loose, it brushed his shoulders, and he looked so insanely dangerous and sexy, Sera's legs almost buckled again.

Struggling for air, she yanked her bra in place and her top back as Ryan strode to the door. There, he paused, glanced back at her to make sure she was decent, and she gave him a short nod as he set his eye to the peephole. He groaned, then released the chain and yanked open the door.

Manny strode in, bald head and both earrings gleaming in the faint lamp light.

Sera quivered from head to toe, pressed her lips together. Manny seemed oblivious.

"What the hell do you want?" Ryan growled rudely.

"I don't have a room." Manny threw himself down into an armchair.

"What?" Ryan stared at him, a hand to the back of his head. Sera's eyes dropped to his jeans, to the obvious bulge, and she pressed her own thighs together. She'd been so close to coming, if she squeezed hard enough she could probably send herself over. She laid a hand on her stomach and struggled for control.

"I don't have a room, man. Gonna have to bunk here tonight."

Ryan lifted his eyes and met Sera's.

She could only stare back at him, mesmerized by the heat and lust she saw there, knowing it reflected her own. She swayed a bit, reached behind her for the dresser to steady herself. She took in a long, deep breath.

It was just as well. They'd been on their way to having hot, animal sex and that would be such a bad idea. God, words couldn't even express how epically inappropriate that would be. Except...like Ryan had said...maybe they just needed to get it over with.

Tension was a part of their jobs. Every minute, with violence and sex surrounding them, they were on edge, putting on an act, hyperaware of everything going on around them. It was only natural that it would get to them, and maybe they did just need to take the edge off, to let loose with a screaming, toe-curling orgasm. Or two.

Or not. What was she thinking? Sex wasn't going to relieve any tension, it would just create more. Just what they *didn't* need.

Manny slumped in his seat and Ryan stood there looking hot as hell, and frustrated. "Isn't there another room?" he demanded.

"Nah. Hotel's booked. I had engine trouble on the way here. Don't even ask." His scowl put a halt to questions about that topic. "So I got here late and they fucking gave my room away." He blew out a breath. "Don't worry. I can sleep in the chair. You two..." For the first time he appeared to notice the one bed in the room. "Uh...you two...can take the...uh...bed."

His eyes flicked back and forth between them and awareness flared. "Oh...uh..."

Ryan closed his eyes and shook his head. "Fine. No problem. You take the goddamn chair."

"Uh..." Manny looked at the carpet. "I could...uh..."

"Never mind." Sera spoke, stepped forward, hoping her top looked decent. "We all need a good night's sleep. There are lots of pillows." She jerked her chin at the bed. "You take the spread and a pillow and sleep on the floor, Manny. You can't get a good night's sleep in the chair."

He nodded, heaved his big body out of the chair, and between the three of them they created a makeshift bed on the floor in the corner. Sera retreated into the bathroom, carefully closing the door tightly behind her. She sank down onto the toilet and buried her face in her hands.

Dear lord, she'd been so close to coming all over Ryan's leg and he hadn't seemed to mind one bit, encouraging her, sucking at her nipples until she was ready to go up in flames. And she still had to share a bed with him, but now...there was someone else in the room with them.

Good. Or bad. She lifted her head, stared at her reflection in the mirror that covered one wall. Good heavens. Her hair tangled in a dark cloud around her face, mascara smudged beneath her eyes and her swollen lips all combined to give her a sexy, trashy look. She licked her lips. Swallowed. Her breasts ached, nipples tingled and her pussy clenched hard, drawing up. She pressed her hands to her breasts. She needed an orgasm like she needed oxygen.

She washed her face, body still quivery with need, brushed the tangles out of her hair and changed into the pajamas she'd packed. Long pants in striped candy colors with a drawstring waist and a pink T-shirt. They'd seemed safe enough, but now she knew a suit of armor wasn't enough to keep her safe from Ryan. Or rather, to keep her safe from her own lustful hunger. Or maybe both. Because his hunger had certainly seemed to match her own, degree for burning hot degree.

She emerged from the bathroom and left the light on. "Next."

Ryan passed her, eyes snagging hers and holding them, still hot. She melted into her pajama pants and slid under the covers of the bed in a puddle of trembling, simmering desire.

She heard Manny's breathing across the room, the water running in the bathroom. Then light sliced the darkness as Ryan opened the door. He turned out the light, and in the inky darkness she felt the bed shift as Ryan climbed in.

They lay there, side by side, not touching, Sera staring up into the obscurity, still quivering with need. Then Ryan shifted under the covers, turned on his side and laid his hand on her stomach. The muscles there leaped at his touch and heat radiated from his palm over her body. She tried to push him away, but his mouth, right at her ear, whispered, "Don't."

She trembled, silent, knowing in the heavy quiet Manny could hear everything— even a whisper. Ryan's hand slipped under the T-shirt to bare skin, caressing her stomach. She shivered. His breath was a warm rasp in her ear. Then his fingers dipped lower, under the drawstring of her loose pants, tickled through the patch of curls above her mound, probed between her thighs.

She tightened her thigh muscles on his hand, and she felt his head move on the pillow beside hers as if he was shaking his head no. "Open," he breathed.

Sweet god in heaven. She needed to be touched there so bad it hurt. She ached with the need to orgasm. And her thighs parted. Ryan's fingers stroked through sensitive, swollen folds, finding her wetness, sliding easily through the silky moisture. She trembled more, and when he brushed over her clit, she jumped at the jolt of sensation. She swallowed a noise.

He dipped slowly into her liquid center, then back up to her clit, brushing over the hard nub, sending exquisite sensations shimmering down her legs. Weakened, they fell apart even farther, giving him wicked access to her most intimate region. He stroked and rubbed, sensation building, tightening. Sera squeezed her eyes closed, arched her neck, lifted her pelvis into his hand. Her breathing quickened, her lungs tightened, and she struggled to keep quiet, her heart racing. Her hands fisted in the sheet, and then pleasure streaked from Ryan's fingers to every nerve ending, exploding in tiny bursts of fiery sensation.

She grabbed his arm, his strong forearm and wrist, and held on until the pulsating slowed and stopped, his hand pressed over her pussy, absorbing the waves of her orgasm. God, she wanted to cry out, noises backing up in her throat, almost choking her. She turned her face toward him, and pressed it into the side of his neck, all warm and delicious smelling. She inhaled long, slow and quiet, knowing Manny probably had heard every quickened breath, every swallowed gasp.

Ryan drew his hand back up to her abdomen and rested it there, warm and damp and heavy. When her breathing had slowed to more normal, he slid his arm across her stomach, curled his fingers around her waist and pulled her closer into his body. Heat poured off him, and she felt his heart pounding too.

"Sleep." The whispered word teased her ear, and she relaxed against him, knowing she shouldn't, but drowsy languor stole over her, softening muscles and bones.

Chapter Eight

"I got tons of good surveillance stuff," Sera said, slicing through her room-service muffin the next morning. "I'm going to get Zocco to introduce me to Casas, and Carly thinks I can offer to sell some of his angel sugar in L.A. They'll want their cut—they'll likely be only too happy to have one more addict offering to sell the stuff, knowing I'll be using it myself and needing to support the habit. That stuff is so highly addictive they're going to know I'm addicted soon."

Ryan frowned.

"So I'm one step closer to finding out if he's the one running the lab. And wait till you hear all the stuff I got," she continued excitedly. "What were you doing all night?"

"Vince wants me to do some deliveries for him. Starting next week. Along with my motorcycle parts."

She gazed wide-eyed at Ryan across the small table. "Really? Oh wow! That's amazing."

"Yeah. Unbelievable, actually."

She grinned. "So we both did good."

"Yeah. Sounds like." But he still scowled. She wanted to roll her eyes at him.

"Good work, guys," Manny said. "What's up for today?"

"I want to find Sam Cogan," Ryan said. He told them about the conversation with Vince and A.J. "I want to know what they wanted him to do."

Manny frowned. "That doesn't sound like a good idea. What if someone sees you talking to him?"

Ryan took a bite of his toast. "I'll play it by ear." He shrugged. "If I can find the guy and get him alone, fine. I'll judge if it's safe to talk to him or not."

Sera glanced between him and Manny and nibbled her bottom lip. It sounded risky. Ryan seemed almost pleased by that. And dammit, she could relate. Risk equaled adrenaline, and the bigger the risk, the bigger the high.

"Okay," she said. "I'm going to meet Casas today. That's my main goal."

"Great." Ryan glanced at his watch. "Everyone else will be sleeping for hours. Maybe I can find out if Cogan is staying here at the hotel."

He picked up the phone and called the front desk, then asked for Sam Cogan's room. After a pause, he quickly disconnected. "He's here," he said triumphantly. "Don't know his room number—yet—but if he's here, I'll find him."

"Be careful, Ryan." A shiver ran over her.

He shook his head briskly. "Who wants to shower first?"

After eating and showering, Ryan and Sera left Manny in the room and went down to the lobby to see what was happening. Things were still pretty quiet. No doubt a few people were tending hangovers.

As they passed the restaurant off the lobby, a man sitting at a table just inside the door grabbed her attention. She took a second look. Dominick Casas.

She clutched Ryan's arm. "Is that him?"

"Who?" His biceps flexed beneath her fingers. Enough to distract her for a fleeting second to admire his muscles.

"Dominick Casas. Right there at the table just inside the door."

Ryan looked over. "Yeah. That's him." A frown tugged his brows down. "How'd you know that?"

She shrugged, not meeting his eyes.

"I guess I can't just walk up to him and start talking to him," she murmured. "I'd better wait for Carly."

"I know him," Ryan said. "I met him with Vince. Let's go say hi."

She wanted to hold back, but knew that would only arouse Ryan's curiosity, so she went along with him as he strode into the restaurant and walked up to Casas' table. "Hey. Dominick."

The man looked up. His moustache and long beard hid most of

his face. Small, dark eyes peered out from beneath the bandanna he wore on his head. He looked at them blankly at first, then recognition surfaced and he smiled. "Tommy. How the hell are you?"

They exchanged small talk, Sera still hanging on Ryan's arm like the good little girlfriend she was—*not*. Then Ryan drew her forward. "Oh, this is my girlfriend, Sara."

Dominick laid his eyes on her. His eyes narrowed, his mouth drew in. Surely to god he couldn't recognize her. She wanted to turn and run. This had been a mistake.

"Sara. Nice to meetcha."

"Hi." She smiled, trying to look normal. Casual. Hoping Ryan couldn't feel the tremors in her body.

"Sara's working for me now," he told Dominick. "With my deliveries."

"Ah. Good. Nice little business you got going, I hear." His tone was patronizing. He had a pretentious air about him, as though he thought he was better than anyone else.

"You see Vince this morning?" Ryan asked.

"Not yet." Dominick's eyes were still fastened on Sera's face. Her fingers tightened on Ryan's arm. Her stomach muscles clenched.

Ryan laughed. "He was pretty shitfaced last night, so I guess he's still sleeping it off. We'll probably see you later."

With a nod he and Sera moved off, back out to the lobby.

"What the hell was that?" he muttered once they were well out of sight and earshot.

She shook her hair back. "No idea. He's a creep, though."

He studied her. And she knew he'd picked up on something. Damn his perceptiveness. Again.

The elevator doors opened, and they stepped in, alone, to go back to the room. Ryan turned and pushed her up against the wall, his body pressing hers. She gasped and turned her eyes up to his face.

"What aren't you telling me?" he ground out.

"N-nothing. Why are you asking that?"

"Dominick was looking at like he knows you. Do you know him?"

"No," she whispered.

"Are you sure? He was looking at you kind of weird."

"I don't know him. Other than what I've researched about him over the years."

He pinned her in place, and his big body pressing into hers felt way too good. He stared at her. "I don't believe you."

"You don't trust me, do you?" She lowered her eyes. "I thought we went through all this already."

The elevator doors slid open with a ping announcing their floor and he stepped back, releasing her. She stalked out ahead of him, chin pointed up. She could not tell him her fears about what had just happened.

In the room, Manny was just coming out of the shower. He walked out of the bathroom in his boxer shorts. Sera took in his muscular body. In his biker gear, Manny just looked big. Naked, he was ripped, with a six-pack of abs, slabs of pecs and bulging biceps. Sera blinked, bit her lip at the masculine display.

"Put some clothes on, for Chrissake," Ryan snarled at Manny, who shot him a look of puzzlement.

"I am, man, I am." He stepped into jeans, one muscled thigh at a time, unconcerned with Sera's presence, zipped his fly and adjusted himself. Ryan looked like he was going to blow a gasket and she almost laughed, despite the tension still quivering inside her.

When Manny was dressed, Ryan told Sera, "Stay here. Manny and I are going hunting."

"For...oh. For Sam Cogan?"

"Yeah."

She watched them leave with a crooked smile. "Do what I say, little girl," she muttered, moving around the room to pick up her things and stuff them into her bag. She occupied herself by packing so they'd be ready to go when they had to check out.

She looked at the bed and took a deep breath. She still couldn't believe what had happened between them last night. If Manny hadn't shown up, they probably would have had sex in that bed.

They'd *had* sex in that bed. Sort of. Eyes-rolling-back, heart-pounding, very one-sided sex. Heat shimmered in her and she pressed a hand to her abdomen.

When Ryan walked back into the room their gazes collided and slid away from each other.

Sera dropped her bag on the floor near the door. "Any luck?"

Ryan shook his head. "Nah. Not yet. We sweet-talked the girl at the front desk into giving us his room number, but he wasn't there."

"Maybe he left," Sera said.

"She would've told us if he'd checked out."

"Yeah." She could only imagine the girl at the reception desk responding to Manny and Ryan's bad-boy charm, and resisted the urge to roll her eyes. "Hey. Have you checked in on your mom?"

His eyes shadowed. "No."

"Wanna do that? While we're up here?"

He nodded and used his cell phone to call the hospital. She sat on the edge of the bed and listened to the short conversation he had, facing away from her as he looked out the window. She studied his back, the width of his shoulders, the strength in the muscles, her gaze tracking down his back to his ass, so tight and perfect in his jeans, then back up to the nape of his neck where his hair was tied. For some reason, the softness of his neck there looked so vulnerable, and as he spoke in low tones, asking questions about his mother's care, she swallowed through a tight throat.

When he ended the call, he turned to face her and she dropped her gaze to her knees. "How's she doing?" she asked.

"Okay. I mean, she's hanging in there." His jaw tightened. "They're increasing her pain medication."

"Oh." She hesitated, unsure what to say. "You wouldn't want her to be in pain."

He shook his head. "No. Of course not. But they're giving her really high doses now, which means…it's probably near the end."

Shit. She wiped her palms along her knees, her heart squeezing for him. "I'm sorry, Ryan."

He gave a short nod but said nothing, his eyes shuttered, his mouth tight.

"Well." She rose to her feet. "Come on, let's go. We've got work to do." Then she paused. "If you want to talk more about it...I'm here."

He gave her another terse nod, but she caught the softening of his mouth as he turned toward the door.

They all went back downstairs and this time found Vince and Carly and several others sitting by the pool eating breakfast. Sera and Ryan took seats and ordered coffee. Yeah, the guys looked rough today. Rough and mean. Sera's eyes shifted to Carly, very quiet this morning, and she frowned as she took in a faint discoloration on Carly's cheekbone. Was that a bruise? Shit.

Her stomach felt like it was falling. Lord, she hated to see things like that. She tried to keep her face expressionless as she studied her coffee.

Why did some women put up with that? It made no sense. If any man ever laid a hand on her, he'd be flat on his back on the floor.

She tried to feel her usual contempt for anyone who would put up with being treated like that, but somehow Carly only aroused feelings of protectiveness in her. She glanced at Vince and felt an urgent need to kick his ass. Anger vibrated through her.

"Hey, Dominick!" Vince stood up and held up a hand to the man paused at the edge of the patio. "Over here, man!"

They greeted each other and Sera watched, the tension inside her dialing up several notches. She sipped her coffee, hoping she wouldn't choke on it.

Dominick greeted the others and they pulled up a chair for him at the table. When his eyes fell on Sera, he paused. Then smiled lasciviously at her. Eeew.

Somehow she had to get things going. She wanted to spend as little time with Dominick as she could, but if he was attracted to her, she could make that work for her. Her stomach rolled at the thought and she fought it back. She had to talk to Zocco, and get him on board with her selling the sugar. And then he would get Dominick on side.

She would sell lots. She had to convince them that she would. She'd be a major player and then...she closed her eyes briefly, willed the pinwheels spinning in her stomach to settle down. It would work. It had to work.

But she couldn't seem too eager. Couldn't push too hard. This was absolutely critical to her success. This moment. This chance.

She looked at Ryan. He was watching her, amber eyes dark and steady. Steadying.

She licked her lips and turned to Carly.

"Did you say anything to Zocco?" she asked the other woman in a low voice.

Carly stared back at her blankly for a moment. "Oh. Yeah, I did." Carly tugged at Zocco's arm. He was talking to Dominick, and he tossed her hand off with a scowl.

"Hey, don't bug me."

Carly bit her lip, eyes flicking to Sera, who smiled reassuringly.

They both waited quietly as the men talked until finally Zocco turned to her. "What'd you want?" he asked.

Carly smiled at him. "Hey. Remember I was talking to you yesterday about the angel sugar?"

Zocco's eyes narrowed. "Not here," he bit out, eyes shifting around.

"Oh. Okay."

Sera sighed inwardly. Carly was nice, but not the spiciest taco. Again, she wanted to lean forward and step in, to save Carly from herself.

Zocco's eyes moved to Sera. "We can go talk inside. If you want."

"Yeah." She nodded, rose from her chair. She felt Ryan's gaze on her, sensed his desire to come with her. She smiled at him and put a hand on his shoulder as she passed behind his chair. "I'll be back in a few, Tommy."

He nodded and she followed Zocco into the hotel. He took a seat on one of the couches in the lobby. Nobody else was around except the hotel staff working the front desk, and they were too far away to hear anything.

"Carly says you want to sell sugar."

She nodded. "It's good stuff. I have lots of friends in L.A. who'd like it."

He studied her, a hint of suspicion tightening his face. "You know what you're doing?"

"Yeah." She met his eyes.

Again he was quiet. "How do I know if I should trust you?"

She frowned. "Why wouldn't you trust me?"

"Babe, anyone could be a cop."

"I bought stuff from you already."

"Yeah."

She shrugged. "So check me out. I got nothing to hide."

He nodded, stroking his chin.

"I'll talk to Dominick," he said finally. "See what he thinks."

Her insides shifted. Perfect.

"Okay." She smiled. "Great. Thanks, Zocco."

They returned to the group and Sera slid into her chair beside Ryan who was talking to Vince and Dominick. Sera remained quiet, in the background, like the other women at the table, although it irked her no end.

Soon, music started, loud and thumping, and the bar opened. Drinks flowed and the atmosphere became less mellow, more hardcore. Energy pulsed in Sera's body in response. People got up from tables, moving around to talk to others. She watched Zocco, hoping he'd talk to Dominick, as he moved from table to table to the bar. She felt Dominick's curious gaze on her too, her skin tingling under his intense scrutiny. She stuck close to Ryan, letting him put his hands on her, nuzzle her neck, acting all lover-like, hoping the sexual energy between the two of them would blur out whatever else it was Dominick sensed about her.

When Ryan leaned against the bar, spread his legs and pulled her between them close enough to feel his erection, she realized her strategy had backfired just a little as hot molten desire flowed through her belly down to the ache between her legs. They couldn't act like that around each other without getting turned on. She laid her hands on his chest, tipped her head back and met his eyes.

"Wanna make out?" he asked.

She choked on a laugh.

His eyes glinted and his hands slid over her ass, into the back pockets of her jeans, and rocked her closer. Oh yeah.

"Do you want to ride all the way back to Clover City with a hard-on?" she murmured.

Now it was his turn to laugh. He bent his head and kissed her mouth. "Smart ass."

It felt natural, sizzling hot yet comfortable, and she couldn't help but wonder how it would feel if Ryan was teasing her and looking at her like that because he really felt something for her. Something more than physical arousal layered over disdain for her lack of experience, and annoyance that she was even there.

She hitched a shoulder. "How's it going?"

"Good. You?"

"Dunno." They couldn't really say much. "What time are people going to leave?"

"I don't know." He looked around. The party seemed to be just getting started. He grimaced. "I don't like thinking of all these guys on the road on their bikes with a blood alcohol level high enough to breathe flames."

"I know."

They stuck around as long as they could but Zocco never approached Sera again and she didn't think he'd talked to Dominick either. Disappointment weighed heavy on her as she and Ryan mounted his Harley for the drive back to Clover City. She hadn't accomplished the one thing she'd set out to do that weekend.

Sure, she'd gotten hours of incriminating recordings. That was something. It just wasn't what her goal had been.

She hung on to Ryan as they roared along the highway, the desert flat and wide on either side of them, baked golden in the sun. Heat shimmered off the highway stretching out in front of them. She tried to clamp down on her jittering nerves.

When he dropped her off at her motel, he turned off the motorcycle. "I should come in," he said. "We need to talk about a few things."

"Sure."

Ryan coming into her motel room shouldn't have been any big deal—they'd just shared a hotel room, although Manny's presence had likely prevented them from getting naked together. It hadn't been enough to stop Ryan from giving her a spine-sizzling orgasm, though. What would happen when they were alone in her room?

She unlocked the door and pushed inside, the air quiet and flat after being closed up for two days. She flicked on the light and dropped her bag on the bed.

"You never found Sam Cogan."

He shook his head, frowning. "No, dammit." He shrugged. "Maybe he wouldn't have said anything anyway."

"What do you think they wanted him to do?"

He met her eyes. "I think they wanted him to kill someone."

She gave a short nod. "Any guesses who?"

He rubbed the back of his neck and sat down on the bed. "There are a couple of unsolved murders with ties to the DAs. Could have been one of those."

"But if they beat him up and kicked him out because he didn't do it, then he might not know who did."

"No. But if he told me who was killed, I could dig deeper and maybe find out."

"Ryan."

"What?"

"This isn't about solving murders."

"Sure it is. It's about whatever we can find. I know they're trafficking drugs and guns. We have lots of evidence of that. Enough for several arrests."

"You want more."

"I want enough to nail the DAs. Not just individuals within the gang, but the gang itself."

"RICO."

"Yes."

She nodded. Ryan blew out a breath. "Okay. We need to go back to L.A. tomorrow."

"Yeah."

"They'll think we're working. We can take off for a few days."

"Fine."

"When we come back, you're moving into the house with me. So, you can check out of here."

Her stomach clenched. "Okay."

That had been the plan. If things went okay and everyone seemed to be accepting her as Ryan's girlfriend, she would move into the house the ATF was renting. She would be living with Ryan, twenty-four seven.

"So," Ryan said. "Tell me why you were acting so weird around Dominick Casas."

"I wasn't."

"Yes, you were. You were almost...nervous."

"I was not!" She stood up straight and glared at him.

He shook his head. "I can't put my finger on it, but he was looking at you funny too." His brows lowered. "You're not setting us up, are you?"

Chapter Nine

"Whaaaat!" Her mouth fell open and she stared at him as if he'd just slapped her face. Her insides constricted. "Jesus Christ, Ryan. I know you don't totally trust me, but that is...that is..." Words failed her. She could not respond to such an egregious accusation. "You are such an asshole," she said, shaking her head. She stalked to the door and flung it open. "Get out."

He didn't move a muscle. Just looked at her with narrowed amber eyes.

"Get the fuck out," she spat at him. "I will not be insulted like that."

"It's not impossible," he said evenly. "It's happened before. Agents turn. Or maybe you've been connected with him the whole time, working your way up through the DEA for some purpose of your own. It wouldn't be the first time gang members infiltrated the police."

She just stared at him, her body rigid and quivering. She felt as if sharp blades stabbed inside her. Did he really think that? But she was tough. He could think what he wanted, but she knew the truth.

How she was going to convince him of that was another matter. She could tell him the whole story. And he'd think she was crazy. Or she could tell him part of the story.

But at that moment anger and hurt ricocheted through her and she didn't want to tell him a damn thing.

"I want you to leave," she said again, voice tight.

"Make me." He folded his arms across his chest and met her gaze squarely. "I want answers."

Oh, there's what she wanted. A reason to kick his ass. Oh yeah.

She marched over to him, grabbed his shirt and hauled him up off the bed. His eyes widened, hands flung out to the side as she almost pulled him off balance.

"Hey!"

"Make you?" she said through gritted teeth. "Did you just tell me to *make you*?"

"Uh...Sera, you're gonna hurt yourself..."

Still gripping his shirt, she whirled him around so his back was to the door, then gave him a shove. He stumbled back. She took one step back with her right leg, planted her left foot firmly onto the floor, and brought her knee up. With a sharp extension of her leg, she laid the ball of her foot into the center of his chest in a stop kick just as he made a move toward her.

Ryan landed hard on his ass. He lay on the floor, eyes closed and she stood there, breathing heavily, hands on hips, staring down at him. She sucked her bottom lip in. Shit. Had she hurt him? He wasn't moving.

Then his eyes opened and blinked. He looked a tad foggy.

"What the fuck was that?" he demanded hoarsely. He pushed up onto his elbows, looked around him. His forehead creased, and he bent his legs and struggled to his feet.

She stood in front of him, mouth firm, hoping she looked appropriately scary and confident. Her nerves shimmered with adrenaline.

"I said, get out."

"Oh no." He shook his head, rubbed his butt with one hand. "You're gonna pay for that, angel."

Ryan was ready to chew bullets and spit them out. There was no possible way she could have done that. But she had. That was gonna leave a bruise on his ass. A girl had just knocked him on his ass. Jesus. The humiliation stung more than his butt.

Clearly she'd just caught him by surprise.

"I can make you leave," she said. And he started to believe her.

"Okay, I'm sorry I said that." He didn't move toward her. Probably best to keep his distance until she calmed down a little. He eyed her arms. She had muscles, nice firm biceps and delts on slim, curvy arms that he'd noticed before as attractive when she bared them in a tank top, but...wow. Strong.

And her legs...also strong. She was in awesome shape. In more ways than one.

He swallowed, shoved a hand through his hair. The elastic holding his hair back had loosened and strands hung around his face. Much as he wanted to turn her over his lap and spank her cute, little ass for that, he knew he couldn't.

"I'm sorry," he said again. "Could we just talk about this?"

"Let's not." She glared at him, tipped her chin up. Her fiery combativeness intrigued him, goddammit. More than that, it fucking turned him on. He wanted to close his eyes against that realization. Oh man.

"All right. I'm sorry I said that. About you setting us up. That was out of line."

She continued to glare at him.

"That's what's going to happen, Sera. If you don't tell me everything. I'm going to wonder about it...worry about it...and consider the possibilities. That's my job."

Her body softened slightly. She blew out a long breath. "Yeah."

"You have to tell me."

Silence crackled between them. "Okay," she finally said. She waved at the chair in the corner. "Sit down."

She sat on the edge of the bed and he took a chair.

Her fingers twisted together and she looked down at them. "I'm sorry I kicked you," she said in a low voice. "I shouldn't have done that."

He gave a jerky nod, lifted a hand.

"When I was a teenager, my father left us."

He nodded. Waited.

She didn't look at him. "My mother started dating this guy. Snake. I guess...she fell in love with him. I don't really know. He was a prospect for the DAs. Into drugs. He used them. He sold them. He got my mom hooked on them."

Okay. It couldn't have been Dominick—the recognition didn't seem that strong.

"What's the connection?" he asked.

She frowned at him. "I'm getting there." She shoved her long, dark hair off her face. "Snake was a prospect for the DAs in Oakland at the time. Dominick's chapter. Dominick wasn't president then, but they were in the club together there. I met him once, when I was a kid."

"Where did you grow up?"

"San Francisco."

"Ah."

"Snake was..." She paused, rolled her lips in as she appeared to struggle with words. "He was an abusive, low-life criminal."

"Like many DAs." He was starting to see some things.

"Yes. And my mom, like many of the DAs women, put up with a lot because she loved Snake. Put up with a *lot.*"

Again, he nodded, not knowing the details but he could imagine a helluva lot, based on his experiences.

"My mom became addicted to meth. It was...awful. She needed it more than anything. She loved that drug, more than she loved me. She'd do anything to get it. Snake controlled her with it, got her to start...selling herself...for drugs."

"Jesus."

"And..." She lifted eyes dark with torment. "She was going to sell me."

Ryan surged to his feet, barely aware he had risen. He clenched his fists. "How old were you?" he demanded.

"I was fifteen."

"Jesus Christ. Did you...did she...?"

Sera shook her head, hair sliding in a silky fall over her shoulders. "She didn't do it, because I tried to commit suicide."

"Whaat?" He gazed at her, his heart a hard ball in his chest. "Oh fuck."

"I didn't succeed. Obviously. I took some of her stuff, tried to overdose."

"Oh, Sera." He stared at her.

"In many ways it was the best thing that could've happened. I ended up in the hospital and there was no hiding what was going on in my family. Social workers were all over me. I ended up in foster care."

"What about your brothers?"

She stared at him blankly. "My brothers?"

"You said you had brothers."

Huh? Then the fog cleared. "Oh! That first night we met!" She shook her head, unable to stop the small smile that tugged her lips. "I made that up. I don't really have any brothers."

He frowned. "Oh." He shook his head. "What about your father? Couldn't they locate him?"

"No. It was like he disappeared. At first my mom told me he was just gone for a while, that he'd be back." She twisted her fingers together. "I kept asking and asking when. And then one day she told me she'd talked to him and told him never to come back again. I didn't believe her. I thought if he'd come back, he would have come to see me. But he didn't. Or maybe..." She shrugged. "Maybe he did come back and she gave him the boot and he didn't bother trying to see me. I don't know, and it doesn't really matter."

Ryan wanted to curse again, but just shook his head, fists still clenched. He forced himself to relax his fingers.

"The foster home I ended up in first was...dysfunctional."

Ah hell. He could guess what that meant. The tightness in his chest intensified.

"The next one was better, but then I turned eighteen and I was on my own."

"How did you...Sera. To become a DEA agent...all on your own..."

"I was determined." Her small chin was firm, her mouth pressed together, her eyes steady. "I felt...you'll think this sounds crazy...I felt a calling. Like I had to do this."

He shook his head. "No. I understand."

"I thought about becoming a social worker. So I could help other people. But I..." She paused, swallowed hard. "I decided this was what I wanted to do." She lifted her gaze to his. "My mother died shortly after I was taken away from her. I've always held Dominick Casas partly responsible for that. He and his drug dealing have killed so many people, Ryan. He's one of the biggest players in northern California, and now with this new drug, targeting young girls...his influence and power are spreading."

"Yes." He processed everything she'd told him. "But why did Casas look like that at you? Did he recognize you?"

"I...don't think so. I think he just thought I...he was attracted to me."

"Fuck." He paused. "You sure that's it?"

"That's too hard to believe?"

"No! That's not what I meant." He growled. "I just want you to tell me everything."

She sighed. "I probably look a little like my mother. She was a few years older than I am now when he met her, but he may have thought I look familiar because of that."

"Shit." Anger flared in him, burning hot. "You could have jeopardized everything by doing that."

"He doesn't know who I am and he never will. I'm well backstopped."

"Shit happens. Christ, Sera. I can't believe you'd be so stupid. Take such a risk."

"Now I'm stupid." She pushed her hair back. "I knew you didn't think much of me, but in the space of a few minutes you've accused me of being a liar"—she stuck out her thumb—"a criminal"—her index finger poked out—"and stupid." She added another finger. "Thank you very much."

He could have growled in frustration. His nerves were on edge with tension and amplifying everything. "You're not stupid. But if he recognized you..."

She shrugged. "So what if he did? I was a kid, on the verge of

Hot Ride

getting into drugs and prostitution just like my mother. Why would it surprise him if I ended up the girlfriend of a gang member, selling drugs?"

True. "But then how do you explain the alias and the bogus background?"

She blinked at him. Kept her face carefully controlled, although he saw he'd scored a point with that one. Ryan rubbed his face. Sucked in a breath, let it out slowly. "Sera, if you're going to be part of this mission, you have to be a team player. You have to think about the big picture, about the entire operation. You can't just do your own thing. The consequences of your actions affect everyone, not just you."

She just sat there, hands in her lap. He waited for an apology that didn't come. Shit, she was stubborn. But now he understood better where she was coming from. Why she was so tough and independent. Why she was so determined to nail Casas and his lab.

"I'm sorry," she finally said, voice tiny.

He cleared his throat. "I'm sorry too. I shouldn't have accused you of setting us up." He moved to the bed beside her, the urge to pull her into his arms and comfort her almost overwhelming. "Thank you for telling me that."

She stood. "Don't get all mushy," she said. "I'm fine. I've made it this far. I can look after myself."

"Yeah. About that...you knocked me on my ass, Sera."

She rubbed her upper arms. "And I'll do it again if you don't watch it."

"Not likely, sweetheart. You might have caught me off guard once, but never again."

She smiled. "You'd like to think that. Remember, I know taekwondo."

"Right. Fourth degree black belt. But..."

"It's all in the technique. Anyway, now you know I can look after myself. With you. With anybody. Right?"

He studied her. Sure, she had the grace and lean muscles of an athlete, but still... "Right."

93

"Then we're good. I'll see you back in L.A. next week."

He continued watching her. He didn't want to leave. Didn't want to leave her. Which was completely crazy. Thank god she was moving into the house next week and he could keep an eye on her all the time. And yet, clearly she didn't think she needed any protection, any guidance.

Slowly he rose to his feet. "Okay. Yeah."

And he left her motel room with mixed-up emotions about Sera and her role in the operation and her surprising abilities. And her past.

Shit. She'd really had a crap life as a kid. Thinking about what had nearly happened to her made his guts twist into knots. And her suicide attempt... Christ.

In the past he'd always thought of suicide as cowardly. Maybe taking the easy way out. But when he thought of fifteen-year-old Sera being pimped out, knowing the kinds of things that could have been done to her—his stomach roiled to the point of nausea. She had to have been terrified, and maybe the option she'd tried to choose was better than what she could have faced. And clearly, she wasn't weak and cowardly. He'd like to say she was stupid rather than brave, but in all honesty he couldn't say that. Inexperienced, yes. And she was definitely strong, physically anyway. She may have gotten lucky, managing to get him off balance and then landing a kick dead center, but that wouldn't always happen. Even killer moves in martial arts couldn't protect her from everything, and she could get herself into serious trouble with a misplaced sense of confidence, with that damn streak of risk-taking he recognized only too well.

Hell. She kept saying she could look after herself and he was beginning to believe her but even so, even though she'd knocked him on his ass, he found himself feeling unaccountably and annoyingly protective toward Sera. Dammit.

Chapter Ten

"You guys are pissing away money."

Ryan glared at his SAC. "We have to."

Darren ran a hand through thinning hair. "Not that much money, for Chrissake. Now you want to buy stolen Harley parts?"

"We think these are the motorcycles that were stolen in Clover City. They're breaking them down into parts and selling them. This is probably only the tip of the iceberg."

"Let's just concentrate on one thing," Darren said. "You're losing focus."

Ryan scowled and glanced at Manny, slouched down in his seat, office lights gleaming on his head, slowly chewing his gum. Nothing ever bothered Manny.

Then he looked at Sera, who appeared a bit confused, brows drawn down, gaze moving back and forth between him and Darren.

"I thought we needed to get as much evidence as we could, about any criminal activity," she said.

Yay Sera.

Darren shot her a you-don't-know-what-the-hell-you're-talking-about look.

Waaaaait just a minute. Darren couldn't look at her that way.

"That's right," Josh said. "We've got guns—trafficking and possession—drugs, stolen motorcycles. Possibly interstate. Extortion. Assault."

"Possibly homicide," Ryan added.

"Homicide!" The word exploded out of Darren's mouth.

Ryan sent a sidelong look at Sera. "Not for sure on that one."

Manny nodded.

"And we're damn close on RICO. Come on, Darren. It's worth it to spend a few bucks. The arrests we're going to make…"

Darren sighed. "Fine. But this can't go on forever. And no cowboy stuff." He frowned sternly at Ryan. "You follow the rules. Hear me?"

"I hear you." But he wasn't listening.

Rules were made to be bent, as far as Ryan was concerned. Which caused a large part of the friction between him and his SAC. Would Darren's retirement ever come? Not likely before the end of this op.

When the meeting ended, Ryan, Manny and Sera retreated to offices to work on the paperwork. There were tons of surveillance reports to write, tape transcripts to verify, timesheets to do after the weekend they'd had. Josh, too, typed madly with two fingers on a keyboard at a desk.

"You didn't say anything about the angel sugar lab," Sera said quietly to Ryan, below the clicking of keyboards and the warbling of telephones.

He didn't even look up from the computer at her. "That's because that's not part of this op."

She slapped a hand down on the desk and his ass lifted off the chair, head jerking up. "Yes, it is part of this op," she said through clenched teeth, leaning down to him. "That is my goal—the DEA goal—and we're helping you with your goal. Remember? Remember the lecture about being a team player?"

"Uh…" Shit. She was right.

"We could be getting close to busting the biggest drug lab in California!"

"He calmed down, so don't worry." Ryan resumed typing. "Next time, we'll use that to convince him to keep going."

"Next time?"

He met her eyes. "Yeah. You don't know Darren. He's always threatening to pull the plug. Hates it when things don't go perfect. And you'd think we were spending his personal money."

She blew out a breath. "Great."

"Do your reports."

Hot Ride

She retreated to another desk and began typing. He watched her fingers fly on the keys. She'd be done in an hour and he'd be there all week. He scowled.

He wanted to finish so he could get to the hospital and see his mom. He'd called as soon as he was back at his L.A. apartment. She was holding on, but still not expected to last much longer. He had to get there to see her. That familiar guilt settled on his shoulders like a weight once again. He'd been playing all weekend, drinking beer, having fun—sort of—playing at working. He knew what he did was important, but sometimes he regretted the things he had to give up for his career.

He pounded the keys, watched in frustration as Sera walked to the printer, tapped papers together and signed her name. She glanced his way as she left with a wave.

Damn, he should have taken that keyboarding class years ago.

Sera felt a swell of relief at walking into her apartment. Her own space where she didn't have to pretend to be someone she wasn't, didn't have to be on guard, on edge every second of every minute, trying to think three steps ahead of where they were. And didn't have Ryan tormenting her every way he could.

She tossed her bag onto her neatly made bed then sank down to sit there. Blew out a long breath. She shouldn't have kicked Ryan like that. Sometimes her physical strength made her forget that it was really better to use her brains rather than brawn. But he just pushed her buttons, over and over again. Like that talk about being a team player.

Okay, she wasn't used to being part of a team. But she could do it.

And then she'd confided to him about her grievously messed up childhood. She sighed and ran a hand through her hair. Well, he might know details about her background that few people did, but they were only coworkers on a case, doing a job. That was it.

She needed to get to the gym for a workout, but first she had to do laundry, pick up a few groceries so she had something to eat for dinner, and pack again for her trip back to Clover City. This time she'd be gone for longer. More time with Ryan.

Stomach tight, she emptied her bag and sorted through it. As she dumped clothing into the laundry basket, her door buzzer sounded.

Damn. She was so happy to be alone for a little while, just herself at home, she didn't need someone bugging her.

She looked through the peephole and saw Leo standing there. She sagged against the wall for a moment. He just didn't give up. Then she straightened and opened the door.

He stood there with a bundle of newspapers in one arm and a few envelopes in the other hand.

"Your mail." He handed her the envelopes and she automatically took them.

"I didn't ask you to do that."

"I know. I just did it."

They stood there looking at each other then Sera shook her head. "Come in." She stood aside and he walked into her apartment.

"It was just the weekend newspapers," he said. "And one day of mail. But I thought I'd just grab it and keep it for you."

"Thank you."

"How's work going?"

"Fine. I...I'll be going away again. Later this week."

"They have you traveling?"

"Sort of."

"I guess you can't say much."

"No."

"Will you be gone long?"

"I don't actually know." She walked over to her kitchen table and dropped the letters there. Leo followed and laid the newspapers down.

"I'll get your mail again," he offered. "And if you gave me a key, I could come in and water your plants."

"If you did, that'd be more than I do for them."

A smile flickered on his face as he took in the wilted philodendrons and dieffenbachia. "Yeah, it looks like they could use some lovin'."

Sera repressed her smile. "I don't have time to look after plants."

"What *do* you have time for?"

She tipped her head to the side.

"I just mean, what other things are you interested in? What do you do when you're not working?"

"All I do is work."

"That's not a life, Sera. You should have a boyfriend."

As if. That was the last thing she needed.

"You're twenty-eight years old. Beautiful. Smart. You should be going out, dancing, having fun..."

"Dancing?" She lifted a brow.

He shrugged. "I don't know. Whatever kids do these days."

"Kids." She couldn't help the laugh that pushed out of her. "I'm not a kid."

He smiled too and her heart softened. "I know, but you're young compared to me. You should have someone to do fun things with."

"I don't need anyone."

"Everyone needs someone. You can't go through your whole life alone."

And yet, *he* was often alone. Her heart ached a little at that. She should call him on it, but...she couldn't. Not if he was really lonely.

"Sure I can," she said lightly. "I've done it till now, and I'm doing fine." His eyes shadowed. She pasted on a smile. "Don't worry about me, Leo. I'm good."

He gave a short nod. "Sure. Well, I'll be going."

When he'd gone, she locked the door and slumped against it. Why did he arouse such confused feelings in her? He was just a neighbor, someone she barely knew. He was lonely and she kind of felt sorry for him, but she wished he would just give up on this crazy idea that they should get to know each other. She gnawed on her bottom lip as she went to get her laundry.

Later, after she'd worked out at the gym, returned home and eaten her dinner—roasted chicken and coleslaw from the supermarket deli—and taken her laundry from the washer and shoved it in the dryer, she decided to have a bath. A long soak in the tub would be wonderfully relaxing.

But as she lay there submerged in warmth, steam curling around her face, an overwhelming wave of...something...swept over her. Her throat tightened and she slid lower in the water, letting its heavy warmth embrace her. Was she feeling depressed? That was crazy. Sad? What did she have to be sad about?

And then she realized what she was feeling was—lonely.

Chapter Eleven

Sera pulled up in the driveway of the small bungalow in Clover City. She'd been there before with Ryan and Manny, but she was about to move in. A couple of Harleys were parked in front.

She left her things in the car—an old Camaro owned by the ATF but currently registered to Sara Lambert—and walked into the house.

Ryan, Manny, Vince and A.J. sat in the living room on the cheap beige furniture hastily purchased by the ATF, the fake wood coffee table strewn with half-eaten bags of chips and empty beer bottles. WWE Raw blasted on the television.

Ryan looked up as she walked in. The smile that broke over his face seemed so reflexive, so genuine, it made Sera go warm inside. "Hey, babe," he said, rising to his feet and sauntering over to her. He threw an arm around her neck and pulled her against him for a kiss. Heat sparked and sizzled over her body as his lips met hers. "You're here."

"I'm here." She smiled up at him. "My stuff's in the car."

She realized her mistake when his eyes flashed.

"I'll go get it in a minute," she added, realizing that Ryan could not make a gentlemanly offer to get it for her. "Hi, guys."

They all greeted her, barely taking their eyes off the television. She lifted her brows at Ryan. He grinned. "We're watching Raw."

"Ah."

He pulled her over to the chair he'd been sitting in and sat, tugging her onto his lap. She tensed momentarily then softened into his embrace, dropping her purse to the carpet between the chair and the couch. He settled her comfortably onto his big solid thighs, one arm wrapped around her. The other hand reached for his beer and he raised it to his lips.

"This'll be done in a minute," he murmured to her.

It was the weirdest thing, but she felt like she'd just come home.

She watched along with them, trying to relax, although the feeling of Ryan's hard thighs beneath her own sent shivers through her. The guys all cheered and made comments on the fight they watched, some of which made her smile. Manny lifted an empty bottle. "Another beer, here."

Sera sat there. Then...oh hell! He expected *her* to serve them. She lowered her chin. Ryan helped her off his lap with a smack on her butt.

"Me too," the others added. Sera smiled sweetly as she strode into the kitchen, seething inside, then returned with several bottles clasped in her hands. Ryan took one from her.

"Thanks, babe," he said with a wide smile, and she resisted the urge to pour it on his head as she handed it to him. When she'd served the others, she picked up the remaining bottle, popped the top and drank thirstily, the fizzy lager tickling her nose and mouth.

Ryan patted his knee, and holding his gaze unsmilingly, she sat down again stiffly. He shifted her on his lap. She resisted but then couldn't help but soften and relax into him.

When the match ended, Ryan lifted her off him and stood up. "Come on, I'll help you bring your things in."

"Okay."

They went outside and she popped the trunk. This time she had two suitcases, one large, one small. Not knowing how long she'd be there, she'd packed enough for a couple of weeks. They'd likely have some time off before then, but it had to look like she was moving in for good.

Ryan heaved the large suitcase out easily and slammed the trunk shut. "Remember. The house is wired to the max. Everything we do and say is captured."

"I know. How's it going?"

"Good. Did my first job for Vince today."

She met his eyes and they exchanged a wordless message. "That went okay?"

"Went perfect." A smile curved his lips. "Come on."

When they walked into the living room, Sera stopped short at the sight of A.J. going through her purse. "Hey."

He looked up. Didn't even look guilty or apologetic.

"What are you doing?" she demanded, walking toward him.

He rifled through her wallet, scanning everything in there. "Checking you out."

She stood in front of him, hands on hips. "Why?"

He shrugged, closed the wallet. "Just because."

It amazed Sera how fast thoughts could fly through your head. In the space of seconds, Sera considered how she—or rather how Sara—should react to this invasion. She wasn't a passive mouse like Carly.

"You got questions for me? Just ask." She cocked her hip aggressively. "I have nothing to hide."

A.J. tossed the wallet onto the coffee table among potato chip bags and beer bottles, then dug around in her purse. He pulled out her cell phone.

"What's this?"

"A cell phone, moron." She scowled at him. Inside, she tensed. Outside, she maintained her pissed-off attitude. The recorder was carefully hidden in the phone, but still...

He opened it and started thumbing through her contacts. She sent a glance Ryan's way. He was frowning too, and she sensed the tension tightening his body. She willed herself to relax. Everything was cool.

"Who's Cheryl?"

"A friend."

"She who you gonna sell the sugar to?"

She lifted her chin. "Maybe. One of them."

He kept clicking through. "Jack?" A.J. looked at Ryan and smirked. "Old boyfriend?"

"Yeah. So?"

"Let's call him. See how he's doing." He pressed a button. Sera sensed Ryan's increasing anxiety. She knew A.J. could call anyone on that list and he'd get a voice mail recorded to match the name and number, carefully planned by the DEA. But still...she had to protest.

"Don't call him, you idiot." She looked at Ryan as if worried about his reaction.

"Call him," Ryan drawled. "I'll talk to the asshole."

"You don't even know him," Sera snapped. "Come on, you guys, this is so juvenile." But A.J. snapped the phone shut after getting the recorded message from "Jack".

"Give me the phone." She held out her hand. A.J. shoved it back into her purse and tossed the purse to her. She caught it. "Stay out of my stuff," she snapped and stalked into the bedroom.

"Hey, man," she heard Ryan say. "You pissed her off. Thanks a lot."

"You worried you ain't gonna get any tonight?"

"Hell yeah. I'm going to talk to her."

"We'll just watch more rasslin'."

Ryan came into the bedroom and shut the door behind him. "Okay?" he asked quietly.

She nodded, breathing a little fast, pulse skittering. Even though she knew they couldn't tell the phone was a recorder unless they actually took it apart, even though she knew every number in there was planned and covered, including a number for Uncle Bill, which was for her emergency use, she couldn't help but be a little nervous when A.J. had started playing with the device.

"Who's Jack?" Ryan asked.

Sera laughed. It released all the tension from her body and she sank down onto the bed. "All those numbers are made up. They're all DEA numbers, with recorded messages. Jack is actually Ward Tanner. My SAC."

Ryan's slow grin spread across his face. "I should have known."

"Yeah. There's nothing in there they could find that would hurt us."

He shook his head and his intense focus on her started to make her feel warm. "You handled that well."

She stared at him. "Thank you." The admiration in his eyes sent shivers through her, hot and sparkly.

"Sorry they're here your first night."

She shrugged. "Makes no difference to me."

"Get used to it. They tend to drop in pretty much any time."

She nodded. "Which means we need to be ready."

"Yes."

Their eyes met and held. "So I guess I bring my stuff in here."

The house had two bedrooms, one for Manny and one for Ryan.

"Yeah. But I'll sleep on the couch."

"What if...they drop by early one morning?"

"Not likely. But if they do, I'll tell them we had a fight and you kicked me out of bed."

She laughed. "Okay. Except—you probably won't be too comfortable on the couch. I could sleep there."

"Nah, it's okay."

Heat rose as they continued to look at each other. Sera sighed inwardly. She hadn't even been there half an hour and it was starting already.

"How's your mom?"

His eyes widened fractionally. "Still hanging on. Barely." He paused. "Thanks for asking."

"It must be hard staying focused with that going on in your life."

He made a face. "I can handle it."

"I know you can. The offer still stands—if you want to talk."

"You don't seem like the touchy-feely, compassionate type."

She dropped her gaze. "I'm not."

"Huh." He took a step toward her in the small room. "Maybe you are more than you think."

She snorted. "I need to unpack."

"I'll get your stuff."

When they went back out to the living room, the guys were standing up and getting ready to leave. "We're going to The Patch," A.J. said. "Coming?"

"Nah. Not tonight."

A.J. sent him a knowing leer, and Sera almost rolled her eyes. Men. But they could go with that. She slipped her arms around Ryan's waist. Damn. It felt good, warm and strong, and she leaned into him. They waited till the others left, Manny with them, and they were alone, and then she stepped away from him.

"We could've gone to The Patch," she said.

He gazed at her. "I got enough for today."

"Okay. So what's up tomorrow?"

"Another delivery for Vince. And he wants me to pick up those motorcycle parts."

"I'll come with you."

"No."

She frowned and set her hands on her hips. "That's what I'm here for."

"Not the motorcycle parts. I'm going to some chop shop just outside town. I don't know what I'm walking into."

"What difference does that make? We're partners, remember?"

He shook his head, and folded his arms across his chest, biceps bulging out from the short sleeves of his T-shirt. "Not going to happen."

"Did I not show you the other day I can take care of myself?"

They faced each other, tension shimmering between them. Ryan's face was implacable. Sera stared him down. "Don't make me hurt you," she warned him.

He laughed. "Bring it on," he said, eyes gleaming.

Her breath quickened, and her heart picked up a faster rhythm. This verbal sparring heightened her energy, adrenaline coursing through her. She wanted to put up her fists and take him on physically as well. She needed the release of physical activity.

She did clench her fists, bounced a little on the balls of her feet.

His eyes widened, and he, too, tensed. She lifted her leg in a lightning-fast roundhouse kick, not even as hard as she could have because she was sure she was going to hurt him, but he lifted a leg too, grabbed an arm and spun her around so fast the breath whooshed out of her.

They ended up tangled in a sweaty, panting knot on the floor, their faces only inches away from each other, his knee thrust between her legs, her hands captured in his. She stared at Ryan, noticing the flecks of gold and brown in his amber eyes, each long, dark eyelash, the fine lines fanning out from the corner of each eye, paler in his tanned skin. When her gaze lifted to his eyes, she saw he was focused intently on her mouth. Which made her mouth go soft and pouty, as if wanting to be kissed. Her lips parted. His eyes widened then grew heavy-lidded.

She looked at his mouth, so perfect, the full bottom lip, the curve of the upper lip, the shadow of stubble darkening his cheeks and jaw. Her mouth watered with the desire to taste him. The urge to close the distance between them swelled up almost uncontrollably in her, and his heavy eyes flickered as if he too felt that way. Suddenly, the urgent need to demonstrate her physical strength, to prove herself right to him, to show him she could in fact look after herself, faded into nothingness.

His body hardened even more against hers, his cock swelling and pushing insistently at her groin where they met. His fingers tightened on hers, and then he rolled her under him, her defense moves forgotten, so his heavy body pinned her to the floor. He released her hand and held her head, thumbs brushing the corners of her mouth, and her lips opened further. Turning her head just a fraction of an inch, she sucked one thumb inside and swirled her tongue over it. Ryan gasped.

"Hurt me," he invited her.

Oh dear god in heaven. Everything inside her went hot and soft and quivery. She didn't want to hurt him. But she *did* want to give him such intense pleasure he hovered on a knife-edge of pain. She vibrated against him, arched her pelvis into him, seeking, and he ground back against her. Pleasure poured over her at the feel of his hardness meeting her softness, and they moved against each other in a needy, desperate rhythm. She spread her legs, opened to bring him closer, their clothing a flimsy barrier between the lust surging through them. She nipped at his bottom lip.

"Fuck," he muttered. "You're going to make me come in my jeans."

"Me too." Her voice sounded husky in her own ears. She let out a long, low moan. "Oh god, me too. Ryan..."

"I know, baby, I know." He rocked against her. Electricity sparked through her bloodstream and she arched her spine to press aching breasts against his hard chest. "Is this what you want?"

She rolled her head back and forth on the hard floor. "What?"

"Is this what you want? Rolling around on the floor, getting off on each other. 'Cause we could move to the bed."

"Uh..." She didn't want to move, so much pleasure sizzled through her as she pressed into him. "Just...want...this..."

"You sure?" He bent his head and kissed her, his mouth hot on hers, opening over hers, pushing her mouth open wider. His tongue licked at her and flames streaked through her body, an inferno of lust exploding inside her. And she came. Arched off the floor, her pussy pressed against the hard ridge of his cock beneath his jeans, hard waves of bliss shuddered over her. She cried out and lifted her upper body off the floor, pressing her face to the side of his neck.

"Christ, Sera." He held her, kept the pressure where she needed it as she pulsed against him. Heat and light surrounded her.

"Oh sweet Jesus." As her quivering body relaxed and softened into the floor, torrid embarrassment heated her body and face. She gulped in air, swallowed hard. "I can't believe we did that."

He huffed out a laugh. "Believe it, baby."

And she realized he still throbbed against her, hot and hard. And once again, she'd gotten an orgasm and he hadn't. Tenderness suffused her and she drew her face away from the shelter of his warm neck and put her hand on his face. "Let's move to the bed."

"Thank Christ." He rolled off her in a flash, rose to his feet and hauled her up off the floor by her wrists. Then he all but dragged her down the short hall to the bedroom.

She was strong enough to resist him.

Okay. She was *physically* strong enough to resist him. Mentally, sexually, emotionally...that was a whole different tale. And she shook with fear at what that meant.

Irresistible. It was his fault for being so goddamn tempting. Enticing. Captivating.

It's not that she was weak. Helpless. Powerless. God, no. Never again.

Then what the hell was going on here?

Ryan's dick was about to burst out of his jeans. His balls ached, drawn up so tight he needed to reach for them and tug them down away from his body. Sera's feisty, sexy strength turned him on more than anything he'd ever known. His irritation at her independence and determination only added to the intense arousal.

Inside the bedroom he picked her up and tossed her onto the bed. She let out of soft cry of surprise as she bounced on the mattress. Then he was on her, over her, pressing her down, kissing her mouth with fiery desperation, lips, tongues, teeth connecting. He ate at her with fierce hunger, pressed his hard cock into her softness, warm and damp even through her jeans. She moaned, and her fingers slid into his hair, tugging it loose from the band that held it back. Christ, the sensations of her threading her fingers through his hair, tugging on the strands, scraping her nails across his scalp, sent a barrage of sparks zinging through his blood.

"You drive me crazy," he muttered against her jaw, and he licked her there then nipped. She moaned again. Then she moved under him, rolled and flipped him onto his back. Jesus.

She straddled him and looked down at him, hands on his chest, her hair a wild dark mane around her face and shoulders. He was used to being the one in control, the one on top. The alpha. Not that he minded her riding him like that. Not at all. She just had too many clothes on.

He reached for the hem of her T-shirt, slid his hands beneath it and found warm, soft flesh. The muscles of her stomach quivered under his fingertips. He lifted the shirt, and she cooperated—for once, thank Jesus—and raised her arms above her head so he could pull the shirt all the way off.

The sight of her body squeezed all the air out of his lungs and he went lightheaded. For such a no-nonsense, get-it-done, I-don't-need-anyone federal agent, she wore amazingly girly lingerie. The sheer ivory cups of her bra were embroidered with pastel pink and peach flowers, edged with lace and topped with tiny satin bows at the base of each strap. Her nipples played peek-a-boo with the embroidered flowers and he reached out to tug a fragile cup away to reveal her fully to him, filled with a desperate need to see her. Touch her. Taste her.

Her head fell back as he pulled the bra down and displayed her breasts, full, round, high, tipped with dark pink nipples tightly puckered into mouth-watering temptation. Heat slammed into his balls, his dick twitched hard and he brushed his fingertips over the tight tips of her breasts. She hissed out a breath, eyes closed, back arched, her fingers resting lightly on his abdomen.

"Holy hell, Sera, you're beautiful." His voice came out husky, worshipful.

She reached behind her and undid the clasp of the bra and it loosened. He hooked a finger into each strap and tugged it off. He wanted to toss it aside but first held the delicate scrap of silk and lace in both hands and just marveled at it. Her warm, feminine smell rose to his nostrils. God, if this was just her bra, what secrets did her panties hold?

He set the bra on the bedside table and reached for her again, flicked open the button of her low-rise jeans then tugged the short zipper down. She rose to her knees and helped him push the jeans down her hips. Once again his breathing stalled—uh, had he even started breathing again? He drank in the sight of her smooth hips and slender thighs, the tiny panties barely covering anything. They matched the bra, the same sheer, embroidered fabric a small triangle between her legs, tying in satin bows on each hip. He swallowed.

"Very pretty," he choked out, brushing fingertips over the lacy triangle. His fingers lingered over another tattoo there, a small set of angel wings. He blinked.

The warm scent of her arousal rose around them. He stroked lower and hell, yeah, her panties were damp. He heard her small gasp, felt the faint tremor run through her body as he touched her there.

Somehow they got her out of the jeans, and then he too needed desperately to get out of his clothes. He was burning hot, feverish, his black T-shirt damp, his jeans annoyingly uncooperative as he tried to drag them down over sweaty flesh. When Sera's hands covered his cock through his underwear, he almost came right then. His cock swelled, and need speared at his balls in sharp stabs. Her stroking hands sent sensation racing over his body. His skin tightened and heated.

"Nice," she murmured, then she tugged the elastic of the boxer briefs lower. She paused as she lowered them to look at his left hip. At the tattoo there. "What's this?" she murmured.

"St. Michael." His voice came out hoarse. She lifted her eyes to meet his. They gazed at each other for a long moment and he could tell she was as taken aback by their matching tattoos as he was.

Then she wriggled down the bed to drag them off, over thighs, knees, calves and feet. To his shock, she kissed and licked her way back up, laying gentle sucking kisses on his thighs, as tight as if he'd just run a 10K, and as she got closer, his fever intensified and his body tightened with anticipation. Then she took him in both hands, stroked his quivering cock, so hard and aching he felt he might burst. He dragged open his eyes to watch her, and the lust and admiration shining in her eyes threw him into a swirling cyclone of sensation. When her mouth closed over his dick, he let out a long groan, flopped his head back onto the pillow, eyes closed, and gave himself over to the exquisite bliss of her lips and tongue stroking over him, satiny licks and wet, heated suction.

He fisted the bedspread in his hands, made some noises that he would probably be embarrassed about later, and when her tongue licked over his balls, his hips lifted off the mattress.

"Sera!" he gasped. "Sera, stop."

She lifted her head, his cock still captured in her hands. "Why?"

"Because I'm so close...I'm gonna come...but I want to fuck you."

"Oh. Yeah." Her soft husky voice seeped into his head. She bent and laid a soft kiss to the head of his dick, making him twitch again, and then she slid her long, smooth body over his and kissed his mouth.

He turned his head to meet her mouth and they kissed, long, clinging kisses, drawing on each other, tongues sliding. Then he rolled her, pinning her to the bed on her back, moved over her. She opened her legs and he shoved aside the tiny strip of fabric and found her wetness, slick and burning hot. "Ah," he moaned. "Ah, Christ, Sera." He stretched across the bed to the bedside table, yanked open the drawer and fumbled inside for a condom.

"Good idea," she gasped. He rolled it onto his cock as fast as he could, fingers shaking, then returned to her sweet pussy. Fuck. He curved his fingers around the string of her thong panties and gave a yank. Her gasp mingled with the ripping sound of the fabric and he tugged the scrap away from her body then slid his fingers through her folds. He dipped lower, pushed gently inside her clinging warmth, then stroked up and around the hard, quivery knot of her clit. When he touched it gently, reverently with the tip of his index finger, she jerked against him and cried out. He swallowed her cry, taking her mouth again, and stroked her there, carefully, her body shaking. She seemed so sensitive, he didn't want to be rough or abrasive.

When he felt her body tightening against his, he stopped and she whimpered. "Want inside you, Sera," he whispered, and he found his throbbing cock and stroked it up and down her slit, wet and slippery, found her entrance and thrust inside her. She arched and cried out.

"Christ, you're tight. Okay, angel?"

She nodded and he looked at her face, flushed and shiny, teeth digging into her bottom lip, eyes closed. He pushed in farther, withdrew, pushed in again. Her hot, wet, velvet sheath squeezed him in a sublimely erotic caress and he knew he was going to come way too fast. "Fuck."

He found her clit again and rubbed it as he sank into her. She lifted against him, her hips moving in the same rhythm as his. Her hands clenched his shoulders. He spread his knees wide, got closer to her body, parting her thighs farther.

Hot Ride

"Damn, you feel good," he breathed, and then pressure built at the base of his spine, in his balls. Pleasure slammed through him, rocketing throughout his body. He again made low, guttural noises as he came inside her, gushing hot and hard into her body. She cried out too, wrapping her arms and legs around him, and Christ, her thighs were strong as she squeezed him with them. He *loved* that, and it sent him spiraling deeper as he thrust into her again and again.

They lay there, panting, chests heaving, hearts thudding, a sweaty tangle of limbs. He stroked her damp hair back off her forehead, kissed her cheek and she trailed her fingers up and down his sweat-slicked back.

"I just want to know," she said, fingers dragging along his back. "Why'd you have condoms here?"

He choked on a laugh. "Uh...good question. I guess I just like to be prepared."

"Hmmm." She continued to caress him and her fingers slid lower, to the curve of his ass. It felt so damn good. "We should not have done this."

"Probably not," he agreed. "But you have to admit, it was coming."

"Yeah." She let out a soft sigh. Then she smacked his ass and he jumped.

"Hey!" He lifted his head to look at her and she grinned at him.

"I still could take you," she said. Her eyes sparkled and her pretty mouth curved enticingly.

"I know," he said wholeheartedly. "Believe me...I know."

He lay there staring at the ceiling for a long time. He *was* the complete fuck-up Darren thought he was—he'd gone and done it again, gotten involved with someone on a case.

No. This was just sex. There was no emotional involvement. And nobody but the two of them needed to know about it.

Except...*shit!* The house was wired. It was entirely possible the whole world knew.

Chapter Twelve

Ryan was stubbornly adamant that Sera was not going with him on his delivery and pickup, so when Carly phoned to offer to pick her up and take her to their place for a swim in the afternoon, Sera accepted the invitation, figuring she could work on her own goal instead. Fine.

Carly made lemon drops and they sat beside the pool in the warm sunshine, sipping them. The blue water shifted and sparkled in the sun, and Sera pushed up her sunglasses on her nose. She stretched out her legs on the chaise lounge, and adjusted the top of her black bikini between her breasts.

Carly picked up a newspaper off the table and opened it. "What sign are you? I'll check your horoscope."

"Uh..." Sera didn't know enough about the signs of the zodiac to make something up. The birth date on her new driver's license was December—what sign would that be? "I don't know. I've never checked my horoscope."

"Really? I check mine every day. It's amazing how accurate it is. What's your birth date?"

Sera told her.

"Capricorn. Here's your horoscope for today... You should handle matters of the heart with care today, and don't allow your dreams to run away with you. The planets are suggesting that you may want to postpone any romantic interludes until tomorrow, when improved aspects breathe new life into romance!"

Pffft. Romance. Romantic interludes. "Hmm. Interesting. What's yours?"

"Today should be a big improvement on yesterday, with you back on form again. Romantic matters are likely to flourish today, whether you're single or attached, so even if you're still feeling the effects of yesterday's negativity be assured that someone will make you feel better by this evening." Carly looked up. "That sounds good. Vince was a little annoyed with me last night. He should be over it today?" She smiled.

Carly's habit of making every other sentence a question could get irritating. Sera lifted her drink. The tangy lemon played with her taste buds.

"Oh, here's Jessie! I invited her over too."

Jessie walked around the corner of the house. "Hey, y'all," she said with a wave. Her long, bleached-blonde hair gleamed in the bright sun, huge black sunglasses hiding most of her face. It was probably the first time Sera'd ever seen her sober.

"Hey, Jess. Come on and sit down. We're having lemon drops."

"Yum."

"How's your jewelry making going?" Sera asked Carly.

"Okay, I guess."

"I still think you could sell your work. It's really good."

"Thank you. But...I don't know. How would I do that?"

"In L.A. you could set something up on the beach and sell it, but I don't know Clover City so well. There must be somewhere..."

"On Sunday afternoons there's this flea market thing at Joaquin Park. I could do it there."

"We should check it out sometime and see. Do you have enough pieces to display?"

"I have lots." Carly leaned forward, eyes shining. "But...what if nobody buys anything?"

"So what?" Sera shrugged. "What have you got to lose? Other than a couple hours of your time."

"I'd have to ask Vince."

Sera bit her lip but couldn't stop the question from popping out. "Why do you have to ask him?"

"Well...because. You know?"

Sera didn't know. She would never know. But she nodded as if she did, as if it didn't bother her that a grown woman thought she had to ask her husband's permission to do something like that.

"That was fun in El Mirage last weekend." Jessie changed the subject.

"Yeah," Carly said. She looked at Sera. "Did you talk to Dominick like you wanted?"

"No." Sera tried to not look too frustrated about that. "Zocco said he'd talk to him about it."

"Oh. That's good. Right?"

"Yeah. Sure." Sera smiled at Carly. "I just wanted it before I went back to L.A. this week. I could've sold a lot to my friends. I can't sell the stuff here, this is Zocco's territory."

"L.A.'s not that far away. You can go back when he gets you the stuff."

"True." Sera took another sip of lemon drop. "Dominick's the main guy, huh?"

"I guess. He's kind of scary. A few months ago, he wanted Vince to kill someone."

Sera blinked. "Really? Who? Why?" Dammit. Her recorder wasn't running. She'd never thought she'd be talking about something like this with Carly. Could she reach for her purse and get it going? She eyed the bag sitting on the table across the patio. *Shit.*

"I don't know his name. Apparently he witnessed some of the guys beating up someone else, who ended up dying, so they had to get rid of him."

Sera felt paralyzed. Two murders? "Vince wouldn't kill someone, would he?"

Carly nibbled her bottom lip. "Yeah. He would. But he didn't kill that guy. He tried to get this new prospect to do it, but he wouldn't do it."

Sera sat up a little straighter. "So who did, then?"

"Zocco."

Oh dear god in heaven. She'd just found out who'd committed

Hot Ride

that homicide Ryan had been talking about. And she didn't have it on tape. *Shit, shit, shit.*

"Have another lemon drop?"

Sera and Jessie held out their glasses and Carly refilled them from a pitcher on the table. Carly and Jessie chatted about inconsequential stuff and Sera tried to look interested as her mind raced. She'd tell Ryan and then he'd have to talk to Zocco about it and get him to admit to the murder on tape. God. Zocco probably wasn't the brightest light, but he was street smart and suspicious. He'd taken her to a private place to talk to her about selling the angel sugar.

"We should swim," Sera said after a while. The hot sun was making her sweat. She looked longingly at the cool inviting water of the pool.

"Oh," Carly said. "I don't really like to swim. It gets my hair wet."

"Oh, come on, it's so hot." Sera set down her drink and walked across the paving stones, hot beneath her bare feet, and dipped a toe in. The water was a pleasant, cooling temperature so she dove in. When she emerged, shaking her hair back and blinking water out of her eyes, Carly and Jessie sat on the side.

"I guess I'll get in for a minute," Carly said. She stood up and hesitantly removed the pareo tied around her hips. "I hate wearing a bathing suit." She looked down at herself with a frown. In her two-piece swimsuit there was no hiding the fact that her hips were substantially wider than her top half.

"You look great, Carly," Sera said encouragingly. Carly's pear shape wasn't unattractive, but Carly obviously felt it was. She slid into the shallow end and stood waist deep, still holding her drink. Sera swam a few laps, enjoying the opportunity to use her muscles, stroking easily through the water. She loved swimming. She'd always been athletic and loved most sports.

After their dip in the pool, Carly took Sera and Jessie inside and showed them the bedroom she used to make her jewelry. "Vince calls it my 'arts and crafts room'," she said with a smile. "He used to use it for his drugs, but now he uses the room next door."

Sera filed that information away for the day it would be needed on a search warrant.

"You have lots of pretty things," Sera said, picking up a silver wire curled into attractive curves and strung with mauve, periwinkle and blue beads. "I like this."

"Take it," Carly said. "It looks beautiful with your eyes."

"I'll pay you for it," Sera offered. "I can be your first customer."

"No, no, I want to give it to you." They argued back and forth for a moment and then Sera relented. It seemed to give Carly so much pleasure to make a gift of the necklace.

"Oh my gosh," Carly gasped, glancing at her watch. "I didn't realize what time it is! Vince will be home soon and I haven't even started dinner!"

"I'd better go," Jessie said.

"Are you driving?" Sera asked.

Jessie smiled sloppily. "Hell yeah. Don't worry, I'm fine to drive."

She *so* was not. Sera had to grit her teeth.

Carly glanced at her watch. "You and Tommy want to stay for dinner? Vince will be home around six. He told me to invite you."

"I have to check with Tommy. Let me call him." She dug her cell phone out of her purse and hit the button to call Ryan. He agreed to meet her there around six and she flipped her phone shut, but started the recorder. Too late, but just in case...

Ryan would die when he heard what she'd just learned. She couldn't help the smile that plucked at her lips.

Carly hurried out of the bedroom and down the hall to the kitchen. Sera trailed along behind her. Carly'd had quite a few lemon drops. Sera had better help her get dinner.

"Does Vince expect dinner ready the minute he walks in the door?" Sera asked in the spacious kitchen. The maple cabinets appeared new and expensive, and granite counter tops gleamed in the under-cabinet lighting. Top-of-the-line stainless steel appliances also looked costly, but the clutter on the countertops and the dishes piled in both sides of the double sink detracted from the luxurious decor. Carly pulled open one door of the refrigerator and stared in.

"What are you making?" Sera asked. "I'll help."

"I...I don't know. I haven't gone shopping for a while."

Oh lord. "Why don't we just order pizza or something?"

"Great idea!" Carly slammed the fridge door shut and turned to Sera. "I'll find a menu."

She dug through a drawer packed with junk, including about a hundred take-out menus, from what Sera could see. "Here!" Carly held up a yellow paper. "House of Pizza. Vince's favorite. What kind of pizza do you and Tommy like?"

Good question. Sera had no idea what kind of pizza Ryan liked. He was a guy, probably safe to go with anything meat. "Pepperoni, sausage. Ham."

Carly nodded vigorously. "Vince likes this meat lovers' special. We'll get one of those. I like..." She bit her lip. "I shouldn't have pizza." She looked down at her stomach and hips. "I'm still trying to lose a few more pounds."

"How about a vegetarian? You and I can have that."

"I guess. Sure. You know...I'm gonna do some of that angel sugar. Then I won't eat too much at dinner. You want some?" Carly dropped the menu and headed for her bedroom.

Shit. Now what was she supposed to do?

"I'll be right back." Carly's voice called from down the hall. Then Sera heard a curse.

"What's the matter?"

"I can't find the stuff." Carly returned to the kitchen, the corners of her mouth pulled down. "I thought I had some." She shook her head. "Oh well. Gotta get some more from Zocco. I should call him."

Sera leaned against the counter, relief relaxing her muscles. "Yeah. Call him and ask him if he talked to Dominick about getting me more. Tell him I want about fifty hits of the stuff."

"Fifty!" Carly gaped at her. "You're going to sell that much?"

"Oh yeah, easily."

Carly picked up the phone and dialed Zocco, whose number she apparently knew by heart. "Hey, it's me, Carly. I need more angel sugar. D'you have some?" She nodded, eyes flicking to Sera. "Okay. Yeah. Thursday? Sure. And hey, Zocco, Sera's here and she says she wants fifty hits to sell." She listened, nodded. "Okay. Goodbye."

She hung up. "He's going to Oakland tomorrow to get more. He'll bring back some for me and he says he'll get you some but he's not sure if he can get that much."

Sera nodded. "Okay." Not much more she could do, she supposed.

"I'll order the pizza now." Carly again picked up the phone and placed their order, then glanced again at her watch. She nibbled on her bottom lip. "It won't be here until about six-thirty. Vince'll be pissed."

"He'll survive." Sera wanted to roll her eyes, but resisted. She couldn't imagine living like that. She could see Carly's lack of confidence, her lack of self esteem. She knew for some women, pleasing their man was their way of justifying their existence, giving them a sense of belonging they didn't think they could get anywhere else. She didn't like it, but she knew it existed. She wanted to change things, to encourage Carly to make a better life for herself, but this was just a job and she couldn't do that. She had to watch this woman submit and act like a man's property, and swallow her revulsion and sympathy.

Vince and Ryan arrived at almost the same time, and greeted each other in the driveway. Carly and Sera had returned to the patio beside the pool for more lemon drops. Ryan walked out the sliding doors behind Vince and his eyes fell on Sera.

"Hey, babe." She returned his smile, felt his eyes sweep over her, spreading even more heat than the desert sun as the memories of what they'd done last night flooded back. Just seeing him made her go wet beneath her bikini bottom, and she clenched her thighs together. She'd managed to successfully push the hot sex they'd shared to the back of her mind, but now he was there in front of her, it all came rushing back, wild and scorching. Oh Jesus. What had they done?

She resisted the urge to cover herself against Ryan's heated perusal and held out a hand to him, her lemon drop in the other. She'd had quite a few of them too, and was feeling pleasantly relaxed and fuzzy. She'd better stop drinking.

Ryan took her hand and smiled down at her.

"How was your day?" she asked, truly eager to know.

"Pretty good." He dropped into a chair next to her. "You girls have fun?"

"Mmm. Yeah." And the weird thing was, she actually had enjoyed herself. Apart from the working part, she, Jessie and Carly had chatted easily on different topics. She hadn't had a girlfriend for so many years. That was another thing she'd lost. After her suicide attempt when her friends had thought her a loony-tune, and she'd pretty much felt loony-tunes, she'd turned into a loner. She hadn't realized how much she'd missed the easy companionship of another woman. Not that she and Carly were friends, or ever really could be, but she found she had a spot of softness for Carly.

"Where's the food?" Vince demanded of Carly.

She smiled cautiously at him. "We ordered pizza? It'll be here soon?"

He frowned. "You know I like to eat as soon as I get home."

Carly glanced at Sera and Ryan. "I know, but we have company." She rose to her feet. "I'll get you both a beer and the pizza will be here soon." She scurried off into the house.

Sera was dying to talk to Ryan alone, to find out what had happened with his delivery and pickup, and to tell him what she'd learned. Urgency swelled inside her and made her shift restlessly in her lounge chair. She uncrossed her ankles, and recrossed them the other way. When she looked at Ryan, she saw him staring at her legs.

He looked like a starving man staring at a buffet through a glass window. Heat flared inside her and her tummy did a roll. She licked her lips and swallowed, wanting Ryan to reach out and stroke his hands over her legs. She bent one knee and slowly drew her leg up then slid it back down, knowing he was still watching.

Carly returned and handed him a beer. Then he and Vince talked, but Sera wasn't listening, aware only of Ryan a foot away from her nearly naked body. Her nipples tingled and tightened behind the triangle cups of the bikini top. Sitting in the sun all afternoon had deepened the golden tan of her skin, and the sunscreen she'd applied gave her legs a nice sheen. Inexplicably she wanted Ryan to find her attractive, especially after last night, and she slowly slid one foot up and down the lounge chair again.

She felt his eyes on her, aware of the contrast between reality and the act they were putting on for the benefit of Vince and Carly. They hadn't had to sleep together to add authenticity to their relationship. No, that had been completely unplanned, unnecessary and inexcusable. Every nerve ending tingled and her breasts swelled and felt heavy.

And then he did touch her, reaching out to set his hand on her bare shoulder. He stroked down over her arm, fingertips lingering in the sensitive crease of her elbow, making her shiver, then slid lower over her forearm and stopped at her wrist. His fingers rested lightly there and she knew her pulse kicked up beneath them.

She glanced sideways at him and just as she did, he turned to her and their gazes collided in a mini-explosion of heat. Dear god in heaven. Lust cascaded over her in hot waves. She quivered inside, unable to drag her eyes away from Ryan's warm, golden gaze. He flicked his eyes over her body again, arched a brow approvingly, and she cast him a slow smile of recognition. His eyes darkened, fingers tightened on her wrist and her pulse fluttered even faster.

"Pizza's here!" Carly rose from her chair and set her lemon drop on the table, slopping it over the side of the glass and into a puddle on the table top. Ryan's gaze turned puzzled and Sera gave him a little grimace.

"She's hammered," Vince commented, watching her walk unevenly into the house. He looked at Sera. "Were you two drinking all afternoon?"

Sera wasn't afraid of Vince like Carly was. She grinned and held up her empty glass. "Yeah. These are sooooo good."

Annoyance flashed in Vince's eyes and then worry nudged Sera. She hoped she wasn't making things worse for Carly. "Don't be mad at us." She smiled winningly. "We were just talking girl talk and looking at horoscopes and Carly's jewelry and the afternoon got away from us." She touched the necklace at her throat and turned to Ryan. "See what Carly gave me? Isn't it nice?"

She never wore jewelry, other than the diamond earrings she'd bought herself a few years ago, but she truly loved the necklace—the shades of blue and mauve and the shiny silver appealed to her.

"Very nice."

She swung her legs over the side of the chaise and sat up. "I'll go help Carly."

"And put some clothes on," Ryan said.

She stopped and looked at him over her shoulder. They shared a long look. She so longed to say, "Excuse me?" but held it back, turned and walked away with a deliberate twitch of her butt in the skimpy bikini bottom, snagging up the pair of shorts she'd worn over there. In the kitchen, she stepped into them and tugged them up over her hips, but they were low rise and short-short and didn't cover a heck of a lot more than the bikini. Smothering her smile, she didn't bother with the tank top she'd also worn, and helped Carly carry out the pizzas, plates, napkins and more beers.

Chapter Thirteen

Ryan pulled into the driveway of the ATF rental house, put the truck in park and turned the motor off.

"I'm sorry I didn't have my recorder going when she told me that," Sera said. "I was so mad at myself. I just didn't expect to hear something like that."

"It's okay. I need to hear a confession from Zocco. I have to think about how I'm going to do that." He'd figure it out.

Sera grabbed the door handle and yanked it open, swung her long legs out of the vehicle. Christ, she was fucking sex on a stick. After last night, he'd been half hard all day, try as he might to keep his mind on work. He'd been kind of hoping that having sex with her would finally take the edge off the sexual tension that had gripped both of them pretty much since the moment they'd met, and they could just get on with things. But no, it had just increased it, making him relive every touch of her mouth, every taste of body, the feel of her around him as he came, all damn day.

Then he'd damn near died when he'd walked out onto the patio and saw her lying there in that tiny bikini, her long, smooth limbs all bronze and gleaming. Her abdomen was flat and muscled, and her tits swelled around the little triangles of black fabric barely covering them. It was all he could do to keep himself from jumping on top of her and fucking her brains out, right there beside the pool.

Then she'd flirted with him, as if she'd known how hard his cock was and how much his balls were aching, and she enjoyed torturing him even more. He'd realized she was just a bit tipsy, his amused reaction a little different than Vince's displeasure. He only hoped she'd maintained enough control to not blow their covers.

Then she'd dropped the bombshell on the way home—her conversation with Carly about the murder. Back to business.

Zocco. It had been Zocco. He no longer had to worry about finding the former Angels prospect who'd taken a shit kicking rather than commit a murder for them. Huh.

As Sera slammed her door shut, he too climbed out and started walking to the house. At that moment, a furious barking erupted behind the fence separating their house from the home next door. Snarling growls and barks clamored ferociously.

Sera gave a little screech and launched herself at Ryan, grabbing hold of his shirt so tightly he feared she might rip it. He caught her around her smooth and bare waist, and held her. "Hey," he said.

She trembled in his arms. "Jesus Christ," she said, teeth chattering. "Is that a *dog*?"

Amused, he tucked her against his side and looked over the fence. "Yup. It is."

She rolled her lips in, still clinging to him and trembling.

"Didn't you know the neighbors have a dog?"

She shook her head, and he saw the fear shining in her pretty eyes. "Sera—are you afraid of dogs?"

She said nothing, swallowed hard and started to pull away from him, but he wouldn't let her go that easily.

"Sera?"

"What?"

"You're afraid of dogs. Aren't you?"

She still said nothing and her reluctance to admit she was actually afraid of something tugged on his heart. "It's okay. The dog's on a chain. And he's friendly."

"Oh yeah. He sounds *really* friendly."

The two kids who lived next door came out of the house. "Bingo! Come, Bingo!" the boy called. "Hey, Tommy."

"Hey, Billy."

"That your girlfriend?"

Ryan glanced at Sera, her face a little less tense. "Yeah. This is Sara. Sara, meet Billy and Crystal."

Sera lifted a brow at him and he grinned. "Yeah. I know."

"How come you're not riding your motorcycle tonight?" Billy asked, approaching the fence. The dog leaped excitedly around him and Billy stroked its head. Sera relaxed slightly against him.

"I need a truck for my job," Ryan told him.

"What is your job?"

"I deliver motorcycle parts to garages."

"Oh. That's cool."

Billy's little sister had followed along behind him and was staring at Sera admiringly.

"You have pretty hair," Crystal said to her.

"Oh. Thanks."

"I wanna ride a motorcycle just like you, Tommy," Billy said. Ryan's gut tightened. He'd talked to these kids before and hated how they admired him. "Maybe I'll be a Coyote too."

Ryan cleared his throat, tightened his grip on Sera. "Nah, you can do better than that, Billy."

"You mean, like, be a Death Angel? Like those friends of yours?"

Ryan scowled. "No, that's not what I meant. Being in a motorcycle gang isn't what you should be aspiring to."

"Why not? You are."

He sighed. "Yeah, but...that's because I...uh...made some mistakes. You can do better than that."

Billy shrugged and grabbed hold of his dog's collar.

"Billy! Bring Bingo in right now!"

Billy and Crystal turned. A woman called to them from the door of the house next door and Ryan recognized their mother. He'd only spoken to her briefly once when he'd moved in. She seemed afraid of him. And he didn't blame her. She should be nervous, with the kind of people who visited him at all hours. He sighed.

"See ya, kids."

He and Sera went inside. He noticed the tiny bumps puckering her soft skin and how she rubbed her upper arms once inside the house.

"I'm going to have a shower," she said quietly. He let her go into the bedroom alone to get her things.

Where the hell was Manny? Likely at The Patch. He dropped onto the couch, put his feet on the table and picked up the remote for some relaxing channel-surfing.

He heard Sera go into the bathroom. The pipes clunked as the shower started. Images of her removing the bikini top, dropping it to the floor, then wiggling her hips out of those tiny shorts swarmed in his head, distracting him from the baseball game he'd found on TV. He pictured her in the shower, surrounded by steam, her naked body wet and soapy.

He groaned and adjusted his hard-on. Christ. It probably wouldn't be appropriate to walk into the bathroom and join her. They had some kind of weird relationship going on here. Partners. Now lovers. But not lovers in the true sense of the word. They'd had sex. That didn't entitle him to any expectations of more—sex in the shower, sex on the floor, or even sex in bed again.

Last night they'd slept together in the same bed. But where would he sleep tonight? Manny'd given Ryan a long, faintly amused look that morning when he'd emerged from the bedroom, and commented, "Taking this undercover role to the max, huh?" Ryan had restrained himself from punching out Manny's smile, then growled, "That doesn't leave this house, right?" They'd lucked out the other night discovering the recording equipment was off, and he didn't want all the guys talking about Sera because they'd slept together.

He longed to open his pants and pull out his cock and give himself some quick relief. He eyed the front door. Hell.

He got up, locked and bolted the door, returned to the couch, fingers at his belt buckle. He wrenched it open, threw himself down on the couch and spread his legs wide, drew his engorged cock out and fisted it. The shower continued to run. He licked his lips, leaned his head back and closed his eyes, pulling at his dick with firm, fast strokes. With his other hand, he cupped his balls and gave them a tug. They were up against his body so tight it was as if they were trying to climb inside him. He moaned again, bit his lip, pressure building in his testicles.

He pictured Sera, water streaming over her bronzed, slender body, tipping her face up to the water. Flames licked over his body, hotter, sizzling over his skin, and the urgency inside him swelled bigger. He heard the shower turn off, muttered a curse. He still had time. He pumped faster, harder, his breath stalling in his chest. As his orgasm erupted, he realized faintly he hadn't planned well, and he yanked up his shirt, made a harsh sound low in his throat as jerking spurts of thick white landed on his bare stomach, slid over his hand. He cried out again, low and guttural, body taut, until the spasms ceased and he relaxed into the cushions of the couch, gasping for breath.

He heard the bathroom door open and lurched upright. He grabbed for the box of tissues on the table beside the couch, swiped at his stomach and hastily zipped up. Still breathing fast, he stood and looked down the hall just as the bedroom door closed behind Sera. Whew.

That was all he needed, her walking in on him busting a nut. Christ. He closed his eyes. He could only imagine her reaction.

He could also easily imagine her joining him, replacing his hand on his cock with hers, stroking him with soft hands, and then taking him in her mouth... He twitched again. Fuck! He was supposed to have gotten some relief, and here he was getting hard and horny all over again.

He went into the kitchen, ran a glass of cold water from the tap and drained it. Then he stood there, both hands on the counter, leaning against it, eyes closed. He should be thinking about this operation, how he was going to get a taped confession to murder from Zocco. Solving a homicide would be the icing on the cake for this op, especially if Zocco admitted he'd done it on behalf of the Angels.

Earlier, over at Vince's and Carly's, he and Vince had talked about the delivery, and Vince had said he'd give him more if he was interested. Hell yeah, he was interested. He'd captured every word of their conversation, and then when Sera'd told him what she'd learned that afternoon, he could have kissed her.

Well. That wouldn't be a hardship even if he hadn't been so jubilant about the progress they'd made.

And he had to admit it was thanks to her. The four of them sitting around the pool, two couples having pizza and beers, talking about business—even though the business happened to be illegal—had been invaluable. And Sera's little girl talk afternoon had turned into a gold mine.

He heard Sera come into the room behind him, inhaled deeply and straightened, turning to face her. She was all pink and damp from the shower, dressed in the same striped pants and T-shirt she'd worn in El Mirage. Dark hair hung in damp tendrils past her shoulders, creating wet spots on the pink top.

"Why are you afraid of dogs?"

The words surprised him more than they surprised her.

She frowned at him. "I'm not afraid of dogs."

"Yes, you are. You almost jumped into my arms out there. Not that I minded." He smirked and her scowl deepened. Then he regretted his teasing. She obviously had a hard time admitting any kind of weakness. And while on one level he liked knowing she actually *had* a weakness, on another level, he completely understood. He didn't like admitting weakness, either.

"Never mind," he said gruffly. "I wanted to thank you."

"For...?"

"For being here." He cleared his throat. "This afternoon you got some great stuff from Carly. And then—just the opportunity to relax with Vince, alone like that, just the four of us...I wouldn't have had that if it weren't for you."

She stared steadily at him. "Thank you."

He nodded. Silence swirled around them.

"When I was a kid, I got bit by a dog."

He nodded. "That happens to a lot of people."

"It was a German Shepherd, just like that one."

"Bingo."

"Yes. Bingo." She blinked at him. "It was more than just a bite. I got mauled pretty bad. Ended up in the hospital with a lot of stitches." She pulled her hair away from one side of her neck. "This is one of the scars."

He hadn't noticed that in his frenzy of lust last night. "Oh Jesus." He sucked in air, not sure what to say.

"I'm uh...going to bed now." Thick tension coiled around them, his unspoken question hanging there.

"Okay."

"I put some blankets and a pillow on the couch for you."

Shit. "Okay."

"Just one thing..."

"What's that?" He crossed his arms across his chest, leaned back against the counter. Disappointment at knowing he wasn't going to be sleeping with her that night buzzed in his ears, distracting him from her words.

"I need to go back to L.A. I need enough money to buy fifty hits of angel sugar from Zocco."

Ryan choked. "*Fifty?*"

She nodded slowly. "I told him I want fifty. I want them to think I can sell a lot."

"Why?"

"So I can get to the lab."

Chapter Fourteen

"No fucking way."

Sera stared at Darren Forsythe. She sent a sideways glance at Ryan, who scowled, and at Manny, who placidly chewed his gum. Her body tightened, and she gripped the armrests of the chair so tightly her fingers ached. She forced herself to relax her fingers.

"I need to do this," she said, leaning forward. "If they think I can sell that much, next time I'll ask for more. And then after that, I'll ask for so much I'll want them to prove to me they can supply me enough. If they *are* running the lab, that's how I'll find out. We have to do this."

Darren shook his head. "Too much money. Not going to happen. Surveillance is expensive. It's gonna break us."

She sat back in her chair and studied him. "Look, Mr. Forsythe, I know this wasn't part of your mandate when you started this op, but it *is* the DEA's mandate. This is what I've been working on for two years. This is an unbelievable opportunity."

He too sat back in his chair. "No. We've been forking over dough like this is a bakery. Forget it. I'm not putting my ass on the line with that much cash."

"It's worth it."

He slowly moved his head from side to side.

"Call Ward. They'll pay for it."

He frowned at her.

"Seriously. Call Ward. If you don't want to, I will."

"Go ahead."

Sera pulled out her cell phone and punched a button. In a moment, she talked to her SAC and explained the problem to him. "He wants to talk to you." She held her phone out to Darren. He heaved a sigh, rolled his eyes, but took the phone from her.

"Forsythe." A pause. "Yeah. Yeah." Silence. More silence. He sat up straighter. "Fine. Let me know." He clicked the phone shut and slid it across the table to Sera like a shuffleboard puck. She caught it neatly. Darren's mouth twisted. "He's got a call in to the U.S. Attorney's office."

She resisted the urge to smirk at him. "So?"

"He's going to call me back. In an hour."

"Okay." She looked at Ryan and Manny. "Let's go for lunch, guys."

They levered their big bodies out of the chairs they sat in, and the three of them filed out of the meeting room. "Ryan." All three of them halted at Darren's voice and looked back over their shoulders. "I need you to redo some of the reports you did last week."

"What? Why?"

"Too many typos."

"Oh, for Chrissake."

Darren shrugged, his eyes gleaming. "Hey. They gotta be done right."

"I'll do them after lunch."

"They're on your desk."

With a scowl, Ryan stalked out of the building. Sera followed, Manny behind her. Wow.

"Asshole," Ryan muttered.

Sera grinned. What was that about?

When they'd taken their seats in a nearby restaurant, full of men in expensive business suits and women in designer dresses, power suits and heels, Sera looked at Ryan over her menu. "Why does Darren have it in for you?"

Ryan scowled and flicked his eyes over the menu, then slapped the laminated plastic down on the table. "He doesn't."

Manny snorted and Sera laughed. "Bullshit."

He met her eyes across the table. "It doesn't matter."

She shrugged, studied her own menu. "Okay. Fine."

"What's your SAC got up his sleeve?"

"Just what Darren said. Washington's interested in this case."

"That should get Darren's attention. He likes to suck up to his superiors."

Sera nodded. "I got that impression of him."

They talked strategy over lunch, Sera sharing how she hoped to get into the lab in Oakland eventually, Ryan talking about his hopes for getting Zocco to confess to the murder of that witness on tape. They were getting closer, so much closer, but still so far away. Sera's jaw tightened at the thought that she might not get the money she needed to do what she wanted. That would be just cruel—getting in, getting close and then tauntingly saying, sorry, no cash.

When they returned to the ATF offices, Ryan heaved a sigh and headed for his desk. Sera followed him. He threw himself down into the rolling chair and reached for the stack of papers on the desk. Sera put out a hand.

He looked up at her blankly. She jerked her hand. "Give them to me."

"Give what to you?"

"The paperwork. I'll redo it for you."

He frowned. "Why?"

"Because I type ninety-eight words a minute and I can redo these faster than you can open the file on your computer."

He stared at her, eyes hard and dark. She waggled her fingers. He glanced at his watch. "Here," he said gruffly. "Take these ones. I'll start on these."

She took the papers from him and retreated to another desk and another computer. He was so cute, pecking away at the keyboard with two fingers. Okay, maybe four fingers.

She tapped away, finished the documents she'd taken from him, then went back and took the remainder from him. He only frowned a little, kept plugging away at the ones he was working on. They both finished at the same time.

"Okay," she said cheerfully. "Let's go see if Darren's heard back from Ward yet."

Ryan poked his head into Darren's office. "Yeah, yeah, give me a minute," Darren yelled. "See you in the meeting room."

With a grin, they retreated to the meeting room and arranged themselves around the table with cups of coffee in hand. Sera watched Ryan stick a hand into the pocket of his jeans and pull out a roll of something—antacids again. He popped two in his mouth and crunched them as he shoved the roll back in his pocket.

"Tummy troubles?" she inquired sweetly. She resisted the urge to rub her own fluttery tummy as they awaited Darren's go ahead.

He glared at her, but said nothing. She sipped her coffee, not all that hot and kind of burnt tasting.

A moment later Darren strode in, wearing the perpetual furrow between his brows, his belly swelling over his belt. He flung a folder down on the table and dropped into a chair. "Okay," he said. "You've got the money. Attorney's office wants us to keep going."

Sera resisted the urge to smirk at him, merely nodded and said, "Thank you, Darren. I really appreciate you taking the time to talk to him. I know that the DEA brass will also appreciate all the work you've done for this case."

She couldn't help but notice Ryan gape at her across the table, and Manny's choked cough.

Darren assessed her across the table and nodded. "Yeah. Thanks for letting me know about that, Sera. We wouldn't want to piss off Washington."

"God, no," she agreed fervently, sending a glance to Ryan. His ferocious scowl almost made her laugh. "So I'll buy the fifty hits of sugar on Thursday, and then I'll tell them I want more. Next buy will be even more money. You're prepared for that, right, Darren?" She smiled at him, and his answering smile tickled her inside. Damn, he was easy. She didn't know why he and Ryan rubbed each other the wrong way. You just had to know how to play the guy.

The three of them had driven to L.A. together, and on the way back Sera turned to Ryan, who was driving. "We need to stop at a grocery store."

"What for?"

"Uh...groceries?"

He shrugged. "Okay. Sure."

She'd discovered very little edible content in the cupboards and refrigerator of the house. She knew the two guys didn't cook and mostly ate out. That no doubt accounted for the antacids Ryan kept popping. She was no gourmet cook, but at least she could scramble some eggs or toss a salad.

They waited in the car while she cruised up and down the aisles of VONS, throwing things into the cart without a lot of thought. Just a few basics. She liked to eat healthy. Yogurt. A couple of bags of salad greens, already washed and chopped. Granola. A few cans of tuna. Then she hesitated at the meat counter before grabbing three steaks.

She loaded the bags into the back of Ryan's truck and they finished the trip back to the house. Manny and Ryan carried the groceries into the kitchen and started to help her put them away. Another amusing moment. These guys had to act all macho and chauvinistic around the bikers, but without their presence they were gentlemen to the core, carrying the heavy bags in and helping unpack them without a word of protest or even her asking. Something inside her softened and warmed at that.

"What the hell are these?" Ryan held up a box, a frown creasing his brow.

"Uh..." She'd forgotten those. Embarrassed, she rushed forward to take them from his hand. He held them up, out of her reach.

"Who're these for, Sera?" Ryan grinned, holding up the box.

She wanted to grab for them but knew she'd only draw more attention to her chagrin. So she stood there, glaring at him, cheeks burning.

"They're for Bingo."

Manny turned from the refrigerator. "Bingo? That mutt next door?"

"Yes." Sera looked at the floor. She waited for more teasing, but when she lifted her eyes, Ryan had turned and was sliding the box of dog biscuits into an upper cupboard. He turned back and caught her eye, and he wasn't smirking. His steady gaze once again melted her inside, all oozing and gooey softness and she stiffened her spine. She didn't need any special treatment from him. Nor was she going to explain herself.

"Hey, ice cream," Manny said. "Great idea."

After the Milk Bones, Sera wasn't about to explain that the ice cream was for Billy and Crystal. Ha. Every time she thought about them, their names made her laugh. Had their parents planned that?

So she didn't admonish Manny not to eat it all. If he did, she'd just go buy more, but them seeing one moment of softness on her part was enough for one day.

"You gonna cook for us, Sera?" Manny asked, mouth quirked into a gently teasing smile.

She grinned back at him. "Maybe."

"Are you a good cook?" Ryan asked. The warm huskiness of his tone made her turn to him. If they'd been alone, she'd have drifted closer to him, perhaps touched him, answered him flirtatiously. But they weren't alone. So she swallowed through a tight throat and tipped her head to one side.

"No," she replied, smiling. "But I'm probably better than you two."

"Ha," Manny said. "Doesn't take much for that. I can't even microwave a hotdog without exploding it."

Ryan laughed. "I actually burnt spaghetti one time."

"See what I mean?" Sera put her hands on her hips. "So when I make runny mac and cheese, don't complain."

"Oh, we won't."

Thursday, Sera eagerly awaited the call from either Zocco or Carly. It came from Carly.

"Zocco's got our stuff," she said. "I'll pick you up and we can go get it?"

"Sure."

They went together to meet Zocco at his place, a tiny bungalow in a sketchy neighborhood near the downtown center of Clover City.

"I got you fifty hits," he told her, eyeing her strangely. "You sure you want that much? It's gonna cost you a bundle."

She pulled the money out of her purse and counted it out to Zocco, counting out loud so it would be captured by the recorder in her cell phone hanging off the strap of her purse. "I can sell it," she assured him. "No problem."

"Okay." He handed her over the drugs. Carly had her stash too, smiling happily.

In the car driving home, Carly said, "We should celebrate. How about you and me go out for a drink?"

Sera, nervously watching a police car turn onto a side street in front of them, wanted to get the drugs home. "Okay. But can I go home first? I don't want to carry all this with me."

Carly's smaller purchase was tucked in her purse. "Sure." She turned and drove toward Sera's place.

Inside, Sera hid the sugar in the bedroom, knowing she'd have to turn that in soon. Then she and Carly headed to The Patch.

Carly knocked back a few martinis, while Sera paced herself through one, not wanting to get as tipsy as she had with the lemon drops the other day. Then Carly glanced at her watch. "Better go," she said. "Vince'll be home for dinner soon."

Sera swallowed her sigh. Poor Carly. "Maybe I should drive," she offered, thinking of the alcohol Carly had just consumed.

"But then how will you get home?"

Good question. "I could call Tommy to pick me up."

So Carly let her drive, thankfully, since Sera was pretty sure her blood alcohol content was way over the legal limit. She just wanted to get Carly home and call Ryan.

As Sera drove, Carly poked around in her purse, pulling out her wallet, her keys and then a makeup bag. She flipped down the visor, applied some lip gloss and fluffed her hair. Then a siren whooped behind them. Sera glanced in the rearview mirror and saw the flashing lights of the Clover City Police Department car. *Please, please just let him want to get by me.*

But the cop car pulled in behind her, lights still flashing. Shit. Everything inside Sera tensed. She slowed to a careful stop. She'd had one drink so she wasn't worried about that, but she became suddenly, painfully aware of the drugs in Carly's purse. She glanced at Carly with the contents of her purse still on her lap. "Put everything away," she said tersely.

"What's going on?"

"I don't know. I don't think I was speeding."

She sat, both hands on the steering wheel, and waited for the officer to approach the car. Another office came up to Carly's window as she tried to stuff her makeup bag back into her purse.

"Afternoon, ma'am." The officer beside Sera bent to peer into the car. "You the registered owner of this vehicle?"

"My husband is," Carly said, jamming her wallet into the purse.

"Can I have your registration, please? And your driver's license," the officer said to Sera.

She fumbled in her own purse, knowing it was perfectly fine to be nervous when stopped by the cops, but she had extra reason. She handed over the fake driver's license, praying it would withstand the check this police officer was about to do. They had elected not to let the Clover City Police Department know about the undercover op. The fewer who knew, the better, and there was always a chance the DAs had infiltrated the police. So they were really running a check on her. All she needed was to have her cover blown in Carly's presence. The officer took both documents back to his car.

Sera glanced at Carly, bit her lip, lifted her shoulders as if to say, "I don't know." With Vince being the owner of the vehicle and the cops knowing he was president of the local Angels chapter, they could be in trouble here. The cops could easily want to give them a hard time. Her stomach turned over and tightened, her neck and shoulder throbbed. Her mouth went dry.

When the officer returned, he said, "Did you know you have a burned out taillight?"

Hot Ride

Sera looked at Carly, whose eyes widened. "Oh! I forgot about that!"

"Please step out of the car. Both of you."

They did so, Sera moving carefully.

As Carly stepped out, the officer on her side reached down to pick something up from the ground. When he straightened, he held Carly's bag of angel sugar.

"This fell off your lap," he said.

Sera's heart turned to a stone and sank into her stomach at the sight of the police officer holding up the bag of white powder. *Shit, shit, shit.* Heat raced over her skin, blood pounded in her ears and throbbed in her temples.

Chapter Fifteen

Ryan arrived at the precinct to pick up Sera, who wasn't charged with anything, but Vince had to wait longer to bail out Carly. She'd been arrested for possession and Vince was pissed off to the extreme.

"Let's wait for them," Sera murmured to Ryan. He looked down at her, feeling pretty damn annoyed himself, but it wasn't Sera's fault. He was just relieved Sera'd been released, her newly backstopped identity apparently having checked out okay.

"Why? It could be a while."

"I'm worried about her." Sera's blue eyes were wide and smoky with concern.

"What are you worried about? Were the cops out of line with you?"

She shook her head. "No, they were okay. Kinda of snotty, but okay. It's Vince. I'm worried about what he's going to do to her."

"Ah." Ryan huffed out a long breath. "Yeah. Okay, but Sera..." He glanced at Vince, across the room talking to an officer. "We can't do anything."

She pressed her lips together. "We'll see."

Now Ryan was worried about two things—what Vince was going to do to Carly, and what Sera wanted to do to Vince.

When Carly was finally free to go, Ryan and Sera followed her and Vince outside.

"We'll come to your place," Sera said, flashing a glance at Ryan. He nodded.

Vince was hot, stomping into the house, slamming the door shut. He turned and yelled at Carly. "You stupid bitch! Why didn't you get that taillight fixed?"

Ryan and Sera shared a glance.

Carly cowered. "I'm sorry," she mumbled.

"Isn't it your car?" Sera asked him.

He scowled at her. "Yeah, it's registered to me, but it's Carly's car. Jesus Christ! How stupid can you be?"

Pale and trembling, Carly pushed a hand through her dark blonde hair.

"Get in the bedroom! Now!"

"Uh, Vince..." Ryan took a step forward. "You wanna cool down maybe."

"Fuck off and mind your own business," Vince snapped. He lifted his chin at Sera. "You should be laying a beating on your own woman for getting in trouble like that."

Sera's jaw tightened.

"You can't let them get away with pulling shit like that," Vince said, striding to the bedroom where Carly had scurried. "You better take care of it, buddy."

He slammed the bedroom door shut.

Ryan and Sera faced each other. Sera started toward the bedroom.

Ryan put out a hand and snagged her by her slim but muscled upper arm, and he felt the tension in her soft flesh. "Don't."

"He's going to hit her." Sera tugged away from him. "I have to stop him."

"You can't stop him, Sara. You'll get hurt yourself. And you'll just piss him off."

"I can't just stand here and let him hurt her." Anguish darkened her eyes even more. "I can't, Ryan."

"Tommy."

She closed her eyes briefly.

"Get a grip, Sara. You have to," he continued softly, still holding her arm. He brought her around to face him and held her other arm, holding her before him. "You have to. I know it's crap. So many times during this whole thing I've had to stand by and watch crimes committed."

"You wouldn't let that guy in the bar get hurt."

"He was going to be killed. Vince won't kill Carly."

"How do you know?" She lifted her chin. "Domestic abuse gets out of hand. Jesus, husbands murder their wives all the time."

Ryan's gut clenched harder. She was right, dammit. He stared at the hall to the bedroom. "Fuck." It was going to make a helluva messy situation if he tried to interfere with Vince's punishment of his wife. What were the chances? Vince was a mean sonofabitch, but he didn't really seem like a guy who would lose control that much. He liked to be in charge, definitely liked to control Carly, but kill her...?

They heard yelling—Vince's voice—and then the door opened and Vince stomped back into the room. He stopped and stared at Ryan.

Ryan heard Carly crying, so he knew she was alive.

He grabbed hold of Sera's arms harder and gave her a little shake. Her hair fell across her face and she stared up at him wide-eyed. *Go along with me*, he instructed her with his eyes, even as he tried to look angry and mean. Then he dragged her over to the couch, pulled her down across his lap and delivered three hard swats to her ass.

She struggled, but he held her down, knowing it wasn't in her nature to accept anything physical like this, but hoping like hell she'd be smart enough to know he wouldn't really hurt her.

Her soft wriggling body against his lap wasn't making him angry, though. It was making him hard. Jesus. Was he some kind of pervert?

Her sweet little ass beneath his hand felt damn good too. He laid his hand there for a moment, until she started to move again, and he gave her another smack. Then he heard something that went straight to his dick and shocked the hell out of him—a moan.

She lay across him, limp and breathing fast, not fighting him anymore. Ryan glanced at Vince, who gave him a thumbs-up and disappeared back down the hall.

He palmed Sera's butt through her jeans. "Sorry," he whispered. "I had to do it."

She lifted her head, her hair a dark curtain across her face. "Fuck you."

He almost laughed. He should have expected that from her. She rolled off him and scrambled to her feet, tugging her short T-shirt down and shoving her hair back. Her eyes shot sparks at him, electric-blue flashes of anger. She curled her fingers into fists.

Ryan held up his hands. "Hey, don't kick me across the room again." He glanced down the hall to make sure Vince wasn't standing there. "Come on, hon, we gotta keep it up."

She sucked in a deep breath and her breasts lifted. He couldn't help but notice her pointy nipples sticking out through the thin cotton T-shirt. Was she really angry? Or hot for him? Did that spanking turn her on as much as it did him? And what did her bra look like today? Oh man.

Oh, she'd be pissed off at that, if his spanking had turned her on. He swallowed a grin. Then more yelling erupted from the bedroom.

They both turned to face it. She looked at him. The look on her face almost had him stumbling to his knees—the agony. The anger. The determination.

"I can't, Ryan," she choked out. "I just can't." And she started toward the bedroom.

He started to say no, took a step toward her, hand outstretched, but she brushed him aside and strode down the hall. Hell. Fuck. Shit. He followed her.

"Sera. Wait."

She hesitated and looked over her shoulder.

Ryan sighed. "Let me do this."

Her forehead creased.

He moved up behind her and nudged her down the hall, then opened the bedroom door and shoved her into the room. Hard.

She made a noise in her throat and started to glare at him. He glared back.

Vince had his hand drawn back and he turned to them, a murderous scowl on his face. "What the fuck?"

"Hey, Vince," Ryan said. "Sara wants to apologize."

She blinked.

"She was driving when they got pulled over. This whole thing is her fault. Right, babe?" He gave her a narrow-eyed look.

She swallowed. "Right." She looked at Vince. "It's all my fault."

"Go away, Sara." Carly's voice quivered. Blood trickled from the corner of her mouth, her lip swollen.

"Come on, Vince. Blame me if you want, I was driving."

Ryan's gaze went back and forth between Vince's black scowl and Sera's set chin. His hands fisted. Vince could turn on Sera and take his anger out on her, and there was no way he could let that happen. If Vince tried anything with Sera, the entire freakin' op was done, and they'd be lucky to get out alive. His gut churned. Vince drew back and lowered his hand. Silence expanded around them, marred only by Carly's sniffles. Ryan waited, adrenaline flashing through him, and he had to restrain himself from stepping into the middle of the fray.

"It's not your fault," Vince said. And Ryan's heart missed a beat. "Fuck, Carly." Vince turned to her, his fists relaxing. "Jesus, woman, you just piss me off."

"I know. I'm sorry?"

Sera's face tightened. She left the bedroom, returned a moment later with a wet cloth and pressed it on Carly's mouth. "Put some ice on this," she said in a low voice. Carly nodded.

Sera turned to Ryan. He scowled.

"Meet you at The Patch later?" Vince looked at Ryan.

"Yeah, I'll meet you there. I'll take Sara home first."

"Great."

"You gonna be okay?" Sera asked Carly before she left.

Carly nodded, holding the cloth to her mouth. "Yeah. I think so."

"I'll call you tomorrow. To see how you are."

"Let's go." Ryan gripped Sera's arm and hauled her out of the room, all pissed off and alpha.

But in his truck he let out a long, slow breath. As they drove home in silence, his brain got all backed up with thoughts of her trying to take on Vince, standing up to him. Her courage, her conviction, her...craziness. She could have gotten in serious trouble there. Hell.

Back at the house, he turned to her, intending give her shit for getting involved in Carly and Vince's domestic dispute, but the sight of her face halted the words. Shadowed eyes stared back at him from a pale face. "Are you okay?" he asked instead, taking a step toward her, feeling a clutch of concern.

She shook her head with a tiny movement. "Just a little headache," she said, putting a hand to her brow. "I just need some Tylenol and some sleep."

The look of pain on her face alarmed him, but not as much as the fact that she wasn't ready to fight with him and defend herself against what she had to know was coming. He strode over to her and bent to slip an arm beneath her knees and pick her up.

"Hey," she protested weakly. "Put me down."

"I'm just helping you," he said, starting toward the bedroom.

"I don't need help."

"That's my girl," he murmured. "I know you don't need help."

He laid her gently on the bed, smoothed her hair back off her forehead. She felt cool and clammy. She closed her eyes, not protesting anymore. "I'll get you some Tylenol," he said.

He found the bottle in a cupboard in the kitchen, shook two tablets into his hand and ran a glass of water. When he returned to the bedroom, she lay exactly how he'd left her, still fully dressed, eyes closed, cheeks pallid. "Here you go."

She pushed herself up on one elbow and took the tablets from him with the other hand, then the water. Unfamiliar tenderness stirred inside him. "You get these headaches often?" he asked.

"No. Not often." She lowered herself back to the pillow and closed her eyes again. He stood there, wishing he could fix whatever was hurting her, hating to see her like that. Hell, just a few minutes ago she'd been all strong and protective, determined to help Carly, and now here she was, laid out because of a damn headache.

He swiped a hand across his brow, feeling helpless. He had no choice but to leave her alone to sleep even if he wanted to give her shit for being so goddamn foolhardy. Maybe it was good that he couldn't jump all over her, though. In more ways than one. The memory of her stretched out across his lap, her sweet ass beneath his hands, still heated his blood.

He was supposed to go meet Vince at The Patch, but he couldn't bring himself to leave Sera like that. He sat in the dark living room, only the light of the television casting a flickering glow in the room, no volume on in case the sound disturbed her.

This wasn't the first time things like that had happened while he'd been in his undercover role, as he'd told Sera. How many laws had he seen broken, while he stood by and allowed it for the sake of the operation? How many people had been hurt? The Death Angels could be brutally violent. He'd seen a few things worthy of assault charges, including Vince's behavior tonight, and he hated it.

But Sera hadn't stood by. She'd stepped up.

He checked on her a couple of times, standing and looking down at her beautiful face surrounded by dark hair spread on the pillow around her. With creamy alabaster skin, closed eyes, long lashes feathery crescents on her cheeks, she looked incredibly, perfectly beautiful—angelic, even. He resisted the urge to touch a fingertip to a smooth cheek, or to push aside a lock of silky hair. Her breasts rose and fell slightly as she breathed. Something ached inside him as he watched her.

Was she going to sleep until morning? Maybe he should have helped her undress so she'd be more comfortable. He debated trying to get her out of her jeans at least, the idea making him hard and uncomfortable. With a sigh, he left her again.

But an hour later, she emerged from the bedroom, shoving her hair back and yawning. "Hey," she said, standing in the arched entry to the living room. "What time is it?"

"Ten thirty."

"Oh."

"Feeling better?"

"Yeah. My head's better." She avoided his gaze.

"Do you get migraines?"

"Yes. Sort of." She studied the floor.

"It's nothing to be ashamed of."

She sighed, standing there, shoulders hunched. Then she straightened and looked him squarely in the eye. "I know. I just hate being weak like that."

"Sera. You are so far from weak."

"Still. It's not really migraines. It just happens when I'm really um...stressed." She shot him a glance, looking almost...fearful.

He blew out a long sigh. "Sit down." He patted the couch beside him.

She sat. He felt her warmth, smelled her warm berry-fruity scent.

"It's not a sign of weakness," he said. "I'm eating antacids like they're candy. We all have our triggers." Speaking of...his gut churned and burned. He reached into his pocket for his roll of antacids and popped a couple into his mouth. Jesus. "But are you sure you're up for this?"

Sera laid a tentative hand on his thigh. "Yes! I can handle it."

He sighed. "Sera. If you can't handle the stress, how are you going to finish this off?"

"I can do it!"

He was silent. She shouldn't have stepped in like that. "You're getting personally involved," he said.

"I can still do it. Please, Ryan. I have to do this."

He looked at her for a long moment. "I think we both need a good night's sleep," he said finally.

She nodded slowly, stood there, slim back straight, head held high, still touchingly pale. "Yes. You're right. Good night, Ryan."

And she returned to the bedroom—alone—leaving him to sleep on the couch. Alone.

"I have to go back to L.A."

Sera struggled up from the depths of sleep, her mind foggy, her mouth fuzzy. She pushed her hair back and blinked at Ryan standing next to her bed in the pale, early morning light.

"What?" She squinted at him.

"The hospital just called. My mom's not doing well. I'm going back right now. I just need a few things."

"Oh." She sat up straight. "Oh no."

"Sorry to disturb you." He yanked open a dresser drawer and grabbed some clothes, tossed them into a duffel bag.

"That's okay. God, Ryan, it's okay. What can I do?"

"Nothing." He snagged a couple of shirts out of the closet and a pair of jeans and started to change. Right there in front of her. He turned his back on her as he stepped out of the boxers he'd apparently slept in and tossed them into the laundry hamper. His long, muscular body was entirely naked. She admired the muscles in his legs and his back, rippling and flexing as he moved, her eyes lingering on the two indentations of his lower back just above his round, tight ass, and her hands longed to reach out and touch. He stepped into clean boxers then jeans, and turned back to her as he zipped up and adjusted himself inside the jeans. Her heart picked up speed at the wholly masculine, completely unselfconscious gesture. Then he dragged a clean T-shirt over his head, covering his bare torso with its firm pecs and ripped abs.

His nearly black hair hung loose around his shoulders and he reached for a brush on the dresser, slid it through the silky strands and fastened it at his neck in his usual ponytail. He didn't bother shaving, his face dark with stubble. God, he was sexy.

She shouldn't be thinking things like that when his mother was on her deathbed. How could she be so shallow? She struggled to control her breathing.

"What do you want me to do here?" she asked him.

"Just stay out of trouble."

"But...what about Zocco? Want me to talk to him?"

"Christ, no! Let me do that. I'll take care of it when I'm back."

"But…" It didn't feel right letting him leave like this. "Do you want me to come with you? I could drive…maybe you shouldn't…"

"I'm fine." His jaw tight, eyes narrowed, he flicked a glance at her. "Don't worry about me. I'll call you when I know more."

"Okay."

She sat there cross-legged, the covers across her lap, bit her lip as she watched him finish his packing then grab the bag.

"Bye, Sera."

And he was gone.

She stared at the closed door for a long moment, listened for the sound of his truck starting and driving away, the roar of the engine gradually fading into silence. Then she flopped back down on the bed. She hoped his mom would be okay. Worry gnawed at her stomach.

He was still angry with her. He thought she shouldn't have interfered, shouldn't have cared so much about what happened to Carly. She covered her eyes with her hands for a moment. He was right. She *shouldn't* care so much about what happened to Carly.

She sat up and swung her legs over the side of the bed, then headed to the bathroom for a shower. Her headache was gone and she felt mostly normal. Maybe she shouldn't have interfered with Carly and Vince. Maybe she just should have let things go the way they were supposed to, knowing that if their undercover operation went as it was supposed to, Vince would end up in prison where he belonged.

The thought of how Carly would feel when that happened grabbed at Sera's insides like a fist. Poor Carly. She was so dependent on Vince and being his woman. It made Sera ache, but she had to accept there was nothing she could do about that.

She poured shampoo into her hand and sudsed up her hair, then tilted her head back to let the soap wash down the drain.

She should go back to L.A. too. She had a huge stash of angel sugar she needed to get rid of. Before the cops decided to raid the house after what happened yesterday. Jesus.

She cranked off the taps and shoved back the shower curtain. She wrapped her head in a towel turban-style, another around her body, and yanked open the bathroom door just as Manny emerged from the other bedroom.

"Uh...hi." He eyed her attire.

She rolled her bottom lip in. Oh hell, what did she care? Manny was a gorgeous guy, but there were no sparks there like there were with Ryan. She had no freakin' idea why that was, but it was the reality. "Hi. Need the bathroom?"

"Yup." He looked past her like he expected Ryan to be there and was afraid he'd interrupted something. A smile tugged the corners of her mouth.

"Ryan's gone back to L.A.," she told him, tugging the towel up under her arms. "His mother's not doing well."

"Oh." His brows drew down. "Damn."

"Yeah. He'll let us know how she is."

"Okay."

"And I'm heading back too. I have to log in all that sugar I bought and do my reports."

"Okay. I've got some things up today—possible lead on some guns."

"Great."

She moved past him, a cloud of fragrant steam following her out of the bathroom and returned to her bedroom to dress.

She spent the rest of the day at the ATF offices in L.A. She checked in with her SAC at the DEA to update him on how things were going, leaving out the messed-up emotional parts.

"Where's Thomas?" Darren barked at her at one point.

She stared back at him. "At the hospital. With his mother. Didn't he call you?'

He scowled. "Oh yeah. He left me a voice mail. I forgot. How long's he going to be there?"

"I don't know," she replied evenly. "I suppose until he knows what the situation is with his mother. It's possible...she might pass away."

Darren's scowl deepened. "Great. Just what we need right now.

My ass is on the line with this op and he's taking some personal time. Jesus."

She watched him walk away, his middle jiggling under his shirt, and tucked a strand of hair behind her ear. She no longer worried about being callous. Darren Forsythe had that market cornered.

Her cell phone rang. She reached for it, checked the caller ID. Ryan. She smiled and flipped it open. "Hi."

"Hi."

He said nothing more, so she asked, "How's it going?"

There was a long pause. Then he said, "She's gone."

Chapter Sixteen

Sera's heart squeezed. She leaned back in her chair. "I'm sorry, Ryan. So sorry."

"Yeah. It's okay." Silence again. She pictured him, his beautiful face, the sadness he no doubt felt.

"Where are you?"

"Still at the hospital." Another pause. "I have to make some arrangements…" The low tone of his voice told her all she needed to know.

"What can I do?"

"Nothing. That's not why I called. I just wanted…to tell you…"

"You have to let Darren know."

"Yeah. I will." The despair and hurt in his voice stabbed at her. "I'm going to need some time off. A few days, I guess." She imagined him shoving a hand through his hair.

"That's okay. We can put things on hold for a few. No big deal." She wasn't sure if Darren would echo those words, but whatever.

"Yeah. Thanks. Maybe you could call Vince. Or Carly. Let them know that's why we're not around."

"I can do that."

"And Manny."

"Of course. What else?"

"I…nothing. That's okay."

She wanted to see him. She ached to see him, to touch him, to comfort him in any small way she could. And she realized she didn't even know where he lived. Another moment of irony. They lived together in Clover City, had slept together, but she didn't know where he lived for real. God.

Hot Ride

"When will the funeral be?"

"I don't know." Silence. "I'm going to try for Friday or Saturday. Gotta give the relatives from out of town a few days to get back."

"Will you call me and let me know? Where and when?"

"Sure."

"What are you going to do now?"

"I have a call in to the funeral home. I have to go there and...do stuff. I don't have a hot clue."

"Do you want some help?" Her tone was soft. "I can come..."

She fully expected him to say no. That's what she would do, in the same situation. So she was surprised when he said, "Okay."

She blinked. "Where should I meet you?'

She made arrangements, touched and warmed by the fact that he actually wanted her, wanted her help, wanted her there.

She met him at the funeral home, sat with him while he planned with the funeral director. She didn't know Ryan's mom, couldn't help with any of the numerous decisions that had to be made, but she could support him on the ones he had to make. An only child, like she was, he was on his own with this.

When they emerged from the building into eye-stabbing sunshine, they both slid sunglasses onto their faces. "What now?" she asked him, slipping her hand into his.

"I have to make some phone calls. I'll call Mom's sister in San Diego first, and ask her to pass the news on about the funeral."

"So you're going home?"

He stared straight ahead, standing on the sidewalk. "Yeah. I guess."

He sounded so unenthusiastic, she said, "Come to my place. I'll make us something to eat."

"I'm not all that hungry."

"I know. But you have to eat. Come on."

She gave him her address, in case they got separated when he followed her home, but he pulled up on the street in front of her apartment building just as she parked in her parking spot.

They went in together. Again, the air in the apartment felt stale and flat. She needed to light some of her favorite candles, open the windows, turn the air conditioning down to cool it off.

She attended to those things while Ryan used his cell phone to make the calls to family, giving them details of the funeral. She opened cupboard doors and surveyed the contents, wondering if she had anything at all she could make into a meal for them. Luckily she put her hands on a box of pasta, a can of tomatoes and some dinner rolls in the freezer she could turn into garlic buns.

Ryan wandered into her tiny kitchen as she worked, chopping garlic that had kept well in the garlic jar on her counter. She tossed it into a pan of fragrant olive oil and gave it a stir. "Smells good," he said, sitting on a stool at the counter separating kitchen from living room.

"It's not much, but at least I had something."

She chopped more garlic and mixed it up with margarine from the fridge.

"Do you want to talk about it?" she asked. "About your mom. Did she die this morning?"

"Yeah." He heaved a sigh. "I was with her all night. They didn't think it was going to be long. Then her heart stopped at about two in the morning. They resuscitated her, but I knew she wouldn't want that. It was only a matter of time. So when her heart stopped again, we just...let her go."

Sera paused in the act of spreading the buns with garlic butter. She wanted so much to make him feel better, the words came easily to her lips. "It's not something to be afraid of." At his lifted brow, she added, "Dying. It's peaceful and calm. She's in a wonderful place now."

He stared at her. After several heartbeats of silence, she said, "I told you about when I tried to commit suicide."

"Yeah." His eyebrows pinched together.

"Well, for a while I actually was dead. On the way to the hospital in the ambulance."

"Okay." He blinked. "They resuscitated you at the hospital."

"You could say that. Or you could say I decided to come back."

"Huh? Come back from where?"

She sighed. "I had a near-death experience. I was..." She bit her lip, peeked at him through her eyelashes. "I was outside my body for a while. I was watching them try to resuscitate me, rushing me to the hospital. It was very...weird. I wasn't down there being worked on, I was floating above. I could move around."

"Don't tell me. You saw a bright light..."

She pursed her lips. "Don't make fun of me. I'm not the only person this has happened to; it's an accepted phenomenon."

He shrugged. "Yeah, I've heard that before."

"Yes, I saw a bright light. It was as if I was looking down a long corridor of dazzling light. After I'd watched myself, watched the people working on me, I was tired of it and I wanted to go. But I came back." She hesitated. "It wasn't scary, Ryan. Sometimes it gives people comfort to know that their loved ones have gone somewhere wonderful and beautiful and peaceful, away from the evil and hardships and pain of life. Your mom is okay now."

For a long moment he said nothing, and she arranged the garlic buns on a baking sheet. "Thank you," he finally said, his voice hoarse. "That does help. I want to believe that."

The fact that he didn't argue with her or tell her she was crazy or even get up and leave squeezed her throat. "It's up to you to believe, or not," she said. "I think it helps. If you believe."

She finished making their dinner while he talked about his mom, and Sera felt unreasonably sorry that she had never met the woman who had raised such a strong, moral, determined man. She also felt envious of Ryan for having a mother who loved him that much, unconditionally, no matter what, unlike her own mother who would have sold her daughter to feed her addiction. Her chest tightened uncomfortably as she compared their lives.

And yet they'd ended up in the same place, doing the same thing, fighting the same fight.

"It's weird," Ryan said after dinner. "I always knew she was there, in the background, rooting for me, even when I was undercover and couldn't see much of her. I don't know how I'm going to do it, without her there." One corner of his mouth deepened as he rose from the stool to help Sera do the dishes. "I'm all alone now."

She'd been alone so long, she didn't think much about it. Usually. The image of her father flickered through her mind. Okay, yeah, he was there in the back of her mind too, but it was different. Ryan knew his mother loved him and was there for him. She knew no such thing. Her father had left her and never come back. Maybe he was out there somewhere, but she was never going to know that, so it wasn't worth thinking about.

When the dishes had been loaded into the dishwasher and it hummed away, Sera turned to Ryan, drying her hands on a towel. He looked so lost, so boyishly sad, that she moved toward him without thinking and wrapped her arms around his waist in a hug. His big, warm body felt solid and strong. She pressed her cheek to his chest, inhaled the scent of him, the clean, male scent of his soap mingled with the faint peppermint of antacids. His arms slid around her too, and he laid his face on her hair. They stood like that for a long moment, their hearts beating against each other, breathing in unison.

"Thank you, Sera."

She lifted her head at his whispered words. "For what?"

His lips quirked. "For the hug. For the comfort. The understanding. Mostly, just for being there."

She didn't know what to say, her throat tight and achy. So she just leaned against him again. His hands stroked through her hair, and then he tipped her head back and lowered his face. He paused, their mouths only a breath apart, and their eyes met. He held her captive with his gaze, those endless amber eyes drawing her in and in…and then her eyes fluttered closed as his mouth touched hers in a soft, brushing kiss.

She kissed him back, gentle puckers of her lips against his, once, twice, then he deepened the kiss, his mouth opening wider, his tongue stroking across her bottom lip. She opened for him, met his searching kiss with her own, digging her fingers into the soft fabric of his shirt at his back.

Hot Ride

One hand cupped her head, the other slid down her back to her butt, resting there, spreading heat. Warmth cascaded over her and she pressed herself against him, sliding her arms around his neck and spearing her fingers into his silky hair.

Last time, they'd been hot and panting for each other, sexual need fueled by the adrenaline of their physical fight. Tonight, it started as a comforting hug, a reassuring kiss, gentle warmth and consolation, but it quickly combusted into a blaze of desire, consuming both of them in its heat.

Flame spiraled inside her; fever suffused her. God! They kissed again and again, mouths craving each other, hands ravenous, bodies yearning.

"Sera," Ryan gasped, and held her head with both hands, holding her back from him. They gazed at each other. Her heart thudded, her skin burned. His mouth was wet and shiny, his eyes dark and hot. Did he want to stop?

She closed her eyes. His mother had just died, for heaven's sake, and here she was attacking him.

"Sera," he said again. She opened her eyes. "I know we shouldn't be doing this, but I want you so bad. I...need you." The aching need in his eyes reached deep inside her and squeezed.

She nodded, his hands following the movement of her head, and she slid her own hands to his face, cupped his cheeks, brushed his mouth with her thumb. "I know. I want you too."

Her eyes drifted shut and their mouths joined again, slowly, warmly, and she wasn't sure if she'd pulled him closer or he had moved her face. Her mouth opened wide for him and she tasted the faint mint of the antacids he'd chewed after supper, loving the taste of him, the sweep of his tongue, the feel of his body against her. It was like a drug. Intoxicating. Addicting.

Together they moved from the kitchen to her bedroom, where they undressed while watching each other in the shadowed room. Sera slipped out of the knee-length shorts and sleeveless shirt she wore, down to her panties and bra, and watched dry-mouthed as Ryan shrugged out of his shirt. When his fingers went to his fly, she tracked his movements with her eyes, anticipation buzzing inside her as his body was revealed to her. She tipped her head to one side to watch him step out of his jeans, admiring the muscles flexing in his legs, his lean hips, the eye-catching bulge in his boxer briefs. Her fingers longed to touch, to feel the weight of him, the softness and the hardness of him, and she stepped toward him.

She rubbed her hands over his chest, across flat nipples that hardened at her touch, rough hair between them, over smooth skin and hard bone of his shoulders.

His eyes smoldered at her touch, his hands clasping her hips. Heat surrounded them. She longed to make things better in his world, knew she couldn't make the pain of losing his mom go away. But she could ease it. She could make him feel alive. She kissed his chest, inhaled the warmth of him, the fresh masculine scent that she now knew as his alone. She kissed her way across his flat muscles, licked over the nub of one nipple and felt him quiver. Inspired, she kissed lower, bending her knees, skimming her lips over his abs, loving how they tightened beneath her caress. Then she lowered herself to her knees, the carpet soft beneath her, and kissed him just above the elastic of his briefs, where a thin line of hair dipped lower.

His hands went to her hair and fisted there, the tug sending pleasure streaking through her. She pressed her cheek against the bulge of his cock beneath soft cotton, closed her eyes and again inhaled, his scent there distinctly musky-male. Arousal crashed through her, made her ache down low. With a murmur of pleasure she rubbed her cheek against him, then kissed him through the cotton. Her mouth watered and the need to taste him had her slowly drawing his underwear down, over thick, hair-roughened thighs, to drop to the floor. With small movements, he kicked them off his feet, and his fingers tightened more in her hair.

Burning hot, silky flesh tempted her and she forced herself to take her time, to slow down enough to admire the shape and size of him, to test the weight of his balls in her hand. She loved how tight and firm they were, loved the shape of the head of his penis, the thickness of it. She stroked a finger along prominent veins, then dragged fingers through the thick thatch of dark curls at the root.

"Christ, Sera." She slanted a glance upward, saw his darkened cheekbones and firm mouth. His head tipped back, and eyes closed, he almost looked in pain. Yet his hands held her head there. She licked her lips first then leaned in to taste him, a swipe of the tongue over the head wringing a gasp from him. She swirled her tongue over and around, wanting to get him wet, then licked up and down the shaft.

She felt his reaction in the hardness of his hands, the tremor in his legs, the way his cock jerked and swelled at her touch, and it thrilled her to do that to him. Her mouth ached for him, and she opened wide and drew him in, tongue sliding wetly, cheeks hollowing as she sucked him.

"Fuck!" The pull on her hair sent sharp sensations skittering over her, and she moaned, her mouth full of him. The smarting shimmered through her, intensifying the pleasure she took at having him in her mouth. She loved it.

He didn't stop, tugged harder, and she went mindless and hot. She took him deep, as deep as she could, sucked him, licked him, devoured him. He moved his hips, held her head, fucked her mouth with muffled groans and whispered praise. "So good...Sera, your mouth is so hot...love that."

She caressed his testicles, drawn up tight, and when his body tensed and his hands tugged hard on her hair to pull her head away from him, hot pinpoints of sensation zigzagged from her scalp to her pussy, and with a muffled protest she kept her mouth around him, held the base of his cock with one hand, pumping, cupped his balls with the other until he exploded in her mouth, hot spurts of sharp taste, and she held him there, lips stretched, sucking and swallowing.

"Ah, Christ, Sera, Christ." His fingers released her hair and held her skull, his hips pulsing toward her. Then she slowly slid her mouth off him, with one last swirl of her tongue over the head of his cock. She looked up at him, and their eyes met. The rapture in his eyes and the softness of his mouth sent tender feelings drizzling through her, like sweet, warm syrup. She wiped her mouth and rose to her feet, sliding herself against him as she stood, his hands on her arms helping her.

"Jesus," he gasped, and she kissed his mouth. "That was unbelievable."

She brushed her smiling mouth across his again. "Yes, it was. Mmm, you taste good, Ryan."

He groaned and wrapped his arms around her, squeezed her tight. "I'm gonna need a few minutes, dammit." He picked her up and carried her to the bed.

"That's okay." They settled under the poufy duvet, bodies pressed together, and they kissed again, long, lush kisses. Ryan's kisses wandered from her mouth to her jaw, nipped at her neck, sipped at the pulse at her throat. She tipped her head back, gave herself up to the floating, the heat seeping through her. His tongue tasted her, his mouth stroked her, sensation building and whipping over her body. Her breasts swelled as his beard-roughened chin rasped over her sternum, aching for his touch, and when he pressed a kiss between her breasts, she arched against him.

He slid his hands beneath her to unfasten her bra then tugged it off and dropped it over the side of the bed. He kissed the inside curve of a breast, the under curve, and her nipples tingled in anticipation. She moaned, wanting to encourage him, but unable to formulate words. She pushed her fingers into his hair, remarkably still tied back, and she clawed at the elastic to free the silky strands. They spilled around his face, tickled her chest, and she grabbed his head and pulled his mouth to her nipple. With a muffled chuckle, he kissed the tip of her breast, a closed-mouth kiss, and she groaned again.

This was so crazy, so unbelievably hot, this man in her bed with her. She wanted to do everything for him, everything he needed and wanted. The thought caused a flicker of worry inside her. She'd never felt like that before, about anyone.

But he was hurting and although she was tough, she wasn't unfeeling. And now, she needed him too.

Then his tongue slid over her nipple in a heated, satiny lick. It still wasn't enough. Her whole body quivering, she pressed up, and when he took her nipple into his mouth and sucked, sensation exploded in her, streaming through her veins in hot sparkles. He sucked hard on the tip, and she felt it between her legs. "Oh god!"

He moved to the other breast, his hand covering the one he'd just sucked on, and his fingers played with her nipple, tugging and pinching. The exquisite sensations on both nipples shot a barrage of sparks through her body, coalescing in her pussy in a heated rush of arousal.

She moaned, shifting her legs against smooth sheets, her hips lifting with need. Ryan placed a hand on her lower stomach and held her there as he continued to suckle at her breasts, lips tugging, tongue licking, teeth nipping in sharp little stings, until she felt both her nipples were glowing hot points of sensation.

His hand slid lower, inside her panties, over her curls. She parted her thighs to allow him there, moaned, turned her head on the pillow. His fingers curved over her pussy and at first his fingers just held her, and she pulsed against his hand while he continued to torment her aching, blazing nipples. Oh dear god in heaven, she was going up in flames, heat and need swelling in her womb, making her arch her pelvis into his touch. She needed more, sought relief, and finally his fingers moved, parting her folds and sliding into her wetness.

She breathed out a long sigh, spread her legs farther, let him dip his fingers into her opening, slick her cream all over her pussy in slow, sizzling strokes, up, down, around. It was like that night in El Mirage when he'd stroked her to orgasm with a slow, sure touch. He circled her quivering and needy clit, around and around, down for more honey, back up and around.

"Ryan!" she gasped. Her hips lifted almost off the mattress. He lifted his head from her breast and sent her a wicked smile.

"What?"

"I need...I..."

"Mmm." He turned his gaze to her nipples to survey what he'd done to them, gave each tight, burning tip a last lick, then kissed his way down over her tummy. Settling himself between her legs, he hooked his thumbs into her panties and drew them down over her legs, tossing them aside as he had her bra. Then he pushed her thighs farther apart and studied her. God, oh god. She bent her knees.

She felt his breath feather over her pussy as he murmured her name. He parted her with his thumbs, leaned in and licked her. Hot flames sparkled inside her, built into a conflagration, rising up, and yet she needed more, she needed his tongue, his mouth right *there*...oh sweet Jesus yes, there. He kissed her clit, a firm kiss that made her jerk, and she pressed a hand over her mouth to hold in the noise that tore from her throat.

He kissed her clit again, and wetness gushed between her legs. Then he kissed her folds, a kiss to one side, a kiss to the other, soft, sucking kisses, drawing swollen sensitive flesh into his mouth and releasing it with a brush of tongue. The sensuality of it, the gentle care of it, melted her inside and she dissolved into a puddle of helpless bliss.

Sensation built to an unbearable peak and when finally he did the same to her clit—a kiss, a soft suckle, a brush of his tongue—she spasmed and burst, cried out, body tight and arched. He sucked on her clit with firm but gentle pulls and she felt as though her pleasure poured from her body into his mouth and he swallowed it, took it from her and gave it back.

He slid up beside her, hand cupped over her pulsing pussy, then he swiped fingers deeply through her slick folds and lifted his hand to her mouth. "Taste yourself," he murmured, watching her with hot eyes. "You taste so sweet, Sera, like honey and peaches." She held his gaze, opened her mouth, and in the most erotic moment of her life, she licked her own essence from his fingers. She sucked on him then released him, and he moved over her. His cock had swollen and lengthened to stunning proportions again.

"Need a condom," he muttered. "Do you...?"

"Yeah." She rolled over and fumbled around in the drawer of the table beside the bed, then handed him the package. He held himself and rolled the condom onto his impressive erection, then his warmth enveloped her again as he moved over her and probed at her entrance. She bent her knees and lifted her legs to open for him, still soft and sensitive from the orgasm, and when he pushed into her she closed her eyes with delight, the pushing, stretching sensation of him inside her an exquisite pain.

She clasped his back with her hands, her body tightening and trembling around him, tried to pull him in with every little inner muscle, and he sucked in a breath.

"Tight," he whispered. "Hot. Wet. Sera."

"Yes."

"I love how you feel around me."

"I love it too." She wondered at the wisdom of using words like that to describe what they were doing. Love was an important word. A special word. A frightening word. And yet...the right word.

She wrapped her arms and legs around him as he rocked against her, hot muscles, damp flesh and impaling cock. He drove deep, hitting her cervix, her body hypersensitive, and when he slid his hand between them to stroke over her clit, she came again in long, rolling waves of rapture.

"Ah, Sera." His long groan came from deep inside him as he thrust harder, faster, prolonging the ecstasy of her orgasm as he strove for his, and then he too tightened, spasmed, eyes closed, jaw tight as he poured himself into her in long, hard pulses.

They lay together, legs tangled, arms wrapped around each other, spent and drowsy. Ryan stroked a lazy hand over Sera's silky hair, her face pressed to his chest.

"I didn't tell you the whole story about my near-death experience."

Ryan's hand stilled. Now what? "Go on," he murmured. He was almost comatose with sexual satisfaction but she wanted to talk.

She kept her face averted, stroked her fingers through his chest hair. For a moment he thought she wasn't going to say any more. Then, "There was someone else there with me in the corridor—I couldn't see what he looked like because the light was so brilliant, but I felt so peaceful and accepted. He asked me to think about what I'd done in my life and I started to see my life in scenes like a movie. He told me I had more to do."

Jesus Christ. Those must have been some good drugs she'd taken. "Sera. I think that was likely some kind of hallucination from the drugs you took."

"I should have known you would think I'm nuts," she mumbled against his chest. "Anyone else I've ever told has."

A wash of shame heated him. She was serious. This was serious.

She lifted her head and met his eyes. "I wasn't afraid. Because I was dead, nothing else could hurt me, I guess. I was just...interested. I felt very relaxed, detached, almost. Then he said, 'You know you have to go back. Because of your mom.' And I did know. I knew he was right and that I had to go back for something. I didn't know exactly what it was." Her eyes implored him for understanding. Belief. Faith. "I didn't want to go back. My life was crap and I was scared and it felt so lovely there. But then I realized because of my mom that I was supposed to help other girls who get hooked into drugs. That's why I came back."

She paused for another breath. "My friends thought I was crazy. They all dumped me. Told everyone I was crazy. My family...well, I didn't have much family. I never told any of my foster parents. I learned to keep this all to myself. There's never been anyone in my life who understands it." He held her gaze, her face pale and tight. "And I don't expect there ever will. I don't know why I told you this."

He didn't know what to say. His chest ached, ached for what she'd gone through as a kid, whether it was some kind of psychotropic dream, or a vivid imagination, or...he couldn't come up with much else. Kids could be cruel, and when she said there'd never been anyone in her life who understood and she didn't expect there ever would be, he hurt for her. He could only imagine the loneliness that came from feeling so different and not having anyone who loved you anyway.

He slid his hand into her hair and brought her head down against him again, holding her.

He thought of his mother, how he'd been such a burden to her through his wild teenage years, constantly in trouble, unable to control his temper, fighting with her to the point of making her cry time and time again. And yet...she still loved him. To her dying day, she'd loved him anyway. The thought that Sera'd never had that, and her belief that she never would, felt like a jagged blade twisting in his heart. Had she hoped for that from him? Was that why she'd told him?

"I see women like Carly, and I just...I have to do this," she added.

He nodded slowly.

"Just promise me you won't tell anyone else. If they think I'm working on this case because of some psycho, near-death experience...well, I don't want to get fired."

He'd heard some whacked stories, some truly horrible experiences that had motivated his fellow agents to do the kind of work they did, but this definitely took the prize. And yet, he understood that feeling—that need to fight for something.

She lifted her head to look at him again. "I truly believe that, Ryan, and I'm doing some good here. I'm getting so close... I know Dominick Casas is linked to it, and if we can get to them and save even one life, it's worth it. I just...want you to know why this is so important to me."

She pleaded with her eyes for understanding from him. He stared back at her. Hey, there were a lot of people who claimed to have had a near-death experience. It didn't make them crazy. Right? "I won't tell anyone else."

Chapter Seventeen

A buzzer woke Ryan and he struggled to figure out where the hell he was, why he felt so goddamn good even though he thought he should be feeling bad—and memories of the day before flooded back, his mother dying, and Sera being there.

Sera.

They lay in her bed, their legs tangled together, body pressed to naked body, her soft breast against his chest, her cheek on his shoulder, her long, silky hair draped across both of them.

The buzzer sounded again.

"Your door." He pressed a kiss to her hair. "Sera."

"Mmmm."

"Someone's at your door."

"Huh?" Her eyes flickered open and the buzzer sounded again. She frowned. "Who the hell could that be? What time is it?"

Ryan was shocked to see they'd slept until almost ten o'clock. After several rounds of healing, restorative, life-affirming sex, they'd finally fallen asleep in the early hours of the morning.

"Want me to see who it is?"

She sighed and rolled away from him, and without waiting for her answer, he climbed out of her delicious bed and grabbed his jeans. He didn't bother with underwear or a shirt, didn't even bother doing up the top button, and strode to Sera's door. He flung the door wide, unconcerned about safety or security, to find an older man standing there.

They both stared at each other with matching consternation.

"Uh...can I help you?" Ryan finally said, since the man wasn't saying anything.

"Is...Sera here?"

Ryan tipped his head to one side. "Who's asking?"

Then he heard Sera's voice behind him. "Leo. What are you doing here?"

Ryan looked over his shoulder. Sera stood behind him, doing up the belt on the silky, pink-flowered robe she now wore.

"I just popped by to see how you're doing. I thought you were home."

Who the hell was this old guy?

His eyes moved between her and Ryan, and Ryan's skin heated.

Sera sighed. "Um. Leo, this is my...uh...partner." Her face turned a vivid shade of scarlet. "Ryan Thomas. This is my neighbor, Leo Manchester."

"Hey. Mr. Manchester. Nice to meet you. Come on in." He stepped aside to allow the older man to enter, which he did with an interested look at Ryan.

"You're her partner?" The older man's brows drew together.

"Yeah. On the...uh..." *Shut the fuck up,* he told himself. He resisted the urge to roll his eyes at his own babbling.

"Leo." Sera's voice softened. "How are you?"

He handed over a stack of mail and newspapers. "You really should cancel the newspaper if you're going to be away so much," he told her. She took the papers from him with a sigh.

"I told you, I don't need you to do this for me. And how the hell do you know when I'm home, anyway? Every time I come back, you show up."

He smiled. "Just lucky, I guess." Then he glanced at Ryan. "You're her partner? As in, work partner?" He lifted a brow, clearly inferring more than business from the fact that Ryan was there, in the morning, neither of them dressed...

Ryan's skin heated. He sent a glance toward Sera. "Uh..." *Christ.*

"You told me you had an office job," Leo said to Sera.

"I did. Up till a couple of weeks ago."

"Oh."

Sera frowned. "Geez, Leo, don't worry about it. This is my job."

"I do worry about you."

Ryan looked at Sera, saw the annoyance battling with affection on her face. Who the hell was this guy that he got her so worked up?

"Don't worry about me!" she said fiercely. "I can look after myself."

Leo looked back and forth between Ryan and Sera with interest.

"I'll...uh...go have a shower," Ryan said.

Sera nodded, her lips pressed together. "I'll make coffee."

He took a quick shower in the bathroom attached to Sera's bedroom. The woman was definitely an enigma. He replayed the conversation they'd had about her brush with death. Her experience had been out of the ordinary, for sure, and it killed him that people had rejected her, hurt her, because of it. But she'd told him, risked getting hurt and rejected again. He didn't want to do that to her, but it was kind of hard to accept.

She was so tough and independent. Too independent, goddammit. That was going to get her hurt too. She was driving him crazy! He didn't have time to worry about her! He had enough stuff to worry about. Jesus.

He almost growled as he sniffed the bottle of body wash he found in the shower. Much as he liked Sera's smell, he didn't want to walk around smelling all fruity girly.

He turned off the taps, dried himself on a thick, fluffy towel—way nicer than any of the threadbare towels at his place—and dressed in the same clothes he'd worn yesterday. He hadn't brought his bag in where it still sat in the trunk of the car. A change of clothes was only a few steps away but he hesitated to leave the bedroom.

When he cracked the door open and listened, he heard only silence. The rich aroma of coffee seeped into the bedroom. Christ, he could use a cup of coffee. He opened the door the rest of the way and walked into Sera's combination kitchen- living room. She stood at the counter, slicing a bagel in half.

"Who was that guy?"

She nodded, didn't look up. "I told you. My neighbor."

"Seems like he cares about you."

She hitched a shoulder. "He's just looking for someone to replace his daughter who apparently pays no attention to him."

His chest squeezed at her words and he stared at her slim, stiff back. The silky robe had slipped off one shoulder, and she tried to shrug it back on, but it just fell lower. Her bare shoulder gleamed in the morning light pouring in the kitchen window. He wanted to touch it, press his mouth to it, inhale the sweet, warm scent of her.

"Have something to eat before you go," she offered, dropping the sliced bagel into a toaster. "I'm sure you have lots to do today."

Gee, thanks. Why didn't she just kick him out the door?

"Hey," he said, moving up behind her and setting his hands on her waist. "What's wrong?"

"Nothing."

He grinned and laid his face on her smooth hair. "Are you upset that Leo found us together? Your reputation is ruined?"

She snorted. "Hardly."

He knew what was bugging her. The fact that her neighbor cared about her and worried about her pissed her off. And she cared about that guy too. She talked tough, but underneath the obstinate, rigid exterior was a soft-hearted woman who cared about people who couldn't look after themselves, like Carly and a lonely old neighbor who missed his daughter.

Ryan's chest ached. He was really losing it. He was getting all mushy over a woman—Christ, a *co-worker* no less. A woman he was more attracted to than anyone else in his life. A woman who'd just told him one of the craziest stories he'd ever heard.

Must be all the stress. The job, his mother's illness, now her dying...a man could only take so much before he cracked. And Sera was just so fucking sexy and sweet underneath that prickly exterior, she drove him out of his mind, had his dick and balls in both hands, hers for the taking.

But he wanted her. No. He cared about her. He wouldn't care

about someone who would lie to him. Someone who would invent crazy stories for some unfuckingknown reason. So yeah, sure. She'd come back from the dead with a mission. That was cool.

Chapter Eighteen

When Ryan returned to Clover City Sunday afternoon, he had to drag his ass there. He felt drained, all his resources sapped. The strain of the last months working undercover, always having to be on top of things, one jump ahead of the DAs, compounded by worry about his mother and now the grief of her death and the strain of her funeral, was sucking the life out of him. How much longer could he go on?

He pulled his truck into the driveway behind Sera's old Camaro. She'd gotten back before him. The funeral had been yesterday and he'd been amazed to see her there, after she'd practically booted him out of her apartment, and after another night of flaming sex. They really had to talk about that. He hauled his weary body into the house and followed voices into the kitchen. Sitting at the table were Billy and Crystal and—sweet Jesus, Bingo, tongue lolling out of his grinning mouth. Billy and Crystal were digging into bowls of...what was that? Ice cream? And Sera, standing beyond arm's range of Bingo, was offering him a dog biscuit.

"Good boy," she said, just a hint of a quiver in her voice. She stretched her hand out a little farther and Bingo delicately accepted the treat from her.

Ryan stopped in the door, taking in the scene. Bingo crunched the cookie, spewing crumbs all over the worn linoleum, which he proceeded to vacuum up with his mouth, crunching all the while. Sera looked up and saw him.

"Hi, Tommy."

Damn, she was good. Nothing but a pleasant hello.

"Hi." He looked at the kids. "What are you two doing over here? That's not my ice cream you're eating, is it?"

They grinned at his teasing. "Sara said we could have it!" Billy chortled. Crystal vigorously stirred her spoon through the melting treat in her bowl.

"Well, I guess it's okay," Ryan said with a smile. He walked over to Sara and put his arm around her shoulders. "Hey, babe. How're you?"

They didn't need to put on the act in front of the kids. He did it because he wanted to, and also because he wanted some reaction from her. He wanted to annoy her. He wanted to drive her as crazy as she was making him. He wanted to know what she was feeling, thinking, about them...about the fact that they'd slept together and had off-the-charts hot sex more than a few times. Even if she shoved him away or scowled at him, at least it was *something*.

She leaned into him, flattened a palm on his chest. "I'm good. You?" When he looked into her eyes, he could see the genuine caring in the question.

"I'm bagged." He stroked her hair. "Totally wiped."

She made a soft sound of sympathy.

Ryan jerked his chin at the dog. "You let him in the house?"

The faintest flush of pink rose in her face. "Yeah. So?"

He could only imagine the courage it had taken her to do that, after her terrified reaction to the dog the other day. When he'd pulled those dog biscuits out of the shopping bag, he'd wondered what she planned to do with them, but hadn't said anything. Now he knew.

"You two are friends now?" he murmured.

Her pink cheeks brightened. "Well, maybe not friends. But he's okay."

He hugged her tighter, then released her. "Can I have some of that ice cream? Or did these two ankle biters eat it all?"

She scooped ice cream into a bowl and handed it to him, and he was enjoying the cool creaminess sliding down his throat when the front doorbell rang. Then they heard voices calling out. "Hey, Tommy! You home?"

It was Vince. Ryan cut a glance at Sera. Jesus. Could he not have one night away from them? He'd just gotten back from his mother's funeral, goddammit. But he swallowed his sigh.

He straightened from where he leaned against the counter and sauntered out into the living room. "Yeah, man, I'm here. Just got back."

To his surprise, Vince came up to him and wrapped him a bear hug. "Man, I'm sorry about your mom," Vince said. He squeezed tighter. "Real sorry."

Ryan drew back in amazement and accepted another hug from Carly. "My condolences, Tommy," she said. "That's really shitty."

"Uh...yeah."

He found himself unable to speak. When he'd gone into the office for a few hours on Friday, he'd seen Darren and Josh, and so many others he worked with. Guys he'd worked with for years hadn't said a word of sympathy to him at the loss of his mother, and yet this outlaw motorcycle gang member—a criminal for sure, a wife beater definitely, a murderer even, maybe—was hugging him and telling him he was sorry.

"Zocco and A.J. are comin' over too," Vince told hm. "To pay their respects."

At moments like this, Ryan struggled to separate his real life from his pretend life, the fake life he'd created as part of his job. These guys he was investigating were people too, with emotions and lives, and it was difficult to reconcile the Vince he'd seen lay a beating on Carly only days ago with the man in front of him, sympathy shining in his eyes, almost more of a friend to him than anyone else.

Anyone except Sera. She'd been there for him.

And if all went according to plan, one day he'd be testifying against Vince in court and sending him to prison.

He swallowed hard as he heard Sera saying goodbye to Billy and Crystal and the mutt. Then she appeared and offered beers and they all sat down. Ryan didn't want to talk a lot about his mom or the funeral, just the barest details, and the conversation turned to work coming up the next week and a couple more jobs Vince wanted Ryan to do.

He was happy to take up Vince's offer but he desperately wanted to nail Zocco for that murder. So when Zocco showed up, also gave him a hug and slap on the back and some choked words of sympathy, Ryan had to focus hard on what he was trying to accomplish. The whole house was wired, so any conversations they had were captured, and he wondered if he could somehow get them talking about that murder.

But try as he might, making a conversational leap every time a possible opening came up, he couldn't direct the talk that way without it seeming really weird. Dammit!

When Sera and Zocco disappeared into the kitchen, he considered following them to see if maybe a private convo could be started up with the man, but they returned too quickly. Sera left the room and returned a moment later and Ryan realized she'd just made another buy. How the hell did she get the money for that so fast? She must have done it last week while they were in L.A. Had Darren given her a hard time again? How much had she asked for?

When their guests all left near midnight, Ryan could hardly see straight. He'd had a couple of beers, a bowl of ice cream for dinner, and he was running on empty, digging deep for any energy he could find.

"You're exhausted," Sera told him as she picked up empties and carried them to the kitchen. "You take the bed tonight."

So they were back to separate sleeping arrangements. "The bed's big enough for us both," he muttered through the fog of fatigue, yanking his shirt over his head even as he walked down the hall. "You can sleep there too. I won't touch you, I promise."

She followed him. "That's okay."

"Seriously, Sera. I'm so wiped I couldn't get it up if you stripped and gave me a lap dance right now."

She laughed. He was too tired to argue, though, so after shucking his boots, socks and jeans, he climbed into the bed, rolled to the far side and closed his eyes. There was room for her. She could sleep there if she wanted. If not...he was too tired to care.

Sera slept on the couch.

Tempting as it was to crawl between the sheets with Ryan, to

Hot Ride

press herself against his big, warm body, she knew she had to stay away. Sleeping with him had been awesome but probably not very smart under the circumstances.

She'd been kicking herself about telling him her crazy near-death experience story ever since. In those moments after sleeping with him and having seen him all unguarded after his mother's death, she'd had a moment of weakness too, and had confided her story and her feeling of having a mission. She knew better than to let her guard down like that. It could only lead to trouble.

But she hated to admit how lonely she'd felt in her bed the last few nights without him. She rolled over on the lumpy couch and adjusted her pillow. She'd slept alone her whole life. Ryan was the first man she'd ever spent the night with. They'd really only spent two nights together—one here, one at her apartment in L.A. That was not enough for her to get used to him being there. She was just overreacting to everything, from the stress of the job, compassion for Ryan at his mother's death. It wasn't anything to do with Ryan himself.

She kicked off the blanket, too hot, and rolled to her back, staring up at the ceiling in the darkness. The drawn curtains in the living room kept the room nearly black.

She fell asleep, but her dreams tormented her. She was fighting something, chasing something, frustrated and unsuccessful, and it went on and on until she finally woke up. She struggled to remember what or whom she'd been fighting with in the dream, but couldn't. Only the frustration lingered. She blew out a long sigh and sat up, now wide awake.

She debated turning on a light and reading a book or a magazine for a while, or maybe watching TV. What she really needed was an orgasm. That always helped when she couldn't sleep. She leaned back, slipped her hand inside the boy shorts she'd worn to bed. Her fingers stroked through her soft folds, only slightly damp. She needed a good fantasy... Her thoughts slid immediately to Ryan. To the way he'd kissed her, the feel of his hard cock inside her, stroking deep, touching that place. She relived their last lovemaking, the unexpected bliss of him going down on her. God! She'd had oral sex before, but Ryan's version had been mind-blowing. Heart-melting. The tender way he'd kissed and pulled at her sensitive flesh with his mouth sent shivers over her body all over again and had her wet.

A noise down the hall, the bedroom door opening, reached her ears. She jerked her hand out of her panties.

Manny wasn't there; he'd stayed in L.A. for another night, so it had to be Ryan awake too. She turned to see him walk into the living room, rumpling his long hair with one hand, rubbing his bare stomach with the other.

"Hey, how come you're awake?" he asked.

She fought for casual, her nipples tingling, her pussy aching and protesting at having relief snatched so rudely away. "I was having chasing dreams."

"Huh?" He stared at her, his eyes dark in the dim light. She huffed a little laugh.

"Chasing dreams. You know. When you're chasing something and you can't catch it. Or you're fighting with something, over and over."

He blinked at her.

"Don't you have those dreams?"

"Uh...maybe." He ambled over and sat down beside her on the couch. "What were you chasing?"

"I don't know. I don't remember. Sometimes I have dreams that are so real and I remember every detail. Other times, I know I was dreaming and I can't remember a thing."

"I don't have dreams."

She snorted. "Everyone has dreams."

Silence settled around them. The heat of his half-naked body radiated toward her. He still wore only his boxer-briefs, snug black ones that hugged his tight butt and the bulge of his penis and testicles. She wanted that penis, inside her, wanted him over her, in her, her pussy aching to be filled. The satiny skin of his shoulders gleamed in the faint light and she longed to reach out and touch, stroke, lick...

She closed her eyes.

"So, what do you do about it when that happens?" Ryan asked.

"Uh..." She coughed.

"Huh? What?"

Her eyes flicked to the recording equipment, hidden in the corner of the room. She stood up and walked over to it, pulled it out and flicked a switch. Then she turned back to him.

"An orgasm usually helps me sleep."

The expressions crossing his face were almost comical. His brows flew up, his eyes widened, his mouth opened. He snapped it shut, frowned, then smiled, a devilish, sexy smile. "I could help you with that."

"I'm sure you could."

They moved, were in each other's arms in a heartbeat, mouths joined in a feverish, desperate kiss. It didn't seem to matter that they both knew they shouldn't be doing this. It was way past that. They needed each other and wanted each other and were going to have each other.

Ryan shoved up her T-shirt and palmed her breasts, squeezing their fullness. When he captured her nipples in his fingertips she gasped, her nipples still tender from his attention a few days ago. Sensations shot from breast to womb, and she grew even wetter.

He buried his face between her breasts, his rough beard scraping exquisitely. His hand delved into her shorts, found her liquid core and she lifted her butt off the couch. Fast. She wanted it fast, needed an orgasm *now*.

She pushed her shorts down, reached for him, pulled his hard throbbing length out of his boxers and stroked.

"Slow down," he hissed.

"No." She gave her head a jerky shake, shoved him down onto his back on the couch, one leg off, one foot still on the floor, and climbed on top of him.

"Okay, okay." A smile flickered over his mouth and he gripped her hips as she took his cock in her fist, centered herself over him and lowered herself down onto it. He sucked in a breath and she let one out in a long whoosh, loving the way he filled her. "Here." He reached for her, found her clit, rubbed with his thumb in tight circles. She rode him, rising and lowering, taking him so deep it hurt, but it was a good hurt, a beautiful, fulfilling ache, and then a starburst exploded around her in a shower of sparks and she cried out.

Ryan's hips lifted below her as he thrust up and into her, his fingers firm on her hips, and she blinked the fog away from her vision to watch his face as he too came.

And then she realized they hadn't used a condom.

Chapter Nineteen

"Shit."

Ryan lay there, chest heaving, body tingling from his scalp down to his toes. "What?"

"We didn't use a condom."

"Yeah. Shit." His head lifted off the couch. Their eyes met. And held.

"I'm sorry," he said on a groan and let his head fall back. His cock still pulsed inside her and he could feel his semen seeping out of her. Too fucking late now. "Damn, I can't believe I did that."

"I think it was my fault." She eased herself off him and sat beside him. He swung his feet to the floor. He reached for the box of tissues and offered her some. "Uh...thanks." She snatched a couple of tissues and he tried not to watch as she mopped herself up. He knew the amount of semen had nothing to do with fertility or virility but he couldn't help feel a little pang of masculine pride at the copious amount of fluid oozing out of her. He wiped himself off too.

"I really needed that," she continued. "I, uh...so I'm sorry. But don't worry." She bit her lip and the unfamiliar uncertainty of the gesture tugged at his heart. "I'm on the Pill and I'm not...I don't...you won't catch anything from me," she finished in a rush. A smile pulled one corner of his mouth up.

"Same here," he assured her. "I haven't had sex for a long time. I mean, before you. And never in my life without a condom." Christ, it was true. His first bareback experience and he'd practically missed it, it had been over so fast. He sighed, shoved his hair back. "C'mere." He tugged her up against him and lay back down. She laid her head on his chest, traced her fingers through his chest hair, then skated her palm over the bulge of his pec up to his shoulder.

"Why were you awake?" she murmured. "You seemed so exhausted."

"I *was* exhausted." His hand stroked down over her back to her butt and cupped a curve there. She moved against him, as if she liked that. "I just started thinking about stuff."

"What kind of stuff?"

He moved a shoulder, squeezed her cheek again. "Just stuff."

She lifted her head and propped her chin on one hand to look at his face. "Talk about it."

When he still hesitated, she lowered her chin and looked up at him through her eyelashes. "Hey. I told you my darkest, craziest secrets. Yours can't be any worse than mine."

He met her gaze and held it for a long moment. She was right. She'd exposed herself to him, made herself vulnerable. Why should he be afraid of doing that with her? She was probably the only person he would ever do that with. He swallowed. "I was thinking about..." He stopped, unsure of his words. She waited. "When Vince walked in, the first thing he did was say how sorry he was about my mom and gave me a hug." Sera nodded. "Nobody else did that. Back at the office, Josh, Darren, Manny, everyone else we work with...I've known those guys for years. They knew my mom was sick. And nobody said a word. In fact that asshole Darren seemed pissed that I needed to take time off."

Sera dragged her teeth over her bottom lip.

"Then Vince and Carly, and A.J. and Zocco...they all cared more than my coworkers. These guys are criminals...but they're almost better friends to me than anyone." He closed his eyes briefly, his hands tightening on Sera's body. "You know, one of the things we have to be careful about going undercover is that we don't go so far under we can't come up."

"Are you worried about that? About yourself?"

"No. I know myself. I'm okay. But it did...scare me. When I felt like that, and then I had to remind myself about the scummy things these guys have done, it scared me. And then I thought, I'll be sitting in court testifying against these guys one day. And I almost felt like I'd be betraying my friends." He stopped, swallowed. "That's a really bad way to be feeling."

She smoothed her hand over his shoulder, the gesture tender and reassuring. "Yes. It is. But you know it is, and that's what matters."

"I'm okay," he said again. "Just saying it out loud helps. Thanks for not freaking out. Just sometimes it all gets to you, you know? The stress is almost paralyzing. The fact that we're always in danger, always on edge, always needing to be thinking two steps ahead...after a while it wears on you. Then I was worried about my mom, and now..." He closed his eyes again.

"I know," she said softly. "I feel it too, Ryan. After what happened to Carly, I didn't know if I could go on. If he hurt her again..."

"Yeah. I know. People get hurt. Things get stolen from innocent people. People buy drugs and take them and wreck their lives, and we let it happen just so we can have evidence."

"I know it's all good in the end," she continued. "We have to think that, right?"

"Right." He opened his eyes. "Thanks, Sera."

"For what?"

"For listening. For understanding."

"Yeah, I guess. For me too. In some ways, this is way harder than I thought it would be. If it weren't for you..."

A connection stretched between them, drawing them together, close, inexorably, as their gazes held, warm and poignant.

"You know, I was thinking about something," she said, dropping her gaze.

"What?"

After a long pause, she replied, "My dad."

"What about him?"

"I was thinking about your mom dying, and about Leo and how he misses his daughter, and...I...well, maybe I should try to find my dad."

He went very still, knowing how huge this was for her.

"Okay."

"But I don't know where he is," she said, voice feathery.

He waited a couple of heartbeats. "Want me to track him down?" he asked, oh so casually.

After a short pause, she said, "You would do that?"

"I could try."

"Um. Okay." She pressed her cheek to his chest and they lay together in silence, and he stroked her long hair.

"I didn't want you here," he said after another long silence.

"I know."

"But now...I'm glad you are."

She went very still and silent for a moment. "We shouldn't be doing this." She tried to roll away from him, but he caught her, pulled her back against him.

"Doing what, exactly?"

She hesitated. "We shouldn't be having sex. We're partners."

He sighed. It wasn't the sex that was the dangerous part. It was all the feelings percolating inside him for her. *That* was what should not be happening. Emotions and becoming personally involved with someone on a case were the biggest mistakes he could make when he was trying to prove to his supervisor he could do it without.

Again she rolled away from him and he let her go. She stood beside the couch and looked down at him, all long, tangled dark hair, sexy mouth and shadowed eyes, her body slender and toned.

She was right. They should not be doing this.

"We need to regroup."

Manny, Ryan and Sera sat at the kitchen table the next morning, drinking coffee.

"I need to get Zocco's confession," Ryan said, staring into his black coffee. His insides burned with determination. If he accomplished nothing else on this op, he wanted to do that. He wanted to solve a murder and pin it on the gang. If it could be proved that a murder was committed on behalf of the gang, not only the individual murderer would go down but it would be huge toward indicting the entire gang. Nobody had ever done that before.

"You were dying to talk about that last night, when he was here, weren't you?" Sera clasped her hands around her coffee mug, a small smile playing around her mouth.

"Yeah. Just couldn't work it in there."

"I'm onto more machine guns," Manny said. "I think I can get this guy in Bakersfield to sell them to me."

"And I'm going to do a couple more big buys from Zocco," Sera added. "And then I'm ready to push to meet Casas. To see if he'll tell me about the lab."

Ryan's eyes shot to her. "What was that last night? I forgot to ask." Somehow she'd squeezed more cash out of Darren while he was gone.

"One more buy." She shrugged. "I have to keep showing him that I can sell the stuff. Lots of it. It's getting easier to get big quantities from him."

Ryan looked at Manny. "How'd she convince Darren to give her the cash for that?"

She waved a hand in front of his face. "Hello. I'm right here. Ask me!"

"Uh...sorry." He'd forgotten how much that irritated her. And now he knew the reason why. Holy crap.

"It wasn't a problem." She met his eyes. "The next one probably won't be either, but after that...he's going to have a shit fit when I ask him for a hundred grand."

"Jesus Christ!" He almost choked on his coffee. "You'll never get that from him, Sera."

"Yes, I will." Her small chin firmed with determination. "I have to."

Ryan exchanged a glance with Manny. "Uh...don't get your hopes up."

"That's the whole point of my being here," she said. "To get to the lab."

"Yeah, but...can't you do it for less money? Somehow?"

"We'll get the money back. That last buy will never happen. We're going to arrest them then. When we find the lab and get in there and confirm what they're doing—everyone will move in and we'll make the arrests."

"Uh...that's an idea," Ryan said. His mind raced. "We're going to need to talk more about that. With Darren. And the whole team. You can't just go making your own plans, Sera." She really had to learn that she was part of a team.

She scowled. "I *know* that."

"Okay." They'd cross that bridge when the water was under it, or whatever the hell that expression was. "Meanwhile, we need to figure out how to get Zocco talking about that murder."

"Maybe I can," Sera offered.

Ryan sat back in his chair. "Yeah? How."

"I don't know. It was Carly who told me about it. She knows. Maybe it's okay if I know too. A little indiscreet girl talk."

"You don't want to get Carly in shit with him," Ryan cautioned. "I don't know if I'd do that..."

"Well, you're not me." She stood and moved over to the coffeemaker on the counter to pour more steaming brew into her cup. "I'll see what I can do. No guarantees." She sipped her coffee and her face was veiled by the steam wafting from the cup as she stared back at him.

"Sera..."

"Believe me, Ryan, I won't do anything to hurt Carly. After what happened..." She shook her head. "That's the last thing I'd do."

He didn't know how she thought she was going to do this, and his gut cramped up at the possibility that she could cause more problems than she solved. "I don't like it," he bit out.

She heaved a heavy sigh. "I know. You don't like much that I do."

Memories of the two of them rolling around the bed together and the things she'd done that he'd liked very much invaded Ryan's head, and he almost groaned.

He ran a hand over his face. He'd accepted that her version of reality was different than his, but no less real. It wasn't that crazy. Lots of people claimed to have had near-death experiences, and he'd rather accept her reality and have her there than reject it and have her gone.

Chapter Twenty

They had their opportunity a few days later when everyone gathered at The Patch one night. Beers were flowing, joints were being passed around and everyone seemed in good spirits. Chatter rose and fell around the head-banging rhythm of Judas Priest's *Breaking the Law* and the crack of balls on the pool table. Ryan bought several rounds of drinks, mostly because Zocco was there, part of the group, and he hoped to loosen his tongue with alcohol.

He and Manny had come up with a strategy.

Vince and Zocco dropped into empty chairs with perfect timing.

"So you're saying you'd kill someone for three hundred bucks?" Ryan asked Manny, leaning on the table with both elbows.

Manny leaned back in his chair. "Maybe."

"What're you talking about?" Vince asked.

"Friend of mine just got sent to Legaldo." Ryan named the maximum security prison not far from Clover City. "He admitted he killed a guy. Shot him because the guy owed him three hundred bucks." He gave a short laugh. "I just wondered what would make a guy kill someone. Three hundred bucks doesn't seem worth it to me."

"Seems boneheaded to me," Vince agreed.

"Harsh is an idiot," Ryan said, referring to his fictitious friend.

"No, he's not," Manny said. "He knew what he was doing."

"He's in fucking jail!" Ryan said with a laugh.

"Sometimes you just gotta do these things," Manny said. "Right, guys?" He looked at Vince and Zocco.

"Right," Zocco affirmed with a nod.

"You've never killed anyone," Ryan said to Manny. "What the hell do you know?"

"How do you know I've never killed anyone?" Manny frowned.

Zocco grinned. "Who'd you kill, man?"

Manny's frown deepened. "I'm not gonna say I did or I didn't."

"Why not?" Ryan grinned too. "Pussy."

"I'm no pussy, asshole. I just don't want to talk about it."

Zocco laughed. "Why not? Nobody here's gonna turn you in."

Perfect. Excitement flowed through Ryan's veins. "How about you?" He lifted his chin at Zocco. "Ever kill someone?"

"Hell yeah." Zocco seemed proud of it. Vince sliced him a glance.

"No shit?" Ryan leaned back in his chair.

Zocco started to speak but Vince leaned forward. "Shut the fuck up, Zee."

Zocco turned to his chapter president and gave him an inquiring look. "What?"

"Just shut up."

Shitfuckdamn. Ryan wanted to curse out loud. Vince was smarter than Zocco. But then, that wasn't saying much.

"Hey, I wanna play pool," Zocco said. And he rose from his chair and made his way to the back of the bar where the two pool tables sat.

Hell. There went that opportunity. Vince was supposedly the one who'd ordered the hit, and he wasn't going to talk. It had to be Zocco. And he had to get him away from Vince.

Ryan searched the room for Sera and found her on the dance floor with Carly and Jessie. She always dressed a little trampy when they went out with the Angels—tight jeans and T-shirts, heavier makeup—but tonight she looked especially...well, hot. The same outfit on one of the other woman would've looked mega slutty, but on her it was just sexy.

A short, black skirt showed off her spectacular long legs. She'd told him she was an athlete in high school, running track, throwing shot put and javelin. That must've contributed to those long, toned muscles in her legs, the sleek muscles in her shoulders and arms revealed by the teal-blue halter top tied around her neck. The silky fabric didn't hide the fact that she wasn't wearing a bra, and her tits jiggled enticingly beneath it as she danced. She laughed at something Jessie said, and her bright smile sucked the air out of Ryan's lungs.

Christ. He found himself thinking about her almost all the time. That was bad. Very bad. He needed to be thinking about the case, needed to be on top of his game. His eyes were continually drawn to her, wherever she was in the bar, whoever she was talking to. Then he scowled as a man approached her on the dance floor and said something to her. She shook her head, flashed him a smile, and kept dancing with the other women.

One corner of Ryan's mouth turned down. The guy must've asked her to dance. *Back off, pal. She's taken.* The thought was instinctive and he had to stop and remind himself it wasn't strictly true. He drained his beer, considered having another, but knew he had to keep his wits about him.

Then Vince ordered another round anyway. He'd just have to drink it *reeaaal* slow. His eyes met Manny's and only a flicker gave any sign that he shared Ryan's frustration.

Sera and the girls returned to the table, laughing and breathless, and there wasn't room for enough chairs so Sera sat herself down on Ryan's lap and slung one arm around his neck. She smelled delicious, warm and fruity-sweet. She reached for his beer and took a big drink and he let her. Her breasts pressed into his chest as she reached across him to set the bottle back on the table. His hands curved around her hips. She smiled down at him, dark-shadowed eyes gleaming, lips shiny with red gloss, and once again he forgot to breathe.

"Hey, where's Zocco?" she asked, looking around. "I need to talk to him."

"He went to play pool."

"Okay." She slid from Ryan's lap and the drag of her ass across him made his dick stiffen. She lifted a brow as she looked at him. Hell, she must have felt that. "I'll go find him."

He let her go, even though he wanted to follow her. He knew she was going to tell Zocco she wanted more angel sugar, this time even more. He hoped like hell she wasn't going too fast with this. Zocco wasn't that bright, but he was definitely paranoid about some things. And was she going to try to talk to him about the murder? Hell.

When Sera returned, a faint frown creased her forehead but she smiled at him. When she slid onto his lap again, he pressed his mouth to her ear, and whispered, "What?"

She shook her head, pressed her lips together and he got the message—later. Fine.

"Going to the ladies' room," she said, once again doing a cock-teasing shimmy off his lap. He held back a groan. "Carly, wanna come?"

The two women disappeared through the crowd. Manny and Vince were talking about guns and Ryan forced himself to listen and join in, knowing Manny was counting on getting this on tape and hoping for more incriminating details.

After a while, Sera still hadn't returned. He looked around for her then rolled his eyes at his obsession with her. Christ. Then Carly came back and sat down without her.

"Where's Sara?" he asked her, frowning.

"She stopped to talk to some guy," Carly said. "That guy that asked her to dance earlier...?" Then she glanced at him and her smile faded, her voice trailing off into her usual question, and Ryan pushed back his chair, scraping it along the wood floor, and stood. She'd mistaken his concern for jealousy. Which it wasn't. Whatever.

His height let him survey the room as he strolled casually to the back of the bar. He spotted her, the satiny top she wore gleaming in the light shining down from above her. A man stood close to her, too close, crowding her against the bar. She was talking to him, and had put out a hand, as if trying to push him back from her.

"Hey." Vince's voice spoke from behind him. Ryan glanced at him. "That guy's puttin' the moves on your woman, Tommy."

"I see that." Ryan scowled.

"You gotta stop him," Vince continued. "Let's go teach that asshole a lesson."

Oh shit. Drug-and-alcohol-fueled bar fight in the making. Vince had already started toward Sera and the man, and Ryan hastened after him, knowing he had to stop Vince from beating the crap out of the guy.

And yet—if he let the guy get away with moving on his woman, the other guys would all think he was a complete wuss. He'd lose all respect. Again, shit.

Vince had grabbed the guy's shirt from behind and yanked hard. Sera's eyes flew wide. Vince spun the man around and fisted the front of his shirt, giving him a shake. "Hey, buddy. This chick's off limits."

"Uh..." The whites of the guy's eyes gleamed. "Says who?"

Ryan rolled his eyes, and stepped up. "Says me. She's mine."

Vince drew back a fist, and Ryan grabbed it and stopped him. "What the hell?" Vince turned to him. "You gonna let him do that? He deserves to hurt."

"Yeah, yeah." Ryan was thinking fast, trying to ignore Sera standing there wide-eyed, hand to her chest. She could probably take the guy herself and thank Christ she hadn't or they'd really be in deep shit. "I'm gonna take him outside and kick his ass," he said.

But a crash beside him made him jump and he turned to see Zocco standing there with a smashed beer bottle in his hand, brandishing it like a weapon.

He swallowed a sigh. Goddammit. The guys thought they were coming to his defense, and really, he had to admire their loyalty and friendship, but fuck, they were making his life difficult.

"Put down the bottle, Zocco," he said. "I'll handle it." He grabbed the guy roughly and yanked him away from Sera. But Zocco was drunk and stoned—what else was new?—and lunged forward with the bottle. Without thinking, Ryan put up an arm to deflect the blow, and tried to get the guy out of there. He'd take him outside, give him a little punch on the chin and tell him to get the hell lost.

He dragged the guy through the bar. Luckily Ryan had a few pounds on him and was able to avoid the guy's fists as he tried to defend himself. Out on the street, around the corner where nobody would see them, he gave the guy a hard shove. "Get the fuck out of here," he snarled. "And be thankful I'm not kicking the shit out of you."

The guy started to speak, took a step toward him, and Ryan drew in a deep breath. Christ, the guy wasn't going to try to fight him for real, was he? But then the man's mouth dropped open. He gulped, and said, "Man, you're...bleeding." And then he turned and ran.

Ryan looked down at himself, and to his horror saw that his shirt and pants were soaked with blood. His arm had a huge deep gash across the forearm, dangerously close to the veins in his wrist. He stood there gaping at it. Wow. He hadn't felt a thing. What the fuck? Zocco must have nailed him with the bottle. Jesus Christ.

Suddenly he began to feel a tad lightheaded. He was bleeding like crazy. He leaned against the wall of the building and put his hand over the wound in a futile attempt to stop the flow of blood.

"Ryan?" Sera appeared around the corner. Her eyes flew wide and she rushed toward him through the dark. "Ryan, what happened? Oh Jesus, look at you."

"Fuck," he muttered. "Zocco sliced me with that bottle. Gotta stop the bleeding..."

"Your shirt." She dropped her purse to the pavement. She started at the buttons, then lost patience and ripped at the fabric. Buttons popped off in every direction. In a fog, Ryan vaguely remembered how strong she was. That was good. Very good.

She wrapped the shirt around his arm tightly. Christ she was trying to cut off his circulation. No, that was a *good* thing right now. *Riiiight.*

"Take me home," he said, clenching his teeth.

"Yes. Come on." She grabbed her purse and led him to where he'd parked the truck. She dug in his front pocket for the keys and he laughed.

She frowned at him. "What are you laughing about?"

"That feels good, but this isn't a good time for fooling around."

"No shit, Sherlock," she muttered, unlocking the passenger door and shoving him in.

She climbed into the driver's seat and turned to him. She looked so cute all worried about him. "I should take you to the hospital. You need stitches."

He sighed. "Ah hell. I can't go to the hospital."

"Why not?"

"Think about it. I either go there as myself and use my government health insurance. In which case I've blown my cover. Or I go as Tommy Briscoe, and sit there for hours—probably all night—because I've got no insurance, waiting to get stitched up. You know how they're gonna treat a biker gang member."

"Ryan. You're bleeding. You need stitches."

"Take me home. We'll look at it there and see."

She inhaled a long breath in through her nose as though he was trying her patience, and turned the key in the ignition. With a spray of gravel she pulled out of the parking lot then raced through the dark streets of Clover City to their house, breaking the speed limit all the way.

"Careful," he cautioned her, feeling strangely light-hearted and amused. "We don't want any more run-ins with the law. Remember last time?" He laughed.

She pressed her lips together but didn't slow down until she pulled into the driveway. She helped him into the dark house, led him to the bathroom where she began unwrapping the shirt tied on his arm.

She sucked in a breath when she saw the open flesh. Ryan looked down at his arm. Fuck, it was starting to hurt like a bitch. The room wavered and the floor shifted beneath him.

"Ryan!" She caught him as the floor came up to smack him, and again he appreciated how strong she was, although his weight almost took her down too. He wanted to laugh, but his ears were roaring and the room was going black.

She shoved his head down between his knees and held it there, and he was happy to stay like that while the noise stopped and the darkness cleared. Christ, what a pansy he was. He'd never fainted in his life.

"You have to go to the hospital, Ryan," she said again, her tone urgent.

"Don't want to go there. Can't go there. I'll be fine."

She crouched on the floor beside him, a towel now wrapped around his arm. He hadn't even noticed her do that. "Fine," she gritted out between clenched teeth. She stood and left the bathroom. He frowned. Where the hell did she go? She wouldn't leave him like this...and then she returned with something in her hands. His frown deepened and he shook his head, trying to focus.

She pulled out a needle and thread—fuck! Was she going to stitch him up herself?

She threaded the needle with black thread, then tugged one end of the towel, unwrapped it and dropped the bloody cloth into the bathtub. She pulled his arm across her lap then poured rubbing alcohol all over everything including his arm and the needle and thread. Fire consumed his arm, flames licking over his entire body, and he gasped. The fumes and searing pain made his head twirl even more.

"Sera..."

"Don't worry." She looked up at him, a cute little crease between her eyebrows. "Do you want something? A bullet to bite on? A shot of tequila?"

"Uh..."

She shrugged, bent her head and stabbed the needle into his flesh. He thunked his head back against the tile wall and closed his eyes, gritting his teeth until his jaw ached. He might have passed out, or maybe he just managed to blank out the pain stabbing at him with every poke of the needle through his flesh. When she stopped, he opened his eyes. She sat with her head bent, her hair a curtain obscuring her face from him. She prodded gently at his skin with her index finger as if testing it, pursed her lips, then shrugged.

"There," she said.

"Sera." He reached with his other hand to push her hair aside. Was he dreaming? Had she really just stitched him up? Maybe she'd taken him to the hospital and they'd given him some really good drugs, and he didn't remember. That's what this was. A psychotropic hallucination.

She unrolled a length of gauze and started wrapping it around his arm tightly. Now that the bleeding had stopped, he chanced a look. Huh. Didn't look too bad, considering. Well, the black thread was really ugly, but her stitches were neat.

He reached out and lifted Sera's chin and stared into her eyes. "Thank you, Sera."

Sera sat on the edge of the bathtub, her knees wobbly. A dull throbbing had started at the base of her skull and she knew it was only going to get worse.

"You're welcome," she muttered. She put a hand over her eyes, the glare of the bathroom light like knives into her eyeballs.

"You sewed me up." His words came out in a low, barely audible tone.

"Yes." She put her other hand out to the edge of the sink to steady herself as she rose. "I have to go lie down."

Ryan lumbered to his feet also, his body huge in the small space of the bathroom. He circled an arm around her waist and led her out the door. His strength supported her, his warmth reassured her. The pounding in her head intensified until her skull felt as if it were splitting in two.

Then the floor fell away from her feet and the ceiling tilted, and Ryan had her in his arms. "Don't!" she tried to protest. "You'll make your arm bleed again." He ignored her, strode across the hall into the bedroom and gently deposited her on the bed.

"I'll get the Tylenol," he said before he disappeared.

"Get some for yourself too!" She closed her eyes and sank into the blissful softness of the mattress and pillow, the hammering in her head a steady rhythm. She put her hands to her head and held it. Shit.

She'd known this was going to happen. Every time she saw blood, this happened. Why did she do this to herself?

Most of the time she had no choice. And tonight, well, what was she supposed to do—let Ryan bleed to death?

Possibly she was strong enough to have dragged him into the ER, if she'd driven there instead of home. But dammit, he'd been right. They'd sit there all night waiting for attention without insurance. She knew how the hospital staff would look at them. As if they were bikers. Criminals. They'd both experienced it, in restaurants, shops, with the cops. Or they blew his cover and ended the op.

No choice.

The words echoed in her head to the cadence of the throbbing. Then she sensed Ryan's presence. He pressed two tablets into her hand. "Here." He helped her sit up long enough to swallow some icy water and the pills, then laid her carefully back down. She felt him removing her boots then her jeans, and she knew she was in sad shape when she didn't even get turned on a little by him taking her clothes off. She let out a long sigh.

He tucked her into the covers and she tried to relax through the pain, breathed through her nose, eyes closed. Moments passed and she heard faint rustling noises and she waited for Ryan to leave, but to her surprise the bed dipped beneath her as he climbed in with her, wrapped his arms around her and pulled her up against his naked body.

She snuggled into him, and the hand that cupped her head felt comfortingly strong and steady.

"I'm sorry," she whispered, drifting on a haze of pain.

"Christ, Sera. Don't apologize. Please, don't apologize."

"How's your head?"

Waking up in bed together was extremely pleasant. Ryan pulled Sera against him and wrapped her up in his arms.

"It's fine now. How's your arm?"

"Hurts like a sonofabitch. But I'll live." He rested his cheek on top of her head. "It's blood, isn't it?"

She said nothing.

"It's okay, Sera." He waited but she still didn't speak. "What did you find out from Zocco last night?"

"Oh. I told him I want to meet Casas. Because I want to sell more sugar, and I need to make sure he can deliver. He's going to talk to him about it."

"That's good. But you didn't look happy."

"Yeah." She sighed against his chest. "I tried to talk about that murder, but I didn't get anywhere."

"Neither did we."

"Damn."

"Yeah."

They lay together for a while. Then Ryan said, "Thanks."

"For...?"

"For last night. For...uh...fixing me up."

"Oh. You're welcome."

This woman was amazing him, in more ways than one.

Chapter Twenty-One

"Did you talk to Dominick?" Sera spoke to Zocco in a low voice. They were at the house a few days later, a bunch of guys watching WWE on television again. She'd dragged him away from the television into the kitchen.

"Yeah." He shoved more chips in his mouth.

"Is he going to meet with me?"

Zocco scowled. "Yeah. He said he's coming to Clover City next week. He'll talk to you then."

"You know Tommy's been helping me sell the sugar," she said to him, leaning against the counter in what she hoped was a casual posture.

"Yeah."

"We've got a couple of really big customers lined up," she said. "The Coyotes in L.A. want to sell the stuff for us."

Zocco frowned. "Huh."

She studied him. "We want to meet with Dominick ourselves about this. Make sure he can actually supply that much sugar."

"He can."

"Well, I know he can," she replied and shot Ryan a glance as he walked into the kitchen. "But Tommy's a little more uh...cautious. He wants to make sure before we start making promises to people."

"We do that and we don't deliver..." Ryan spoke up. "Sara trusts you guys."

"But you don't?" Zocco seemed completely unoffended by that.

Ryan grinned. "I'm not stupid," he said. "I value my life. Some of these people aren't very nice, and you know yourself what can happen when a deal goes bad."

"Yeah." Zocco nodded understandingly. "I get it." He thought a moment. "You're still not going to sell the stuff here though?"

Sera shook her head. "No. This is your territory. We had a deal, and I'm sticking to it."

Zocco nodded again.

"I want to know where he gets the stuff," Ryan said in a hard, cold voice. "I'm getting the cash, and I'll front the money. I'll take that risk. But I want to know he's going to be able to keep up the supply before Sara starts telling people."

"This is big, Zocco," Sera said with a meaningful look at him.

"How big?"

She glanced at Ryan and he gave a nod. "A thousand hits. One gram each."

Zocco's eyes bulged. "Holy shit! That's a hundred grand! Where you gonna get that kind of dough?"

"I have my connections," Ryan said. He took another step into the room, hands in the pockets of his jeans. "Sara wants to do this and I think it's a good deal. So I'm arranging to get the money."

Zocco looked from one to the other. She could see the thoughts processing in his mind. He wasn't brain surgeon material, but he was canny and street smart. He was figuring out how much money was in it for him personally. She wanted to offer him a calculator, but instead just leaned against the counter and waited. Breathed. In. Out.

"Okay," he finally said. Greed won out. "I'll tell Dominick."

"Great."

"Hey, man."

Vince and Ryan sat at the bar at The Patch. It was only four in the afternoon, but Vince had called him and wanted to meet for a beer. Ryan had put him off on the pretext that he had one more delivery to do, long enough to get hold of Josh and get surveillance in place.

"Heard about your big plans with Zocco," Vince told him.

Ryan nodded. Caution tightened his muscles. "Yeah."

"You're getting into the drug business."

"Sera is." He lifted a shoulder, smirked at Vince. "I'm just helping her out."

Vince nodded. "Yeah. Well. Zocco says there's a lot of money it. She really have that kind of connections?"

Ryan paused as if thinking it over. "Yeah. I think she does. I wouldn't be putting up that kind of cash if I didn't think she could do it."

Vince nodded again, staring at his beer. "Well. You know. You've been hanging around with us a while now. You've done some good business for me. And now this." He lifted his eyes and met Ryan's gaze. "We want you to consider patching in with us."

Holy shit! Ryan wasn't sure he'd heard right.

He stared at Vince, who grinned.

"Really?"

"Yeah. You'd be a good DA. We need guys like you. You've got what it takes. You're loyal. Tough. Smart."

He still didn't know what to say. On a certain level, Vince's words pleased him, but Christ. He was not a biker.

Vince frowned. "What's wrong? Jesus, man, we don't make offers like that every day."

"No. I know. I just...you surprised the shit outta me, man." He grinned back at Vince. What the hell? What should he say? What should he do?

This was one of those classic fly-by-the-seat-of-your-pants undercover moments, where something totally out of the blue sent him reeling. He had to recover, regroup, buy time somehow. "That'd be great," he said. "Thanks, buddy." He lifted his beer and they clinked bottles together, his mind racing. Jesus Christ! Why now? Why couldn't this have happened weeks ago? As a full patch member he'd have access to all kinds of stuff he didn't now, things that would guarantee RICO convictions. Shit.

It was an unbelievable opportunity. Only a couple of agents had ever actually patched in with an OMG and he could be one of them. He could nail the whole DA chapter here in Clover City and probably others too. But it would take time. He'd have to become a prospect and go through "biker probation" which would take months. And worst of all, they'd likely expect him to kill someone. How would he get around that?

He didn't know if he had it in him. Months of doing this was taking its toll on him. So close. So fucking close he could taste it. Could he do this?

Zocco called the next week and told them Dominick was willing to meet them to discuss the deal when he was in Clover City. They'd meet at The Patch Wednesday night. They knew if they didn't convince Dominick of their ability, not to mention their sincerity and veracity, this would be their last chance to get to the lab. All was riding on this meeting. They had to be ready and their game had to be perfect.

Sera was ready. She looked at herself in the mirror, inspected her hair, the heavy eye makeup, the red lips. She didn't look like herself and sometimes she didn't even feel like herself anymore. Ryan was right. Working undercover was dangerous, for more reasons than just the obvious. You could lose yourself in the role, as he'd said, go so deep you couldn't come out. She pressed her lips together and walked out of the bedroom.

Ryan waited in the living room, jingling the keys to his Harley. "Ready?" His hot gaze surveyed her from head to the toes of her boots.

"Are we taking the Harley?"

"Yeah."

"Oh."

"Sera."

"What?"

He walked toward her and she took a step back at the intensity in his eyes. Since the night she'd stitched him up, he'd acted differently toward her. He treated her as an equal. A partner. The fact that he didn't boss her around, didn't question everything she said and did, made that tiny flame inside her burn brighter. The fact that he trusted her, believed in her, made her feel warm inside. And she knew that was the most dangerous thing of all.

"Why didn't you ever tell me you're afraid of motorcycles?"

"What?" She gave a little laugh and tossed her hair back. "I'm not afraid of motorcycles."

"Yes. You are."

Shit. How'd he figure that out? She'd thought she hid it pretty well.

He moved his head side to side, a smile tugging at his lips. "If you can make friends with Bingo, and you can brave the sight of blood long enough to stitch me up, a motorcycle shouldn't scare you."

She looked at him from beneath her lashes. Sure, he was right. But... "Fears aren't rational, Ryan. I know that. But you know how some people can't go on the Viper at Six Flags?"

He nodded.

"They know it's safe. They know they won't get hurt. But they can't do it. Because they're afraid."

He nodded. They stood there, looking at each other, an invisible spiral of emotion wrapping around both of them.

"Want to take the truck?"

She inhaled deeply. "No. I'm gonna do it."

"You," he said, walking over to her and kissing her forehead, "amaze me. Let's go."

She wanted to throw her arms around his neck, hold on and never let go.

At The Patch, they greeted the people they knew there, acted like the couple they were as they strolled through the bar, ordered drinks, then sat on stools and waited for Zocco and Dominick to make an appearance. Much as Sera thought the alcohol might help ease her jangling nerves, she had a hard time swallowing the icy liquid. Ryan's arm sliding around her waist and pulling her in for a hug was more what she needed. She sent him a quick smile.

She spotted Carly and Vince walk in. Well, that was okay. Then she noticed the look on Carly's face. Like she'd been crying. Oh damn. Had Vince done something again?

She tightened up and sat a bit straighter, pushed her elbow into Ryan's side and jerked her head toward the couple who hadn't spotted them yet. Ryan nodded slowly. Then Carly looked up and saw Sera. Her eyes widened and she immediately rushed forward, pushing her way through the crowd around the bar.

"Sara!" she cried as she closed in on them. "Oh, Sara. Something awful's happened."

"What?" Sera put out a hand and Carly grabbed it tightly. What could it be?

"It's Jessie."

"Jessie?" She stared at Carly. "What about Jessie?"

"She's dead."

Sera froze. Blinked. What? "What...how? What happened?" She swallowed tightly, staring at Carly in disbelief.

"She took some sugar. Too much sugar. She's been..." She swallowed. "She's been trying to lose weight. Especially since Chomp called her fat ass. I think she accidentally took too much." Her wide eyes gleamed with tears.

"Oh dear god," Sera breathed. She dropped her bottle onto the bar and took both of Carly's hands in hers. She knew hers were cold from holding the beer, but Carly's felt even icier. Their fingers wrapped around each others'. "When did that happen?"

"Just a little while ago."

Sera just stared at her, then lifted her eyes to Vince walking up behind Carly. He, too, looked like someone had just laid a beating on him, eyes dazed.

"I can't believe it," Sera said. She glanced at Ryan. His face was hard, but he put a hand on Carly's shoulder and squeezed.

That fucking drug! Curses ran through her mind. Goddammit! Where the hell was Zocco? This was all his fucking fault!

She glanced wildly around the room, but didn't see him. Which was good. She needed to take a breath. She couldn't react that way.

Trembling inside, every muscle tight with restraint, she tried to maintain her composure and act like everyone expected her to act—grief-stricken, sad, shocked—not ready to murder the man who'd sold Jessie those drugs.

Sera kept a tight leash on the rage bubbling inside her, reminding herself Jessie was not the first person to die from the drug, nor would she be the last. But if Sera could do anything—*anything*—to save even one more life, she would do whatever it took.

And right now, it took convincing Dominick Casas that she was who she said she was, that she could do what she said she could. That he could trust her.

But Casas apparently wasn't a trusting individual.

He arrived a short time later and made his way to a back room without stopping to talk to anyone. When she and Ryan entered, Casas sat at a small table, alone. This was the room where she'd made her first buy from Zocco, months ago now. She tossed her head and met his eyes straight on, stood there and waited for him to invite them to sit, the music of AC/DC pounding distantly.

"See if they're wearing a wire," Dominick said to a man standing at the door. Sera turned. The man was huge, as bald as Manny but much meaner looking, with ink-sleeved arms and a bulging gut that might have meant he was out of shape—except his equally bulging biceps displayed some impressive muscle power.

Shit. She did not want to be searched. She frowned, watched as the guy pushed Ryan to his knees, patted him down, everywhere. He found nothing, as she knew he wouldn't. Then he walked over to her, stood in front of her and looked down at her. His dark, slitted eyes gave her the creeps, but she stood her ground. Just let him try anything. Except she had to be careful.

The guy started frisking her, up and down, checked under her shirt. Ryan made a noise and a move toward her, but she sent him a warning glare. Her skin crawled and itched as she endured the search. With a final pat on her ass that totally wasn't necessary, the guy stepped away.

"They're clean."

"Have a seat." Dominick nodded to the chairs at the table. Sera and Ryan joined Zocco and Dominick. "So. Zee here tells me two think you can become big-time drug dealers. With sugar."

Sera nodded. "Yes."

He nodded too, slowly, tapping a package of cigarettes on the table. "You've been selling a lot of the shit lately."

"Yeah. It's good stuff. I have lots of contacts in L.A. They all like how it helps them drop a few pounds."

"Yeah. It does." He smiled, if you could call the curve of his lips a smile. It held malicious evil and cunning. "You know lots of people in L.A.?"

"Yeah. I grew up there."

"Where you getting the cash for this deal?"

Ryan spoke up. He crossed one leg over the other. "I'm not going to give you details. I have business connections. From my other business."

"Uh-huh. You were charged with possession a few times in the past."

He'd checked their records. Sera kept her face calm. That was to be expected. That's why the ATF and DEA had done the full backstop on them.

"Yeah." Ryan smiled. "Possession, but I never got nailed for trafficking."

"Good man." He tipped his head to the side. "How do I know you're not cops?"

Sera laughed. "Obviously you checked us out, if you know Tommy's arrest record. Clearly, we're not cops."

"Anyone can be a cop. I want you to do a line."

Sera froze inside, resisted the impulse to send a panicked glance at Ryan. Fuck!

Casas nodded to the big bruiser at the door.

She held his gaze. "Sure."

Bald bruiser guy walked over and laid out a line of sugar, pulled a bill out of his pocket and handed it to her. Mind racing, thoughts spinning uselessly through her head, adrenaline singing through her veins, Sera rolled it up.

She looked at the line on the table, all neat and powdery white. She could not do drugs. Federal agents could not do drugs. Not only that—since her overdose she hadn't touched anything more than Tylenol and swore she never would again.

She stared at the sugar.

If she didn't do this...they'd never get another chance. In fact, if she didn't do this, their whole operation was at risk. She couldn't do that to Ryan. Or Manny. Or everyone who'd worked so long and so hard on this case.

Jessie's image floated through her mind.

She felt Ryan's eyes on her, burning into her. Now she did risk a glance at him, and his steady gaze calmed her. Just a bit.

She could do it. They might fire her, but maybe not until after it was all done. She swallowed and leaned forward.

"That the stuff you cook in the lab in Oakland?" Ryan asked casually. Flicking her eyes up to Dominick, she saw him jerk his head toward Ryan, frowning. And she quickly bent down, inhaled through the tube— beside the line of sugar, sweeping the powder to the floor with her other hand in a gesture that took a fraction of a second.

Her body was between the bald bruiser and the table so he didn't see. She only prayed Zocco hadn't been looking right at her too. She sniffed, rubbed her nose, dropped the bill to the table and covered the sprinkle of white on the floor with her foot. She glanced at Dominick, who was nodding, then at Zocco, her gut so tight she thought she might puke. But he was watching Dominick.

Casually, carefully, she scrubbed the sole of her boot back and forth along the floor, under her chair, sideways, spreading the powder around on the pale, scarred wood floor.

Had Ryan seen what she did? Or did he think she'd snorted the sugar? Their eyes met and held, his burning hot and dark.

Damn, what had she done?

Ryan stared at her intensely. Then, insides churning ferociously, he turned back to Dominick. Damn, he needed some antacids.

"I can supply all the sugar you need," Dominick said.

Ryan smiled again. "We know you're the biggest dealer around. That's why we want to do business with you."

Dominick's face cleared at that flattery.

"So where do you get your supply?" Ryan asked

Dominick leaned back in his chair, turning the package of cigarettes between his fingers, a smile twisting his thin lips. "I have a good source."

"Yeah. Well, we want to know who it is. Just to make sure."

Dominick leaned forward, eyes alight. "I have a lab. Buncha guys that cook the stuff for me. You got no worries about me being able to supply you. We can make as much as you need. More," he bragged.

Ryan tamped down the triumph that shot through him, resisted the urge to meet Sera's eyes.

"We want to know if it's big enough for us," Ryan said. "Unless we're satisfied, no deal."

"I told you how big this is," Zocco said eagerly.

Dominick nodded, and Ryan could see the greed in his eyes as he weighed things in his mind.

"We want to see the lab."

Dominick looked at him, the corners of his mouth pushed down, eyes narrowed. "It's in Oakland."

"We'll come there."

Again a long pause as he thought about it. "Okay. I'll let you know when."

Relief permeated Ryan's body but he kept his face tight. "Great."

They walked out, Ryan with one hand on the small of Sera's back. He shot an evil glare at the asshole standing by the door who'd dared to feel Sera up under her shirt. It had taken every particle of his willpower to keep from grabbing the guy by the throat.

"That was good," Zocco said behind them. "Now we gotta find Chomp and see how he's doing."

Jesus Christ. Did the man not make any connections whatsoever to the fact that he'd sold Jessie the fucking drugs that had just killed her? Ryan's hands now itched to reach for Zocco himself and wring his goddamn neck. He gritted his teeth.

"Let us know if there's anything we can do," Sera told Zocco. "We're gonna head home."

Thank Christ. The adrenaline rush was subsiding and taking all his energy with it. He felt like he could sag into a heap on the floor at that moment. But he kept his head high, shoulders straight as he and Sera left the bar and climbed onto his Harley.

The speed felt good. He revved the motor, accelerated full throttle out of the parking lot, Sera's hands clutching on to him. He roared down the dark street. He'd head out of town, where he could go even faster. Making a left on Sage Drive, he roared faster, wind whipping past him. Sera's arms tightened on him as he took the exit onto Interstate 40 at a dangerous angle.

Josh was no doubt following behind him wondering what the fuck he was doing, but he didn't care. He was so wound up, so furious, so fucking up to his eyeballs in this shit, he needed the speed, and he went full throttle on the highway, passing cars.

Sera's hands dug into him and he heard her yelling into his ear. "Ryan! Slow down! Please!"

"You scared, baby?" he shouted back, not even sure if she could hear him.

She thumped him on the back with one hand, the other digging into him so tightly she was going to draw blood. "The cops are going to pull you over! Slow down! Don't be an idiot!"

Sober, sane responsibility returned to him, and he eased off the throttle. Dropping his speed to the speed limit, he watched for the next exit so he could turn around and take them back to the city.

Sera's arms remained snugly around him, but she said nothing more until they were back in the driveway at the house. She slid off and removed her lid, shook out her long hair, then staggered a little. Ryan frowned.

She grabbed hold of the fence as if to support herself and he took in the pale face and trembling hands as she tucked her helmet under one arm, and cocked a hip.

"Feel better now?" she asked.

He met her eyes. Fuck. He'd scared the shit out of her. She was shaking so hard she could barely stand, but still she stood there all defiant and cocky.

He closed his eyes and tipped his head back. He'd fucking forgotten she was afraid of motorcycles. Ah shit. He wanted to disappear into the concrete driveway beneath his feet. He slowly opened his eyes.

She should've been pissed off that he'd do something so irresponsible. But she studied him with eyes that gleamed with understanding. His chest got tight as he stood there in an eye-lock with her.

"Not really."

She blew out a long breath. "I know. Come on. Let's go in."

A car pulled up on the street at the end of the driveway and they both turned. What now?

Ryan was surprised to see Josh, sitting in the driver's seat, window rolled down. He gestured to Ryan with a stiff arm movement.

"What?" Ryan strolled down the driveway toward the car, eyes sweeping the neighborhood for any signs of the DAs.

"What the fuck was that?" Josh's face was red and his hair stuck up all over the place. He slammed a hand on the steering wheel. "Have you lost your fucking mind?"

Ryan ran his tongue over his teeth as he contemplated his response. "Yeah. Maybe." He rubbed the back of his neck and looked up at the sky. Only a few stars twinkled in the darkness, the nearly full moon and city lights drowning out most of them. "Sorry."

"Sorry! Sorry, my ass! Jesus Christ, Thomas..."

Ryan sucked in air. "One of the biker's girlfriends died tonight. All hopped up on sugar. Her boyfriend told her she had a fat ass so she accidentally OD'd."

Josh stared at him. "Shit."

"Yeah." Ryan nodded. "I'm going in now." He turned and walked back toward Sera, standing there watching him. Her hair blew back from her face in the evening breeze, long and silky. In the moonlight her face was a pure, pale oval, her light eyes shining, her mouth full and soft. The helmet dangled from her fingers in front of her, her slender shape in black jeans and leather jacket outlined against the white stucco of the house.

The ethereal, pure perfection of her beauty made his steps falter. He wanted to stand and look at her forever. He kept going, one foot in front of the other, until he stood in front of her, their bodies almost touching.

He held her gaze, the glowing crystal blue of her eyes almost eerie in the darkness, emphasized by her sooty lashes. The sound of Josh's vehicle faded away.

He bent his head and kissed Sera. Her mouth moved against his, kissing him back. He wanted more. He needed more. He needed her and the comfort she could provide, the uplifting, energy-giving support she gave him without even trying or knowing.

To hell with Forsythe and him riding his ass about past mistakes. This may be the biggest mistake he'd ever made, but there was no stopping the emotion that surged inside him. With a last lingering touch of his tongue on her lips, he lifted his head. "Come on."

He led the way in, Sera following, dropping helmets, keys, purse and leather jackets along the way to the bedroom. Tonight there was no question for either of them about where they were going to sleep.

Chapter Twenty-Two

As they waited for the others in the boardroom of the ATF offices, Sera looked at Ryan, seated next to her at the long table. She remembered the first time they'd sat in this room together, him across the table from her, glaring at her, refusing to allow her to participate in the operation.

Now they were friends. More than friends. Lovers. He believed her. He was the first person in her life who had ever believed in her.

She could not let that make a difference. Just because he believed in her did not mean he was any different than anyone else when it came to the long term. He wouldn't be there for her. Once they were done working together she'd never see him again.

He slanted her a smile that warmed her insides, and then Manny walked in, lazily chewing his gum. He slouched down into a seat. "Hey," he said.

Sera smiled back at him. "Hi, Manny."

Despite Ryan's lack of success at getting a confession from Zocco about the murder, a sense of hopeful anticipation filled her. They were about to get permission to move forward on the most important part of her goal so far—getting into the lab. She was filled with confident expectation, the knowledge that she was so close swelling inside her. She'd waited so long for this!

Ward Tanner from the DEA arrived and greeted her warmly. She'd been making progress and that made him happy despite the money she was spending. Josh arrived soon after, and then Darren Forsythe, and she felt Ryan's hostility shimmering off him. Darren really pushed his buttons, for some reason. What was that about? Ryan had avoided the whole issue when she'd asked him before, but curiosity spiked inside her. She didn't like Darren either—he was a self-serving, ass-kissing paper pusher—but she knew how to play him to get what she wanted. She felt confident she'd be able to do that today, as well.

Everyone settled into their seats and she, Ryan, Manny and Josh updated their superiors on their progress and what their next steps were.

She already knew Ryan and Manny's. They had their sights set on guns and murder. Ryan just wanted that last piece—a murder conviction under RICO would allow them to charge the entire group of Death Angels. She knew why it was so important to him.

And her goal was important too. Dominick Casas was running that lab, which she was sure was backed by Quintano, and she was going to shut that lab down and save countless lives by doing so.

After that... She drew in a long breath. Quintano was a widespread organization. Maybe she'd move on to something else. It was what she was meant to do.

She smiled as she lounged in her chair, listening to the others talk.

Then it was her turn. She updated them on the buys she'd made, how she'd increased the amounts she was buying and "selling" to impress them that she could be a major player. And they'd bought it.

Now what she had to do was get everyone in on planning the next big step. Because this was going to be huge. They'd move in on the lab, make their arrests and shut it down.

When she outlined her plan, Darren and Ward exchanged glances.

Silence fell as Darren leaned back in his chair, hands folded across his doughy belly. He didn't look at anyone, just shook his head slowly from side to side.

Sera glanced sideways at Ryan. What was Darren doing? Was he thinking? Ryan frowned.

"No can do," Darren finally said. "That's way too much money, Sera. Not gonna happen."

Her eyes widened and she stared at him. "What do you mean? It has to happen!"

She looked at Ward, trying to message him with her eyes, *"Tell him! Tell him this is important!"*

But Ward said nothing.

She nibbled her bottom lip until she realized the gesture spoke of uncertainty, and carefully composed her features into neutrality.

"We're pulling the plug," Darren continued. "I know you all have more you want to do, but we think we have enough for a number of arrests, indictments, convictions even. This is costing us a fortune and it's dragged on long enough. The liability risks are insane. We want it done."

Sera turned to Ryan and met his eyes. He had straightened in his chair, shoulders square and tight, his face a mask of indifference. But the fire in his eyes told her that he was far from indifferent.

Ryan turned back to the others at the table.

"You can't do that," he said slowly. "We're so close to breaking through. They really trust us now, with all kinds of things. They want me to patch in with them!"

Darren shook his head. Sera stared at him in stunned disbelief.

"I know that would take a lot longer than we planned," Ryan continued. "But maybe it's worth it—"

"No," Darren said.

"Sera heard that one of the DAs committed murder," Ryan added. "She just didn't have her recorder going at the time. I can get that."

"And I can get into that lab," she added, leaning forward. "I know I can. It'll be huge. It'll be the biggest bust ever. No one has ever been able to infiltrate an illegal drug lab like this." She looked from one man to the other at the table.

Ward's eyes spoke to her, trying to convey a message, and she understood that this wasn't his decision, but he had to support it. She blew out a long breath and sank back in her chair.

"We can't justify spending that kind of money to get in there," Darren said pompously.

"You can't do this," she said. "Not when we're so close. You know the Attorney General and the administration of the DEA in Washington are interested in this operation. Don't you want to be able to go to them and tell them we did this?"

Darren and Ward exchanged a glance. Darren's scowl deepened. He shifted in his chair.

"Okay, listen," Darren finally said. "It will take a couple of weeks for us to take this to a grand jury. We need to work on the operation plan for the final raids, and for your raid on the lab in Oakland. In those two weeks, you can continue gathering information, especially any known weapons and narcotics locations so we can write up warrants."

Two weeks? She blinked rapidly. Could she do what she wanted to do in two weeks? Could she get to the lab? That was going to be pretty damn rushed. "I don't know if I can get to the lab in two weeks."

"That's it. Two weeks."

She looked at Ryan. Two weeks wasn't enough for him. It would take months to patch in. His face was drawn into tight lines of restraint. Manny's hands, clenched in fists, rested on the table.

But for her...two weeks might be enough. She closed her eyes, tried to control the urge to breathe fast and shallow, adrenaline tingling in her bloodstream.

Was this the best they could get?

She surveyed everyone in the room, the firm, implacable expressions on the faces of their superiors, and she knew—yes. This was it.

Two weeks.

"Thanks a fucking bunch."

Ryan's harsh tone made Sera blink. Sitting with him and Manny in the restaurant on Figueroa near the ATF offices, she closed her hands around the warmth of the coffee cup she held. Was he talking to her?

"What?" She eyed him warily.

His eyes shot sparks at her. Yeah, apparently he *was* talking to her. "For getting the plug pulled on us. Jesus, Sera, you had to keep asking for money. Now look what's happened."

"You're blaming me for this?" Her eyes flew wide. "Hey, wait a minute—"

Manny held up a hand. "We don't need to blame each other. It's done."

"But—" She stopped at the look on his face, then started again. "It's not my fault! They were going to end this anyway!"

Ryan shook his head, his mouth a straight line of grimness.

"You pushed it," he muttered, looking down.

"Dude," Manny said in a warning tone. "I know you're frustrated. But they gave us two weeks to wrap up."

"Fuck." Ryan stared down into his coffee while Sera seethed, anger simmering in her.

He blamed her? She was just as angry and frustrated as he was. Maybe more. How was she supposed to get to the lab in two weeks? She kneaded the crease between her eyebrows.

"We gotta make the best of it," Manny said, looking from Sera to Ryan. "And you two have to get along. For two more weeks."

That thought sliced through her like a knife blade. Lord, she'd been thinking of the time frame in terms of the op, but the sudden realization that she and Ryan had two more weeks together left her sitting back in stunned silence. She picked up her coffee and sipped the hot brew, almost burning her mouth.

Ryan glanced at her. Was he thinking the same thing? Probably not.

And she shouldn't be either. Hadn't she already reminded herself that this was nothing? She had no room in her life for any kind of emotional entanglement, didn't want anyone in her life, didn't need anyone in her life.

Right now she had to focus on the job at hand.

She glanced at her watch. They had just enough time to eat, if their food arrived now, to get back to the one o'clock meeting where they were going to strategize about the plan to take the lab. That was what needed her attention. All her attention.

The waitress arrived and slid plates onto the table in front of them. Sera picked up her fork and waited until Manny and Ryan had dumped ketchup all over their fries before stabbing a piece of her spinach salad.

"You know, if you ate better, you wouldn't have to pop those antacids all the time." She eyed Ryan's plate.

He shot her a disgusted, mind-your-own-business look and picked up his burger. She shrugged.

"I gather you have ideas for how you want this to go down," he said after swallowing his first bite.

"Of course."

She could see his skepticism. After all, she was a rookie at this. But she'd given it a lot of thought. Yeah, she needed advice from the experts, but it wasn't rocket science. She'd been laying the groundwork for weeks now; that had been the most difficult part. She quickly outlined her thoughts about it.

"I don't know, Sera." He lifted eyes full of doubt and apprehension. "Maybe you should just give up on this."

Fire flared in her gut. "No! I'm not giving up now! We're so close..."

"Timing will be critical. We have to raid the lab at the exact same time search warrants are executed in Clover City, and arrests made."

"If it goes wrong, she jeopardizes everything," Manny said quietly.

"That's what I'm saying."

"Don't talk about me like I'm not here," she hissed out between clenched teeth. She shot Manny a not-you-too look. He lifted his brows.

"I'm just saying. We need to be careful. We're this close to being done—let's not screw up. Remember, they won't hesitate to kill any one of us if there's any hint we're not who they think we are."

She nodded slowly. "I know." It was a good reminder though. She'd become so embedded in the lifestyle, she too was almost coming to think of the DAs as friends. She had to remind herself they were criminals, and despite their numerous displays of loyalty, their first loyalty was to themselves. Individual and gang. "I know."

"Sera." She looked at Ryan, brows raised. "I'm sorry." He held her gaze, gave her a wry smile. "I shouldn't have blamed you for them pulling the plug on this."

Her insides melted into a thick liquid. She nodded. "Okay."

It was hard not to push Zocco. They had two weeks and no date from Casas on when they could see the lab. Sera had to curb her impatience and fight for subtle reminders. She worried that Zocco wasn't following up, then she worried that he was and they were pushing too hard.

In the meantime, other details took their attention. They needed to get back inside Vince and Carly's house. They had to have seen the evidence within the last ten days to use it in a search warrant. It had been weeks since she'd been there drinking lemon drops by the pool, getting a tour of the house and filing information away.

She'd finally convinced Carly to try to sell her jewelry at the Sunday flea market, so she offered to help by picking her up at home, helping pack up her creations, driving her to the park. She stayed with her for the afternoon, disturbingly pleased at Carly's sales and the joy in Carly's eyes at being so successful. At being something. Sera's heart weighed heavy in her chest at the path Carly had to follow in life, even as she made careful mental notes about the house as she helped her.

And then, success.

Dominick wanted them to call him on his cell phone.

"When can we come?" Ryan asked him, sitting in the kitchen with Sera and Manny.

"Next weekend."

No good. The plan was to execute search warrants on Friday.

"It has to be before the weekend," Ryan said, holding Sera's gaze. "We can do Friday."

A pause.

He watched Sera's face. She swallowed.

"Okay," Dominick said. "Call me when you get into town."

When they left the house Tuesday night, it was the last time they would ever be there. Sera almost felt sad as she carried her suitcase out to her car, packed with her belongings. Everyone thought she and Tommy were flying to Oakland for a few days, but the truth was they would never be back. She couldn't say goodbye to anyone—not even Carly, still hurting over Jessie's death, still so proud of her jewelry sales.

Sera was just as sad about the fact that this was the end of her and Ryan living together. They had a couple more nights in a hotel in Oakland, but they'd never come back to this house.

The operation plan had been drawn up. The warrants were being written. A crisis center in the downtown L.A. ATF offices had been set up, manned by representatives from both the ATF and DEA, as well as from the U.S. Attorney's Office, Customs, and the Los Angeles County Sheriff's Department. On Saturday, while she and Ryan were in Oakland, search warrants would be executed at over a dozen businesses and residences.

They each returned to their own home and spent the night there. Sera had never felt so alone as she did sleeping in her bed by herself. The fact that she missed Ryan so much was not a good thing. She had to put that kind of emotional crap out of her head. She'd deal with it all later, when everything was done.

Wednesday morning they flew to San Francisco from LAX and were met at the airport by Carlos Lopez, supervisor of the drug enforcement group they'd be working with. Ryan rented a car in Tommy Briscoe's name, and they drove to Carlos's office where he introduced them to his team. They spent the rest of the day reviewing their intelligence along with their own, and going over the plan for Friday. That night Carlos took them out for dinner, then they checked in at the Hilton near the Oakland airport, even though they hadn't flown into Oakland. They spent most of Thursday again reviewing the operational plan in great detail.

Thursday evening, back at the Hilton, Ryan called Casas. "We're here," he told him, eyes on Sera. He listened. "Tomorrow. Yeah. Jack London. Okay." He listened again and his face tightened. She watched him, stomach tight with nerves. "Okay. Sure. Sounds good. See you tomorrow." He snapped the phone shut. "We're going to meet at two o'clock. There's a bar in Jack London Square."

"What else?" She looked him in the eye.

"He says he'll take one of us to the lab."

"One of us."

"Yes."

She turned that over in her head. "Me."

"No."

"Yes." She leaped to her feet and strode across the room toward him. She jabbed a finger into his chest. "Yes, Ryan. Me. This is my mission."

He shook his head, grabbed her hand and held it tightly. "No, Sera. If only one of us goes in, it's gonna be me."

She wanted to scream and smack him. She'd thought they were past all that. Once he believed in her, knew what she was capable of, there was no longer any reason for him to treat her as second class, to treat her like a kid, to feel like he had to look after her.

She tipped her head back and closed her eyes, fighting for patience. "Ryan. It has to be me. You know that." She opened her eyes and looked deep into his, willing him to understand and agree.

He shook his head. Pulled her closer against him. "No." He pressed a hard kiss to her mouth. "We'll talk to Carlos and the guys, and rework the plan."

"Ryan. Don't do this. You know it has to be me. You know I can take care of myself."

The corners of his mouth kicked up. "You know, that could be kind of insulting to my masculine ego."

"You know what I mean!" She pulled out of his grasp and paced across the room, turned and stared at him, talons of aggravation clawing inside her. "I thought you knew now that I can take care of myself. That I can do just as good a job as you can."

"I do know that," he replied softly, crossing the room and standing right in front of her. "I know that, Sera. I'm not being chauvinistic or bossy. I just want to know you're safe." He touched her hair and drew it behind her shoulder.

She looked at him. "Ryan."

He blew out a long breath. His eyes went unfocused for a moment as he stared past her. Then he dragged his gaze back to her. "Okay," he said. "You do it. You go in."

Sera's breath stuck in her chest. It felt like a golf ball had lodged there. "Really?" she choked out. She touched her fingertips to his cheek.

"Yes." He closed his eyes briefly. "You're right. You are the best one to do this. They trust you. And I know you can look after yourself."

She continued to gaze at him, her heart swelling inside her chest, her body softening. Her expanding heart felt like it had cracked, and soft and messy emotions began leaking out. Ryan believed in her.

"I care about you, Sera," he continued. "That's the only reason I didn't want you to do it."

She blinked at him, his words robbing her of speech. She was afraid if she tried to talk, her tight throat would have the words coming out incomprehensible. She wasn't even sure what she wanted to say. She didn't know how to express all the things bubbling up inside her. It was probably better if she didn't.

She flew into his arms it seemed without even moving her feet. The feel of his strong arms wrapping around her undid her even more, and she leaned her face against him, pressed her nose to his throat. She inhaled the warm masculine scent of him. She would never forget Ryan's smell. She closed her eyes and just breathed him in, over and over, while his arms held her, rocked her.

Gratitude, relief, and honor all mingled inside her, warming her from the inside out, and she lifted her head, cupped his lean, raspy cheeks in both hands and kissed him. His mouth moved beneath hers as he kissed her back, and she pressed herself closer, unable to get close enough.

A groan rumbled in his throat, and he hardened against her as the kiss went on and on. When she finally lifted her mouth to meet his eyes, they were both panting.

"Sera."

"Ryan."

The corners of her mouth kicked up and she went up on tiptoes and kissed him again, winding her arms around his neck. "Oh, Ryan."

The heat building between them snapped into an inferno, consuming both of them in licking flames. "Christ," he muttered against her mouth, his hands sliding up under her shirt. His rough touch sent shivers over her body. Then he stroked lower, down the curve of her back and dipped his fingers inside her jeans, as far as he could, cupping her butt.

She wriggled against him, wanting more of his touch, and when they again separated and stared at each other wide-eyed, gasping, she reached for the hem of her top and pulled it off over her head.

"Black lace," he murmured, looking down at her chest. She followed his gaze to where the curves of her breasts swelled against the scalloped edges of the lacy cups. His hot hands burned her bare waist, and she started unbuttoning his shirt, a blue-and-white-striped buttoned shirt so different from his usual black T-shirts.

When she reached the last button, she separated the sides of his shirt to reveal his chest. She trailed her fingers over his flat, brown nipples, the dusting of hair between, the slabs of muscle over his abdomen, and the trail of dark hair disappearing down beneath his pants. He gasped.

Lust escalated in her, and she fumbled at the button and zipper of his pants. He took over, and while he got rid of the rest of his clothing, she wriggled out of her jeans. In a matching black lace thong, she then flattened herself against his hot, naked body and kissed him again.

"Jesus," he panted. "Sera."

"I know, I know, but I need you. I need you right now."

She straddled his thigh and rubbed her pussy against it, knew her panties were wet. With a long groan, he fisted his hands in her hair and tugged her head back to kiss her throat.

He licked and sucked gently there, and sensations whipped over her, building so fast and strong she shuddered helplessly. When he tugged harder at her hair, pleasure pursued pain and excitement sizzled over every nerve ending.

She yanked the elastic out of his hair so she could run her fingers through it too, scraping her nails over his scalp, making him hiss.

His touch was firm, confident. His hands gripped the cheeks of her ass, bared by the thong, and squeezed. Then one hand slid around and cupped a breast, and she swelled into his palm. Her nipples tingled, hardened, ached to be touched, and she pulled the cups of the bra down.

"Damn, Sera," he muttered, staring at her breasts. Then both hands captured her flesh, gave a gentle squeeze, grazed over her nipples. He took each pointy tip between his fingers and pinched them. Her body twitched hard, flames licking up inside her from between her legs.

"Yes," she hissed. "More...please."

She was begging. Begging him to touch her, touch her harder. She loved the edgy feeling of his bold caresses. Her head fell back and he continued to play with her nipples, tugging, twisting, then sucking and nibbling on them until they felt glowing hot. Mindlessly, she reached behind her to undo her bra and let it slide off. When she dragged her eyes open she found him staring at her nipples, deep red and burning, and she ached down low inside with a fierce, urgent need. "Oh Christ," she groaned. She gripped his shoulders to keep from falling, her legs going wobbly, and then he swept her up and carried her to the bed in two long strides.

He tossed her down, immediately fell upon her, kissing her with long, hard, demanding kisses. Her mouth met his, her tongue twined with his, their teeth bumped. He dragged her panties down, and she bent her legs, lifted her hips and kicked her feet to get them all the way off. Then they rolled together across the king-size bed, hands frantic, mouths devouring. Ryan grabbed her wrists, and pinned them above her head, his lower half pressing her into the mattress. He stared down at her with hot eyes, both their chests heaving.

"Fuck me," she whispered. He gave the barest of nods, held both her wrists in one hand and slid the other down between them. He found her center where she was wet and aching.

She stared into his eyes, at the heated emotion there. His firm touch, his dominating posture thrilled her to her very core. Her pussy throbbed and wept, and she parted her legs and arched her pelvis for him.

His cock, long, hard and thick, pressed at her softness. She wanted to touch it, wanted to taste it, but he held her down, hands captured above her head, the position forcing her breasts up and out.

He took a nipple in his mouth again, suckled hard, and she felt it right in her pussy. He nipped with teeth and the burning pleasure shimmered outward from her nipples, suffusing her body in heat.

"I love that!" she cried. "So much."

He moved to the other nipple, while his fingers stroked through her folds. She moved against his hand in an erotic rhythm, needing more, needing his touch right on her pulsing clit, but he circled around it, up and down, dipping into her opening, slicking her juice over her outer lips, then dragging his fingers through the patch of curls between her legs.

"Ryan, please," she choked out. "Please..."

"What do you want, Sera?" He kissed her chest between her breasts, rested there for a moment, breathing heavily. His cock twitched against her and she moved her legs restlessly.

"I want you inside me."

"Mmm. I want that too." He reached down, took his cock in hand. Yes! She arched deeper, ready for him, but then he released her hands and the next thing she knew she was facedown on the bed.

The slippery bedspread had slithered to the floor, the blanket and sheets rumpled beneath them. With a gasp, she felt his hands on her hips, lifting them.

Dear god in heaven, this was the position of ultimate submission. Now he did have her pinned to the bed, his body heavy, his face pressed to the side of her neck. Strong as she was, she wasn't strong enough to throw him off her, even if she wanted to. Which she didn't. Did. Not.

She'd never let a man fuck her like this. Never let a man pull her hair, bite her nipples, pin her down. A flood of moisture between her legs signaled to her that all these things turned her on until she was out of her mind. God!

As she struggled to make sense of it, Ryan's fingers sliding between the cheeks of her ass, down into her slickness, his breath a warm sigh in her ear, she realized the only reason this turned her on was because it was him. Ryan.

Emotions rose in her, threatened to swamp her, brought stinging tears to her eyes and she blinked rapidly. Christ, she didn't cry. She hadn't cried since her father had left when she was fourteen. What was happening to her?

For a moment, she struggled, pushing against Ryan in a feeble attempt to move him off her. He pressed back and she realized she wasn't fighting against him, but rather against the unfamiliar feelings assailing her.

"Hey," he murmured in her ear. "Stay still." And with that, his hand landed on her ass in a smarting caress.

She went still.

He had not just done that!

Warmth spread from where his hand had landed, through her entire body, nerve endings sizzling with it. And then he did it again. And more liquid spilled from her pussy and she cried out with wanting and needing.

His fingers plunged into her roughly and she pushed her butt up to give him access. "Christ, you're wet," he muttered. "You like that, don't you?"

And one more firm smack landed on her butt.

Then he probed her pussy with the head of his cock, drawing it up and down through slick folds to wet the head and ease his way. When he shoved into her she cried out at the intensity of it, the feeling of being stretched and full. His cock touched a spot inside her she hadn't even known existed, something exquisitely sensitive that sent shivers cascading over her.

He pulled her hair to one side, pressed his mouth to the side of her neck, his breath a ragged rasp in her ear. As he thrust into her, pleasure slammed through her and she fought to breathe.

His hand slid around, under her stomach, then lower, finding her clit, and she jerked at the touch on the sensitive flesh. His fingers there combined with the sensation of his cock inside her and the two sensations twisted together into a hot spiral of delight.

"Oh god," she groaned into the sheets.

"Wanna make you come, baby," he murmured, breath teasing her ear. "But first..."

He lifted up, and the removal of his heavy warmth left a cool feeling on her sweat-dampened back. One hand still below her on her clit, the other hand stroked down between the cheeks of her ass, swept lower to gather up moisture then probed at the opening of her ass.

She tensed at the intrusion she'd never before felt, his fingertip playing there, sending so many wicked sensations shooting through her she worried she might pass out. Her clit throbbed, her pussy clenched, and then his finger pushed inside her, into the forbidden entrance no one had ever touched.

She cried out, and then to silence herself, she stuffed the sheet into her mouth and bit down on it. Ryan's cock inside her, his finger inside her and another finger on her clit pulled all those sensations into a stretched out coil of ecstasy, winding tighter and higher and hotter.

She reached for it, blind from it, hearing only a roaring in her ears and Ryan's low words of encouragement. "So tight," he murmured. "Your ass is tight, Sera. Your pussy is hot, gripping me like a fist, for Chrissake. I love it. Damn, I love it."

His finger thrust into her in small pulses. She had never before experienced this feeling of her entire body being consumed by pleasure and it kept building so high, she was afraid she was never going to come down. Higher, tighter, to a peak of sharp, exquisite pain that burst into a shower of pleasure, heat and light surrounding her body. She cried out, her noises muffled by the linen in her mouth, fingers clenched into the blanket, pushing her ass back against him as she came in a dizzying, blinding, deafening orgasm.

His finger slid out of her, his other hand covering her pussy, and he picked up the pace of his thrusts, faster, harder and then she felt him come too, holding her ass tight against him while he spurted hot jets inside her, his cock pulsing.

"Oh sweet Jesus," he groaned as he collapsed onto her, his body a damp, warm weight that crushed the air out of her. She struggled to breathe, and after a long moment, he slid out of her and rolled to the side.

Her head turned to the side. He lay there facing her and stroked her hair back off her face and neck.

"You spanked me," she mumbled, unable to even lift her head.

"Yeah." The satisfaction in his voice was unmistakable. "And you loved it."

"I did not. Don't ever do that again." But her words carried no heat, no conviction, and when she pried her eyes open to meet his, the warmth in his eyes and his half-smile told her he knew she lied. She did love it.

She had no idea why this man dominating her, inflicting sweet pain on her like that, doing things to her that no man ever had, thrilled her right to her very essence.

And then she knew why.

He wasn't dominating her in the sense that he wanted to control everything she did. He believed in her, which no one ever had. He respected her abilities and treated her like his equal. What they did in bed had nothing to do with that—and everything to do with it. It was all about the pleasure she got from the things he did. He knew what she liked, what she wanted, what she needed, and he gave it to her. She trusted him with her life, in any situation, including sex.

She was in love with him.

Chapter Twenty-Three

"Sera." He lay beside her, his body still reacting to the stunning sex they'd just had, his mind reeling. He stroked her hair back behind her shoulder. Realization of the powerful feelings he had for Sera sank in, and he felt like he'd been kicked in the gut.

This was the worst thing that could happen.

Had he not learned his fucking lesson last time? He'd gotten emotionally involved with an informant who had then died from doing some bad meth. He'd screwed up the case against her loser boyfriend/dealer because of his uncontrollable rage.

The feelings he'd had for Lucie Gonzales were nothing compared to what he felt for Sera. He'd cared about Lucie, wanted to protect her and when he couldn't, it had destroyed him.

And here he was now, about to send the woman he loved into a complicated, dangerous operation while he sat outside and waited.

It made his skin itch, made him want to growl and shove his fist into the wall. She was inexperienced and that scared the hell out of him, but she was also strong and capable and smart, and he could only hope that would keep her safe, because if she didn't come out of there and come back to him, he wasn't sure how he was going to survive this time.

What a fucking disaster. He should never have let his personal feelings for her become so intense. He needed to be professional, in control, focused on the job, not scared out of his mind for her.

As the mess of feelings tore their way through him, he continued to stare at Sera, her beautiful face, lips swollen from his kisses, eyes drowsy. Then he thought about the things he'd done to her—the things she'd let him do to her—and he knew she had to have feelings for him too. There was no way Sera would let any man pin her arms over her head and hold her down, or flip her over and fuck her from behind like that, if she didn't care about him in ways he was afraid to think about.

What had they done?

This had gone so far beyond an act, it scared the shit out of him. If Darren Forsythe ever found out about his involvement with Sera, his ass would be grass. And yet, he really couldn't bring himself to care, such was his worry about Sera's safety. That was all that mattered.

He swallowed hard, ran his fingertips over Sera's smooth cheek.

"I love you, Sera." The words just leaked out of his mouth. He couldn't stop them. He felt an urgent need to tell her that before what was going to go down tomorrow.

Her eyes widened, her lips parted. He expected her to say the words too, because he could read it in her eyes, feel it in her touch. But she just blinked at him, and then he saw her eyes had gone glossy. Shit! She was going to cry!

He'd never seen Sera even close to shedding a tear. Not that they'd known each other that long, but she was so tough, so determined, so independent, he just couldn't picture her dissolving into tears.

And she didn't now. Of course not. She blinked hard and smiled at him.

"Ryan. We can't love each other."

"I know. But I can't help how I feel. You feel it too, I know you do."

She didn't deny it. But she didn't agree with him either. She pressed her lips together. "I don't have room for love in my life," she whispered, placing her palm on his chest over his heart. "Anyone who's ever loved me, betrayed me. Left me. I do better just on my own."

"Forever?"

She hitched a shoulder. "I haven't thought about forever."

"I know you can do anything on your own," he told her seriously, smoothing a hand over the curve of her shoulder. "Anything. But...you don't have to, Sera."

Her throat moved as she swallowed. "Oh Ryan."

She pressed her face against his throat, snuggled her body in against him. They stayed that way for a long time, and when he moved against her and made love to her again, it was slow and gentle.

Their eyes met and held as he pushed inside her, a connection between them that was more than just physical, more than just his body inside her, more than his hands in her hair, her hands on his hips. It shimmered between them, surrounded them in heat and light as they drove each other to a peak of perfect pleasure—carefully, tenderly, respectfully, reverently.

When they reached the pinnacle together, they both cried out at the exquisiteness of it, the sublime bliss of giving that to each other.

"Sera," he gasped, pulsing inside her. "I know you're going in alone tomorrow, but know this...I love you. You're not alone. Never alone."

Her eyes fastened on his, serious, aware, earnest, and she nodded her head.

In the morning, they awoke in each other's arms and shifted lazily together. Sera ran a foot up over his leg, and he skated his palm down the curve of her back and over her ass.

She pressed her lips to his throat. "Hey. I forgot to ask yesterday. Have you found out anything about my dad?" She still wasn't sure why she'd agreed to let him try to find her father.

"Oh. Uh...no. Not yet."

His voice sounded funny and she pulled back to look at him. "You haven't?"

"No."

"Yes, you have." She gazed at him. "What? Did you find out where he lives now? I'll call him when we get back."

"No, you won't."

She blinked. "Huh?"

He licked his lips. Her body tensed.

"What is it? Just tell me, for god's sake. He's in detox again? Drying out? In the slammer because they found him passed out on the street?"

He shook his head and put his strong, warm hands on her

shoulders. "He's dead, Sera."

"What!" She stared at him, the breath sucked out of her. "He's dead?"

He nodded, brushing his thumbs over her collarbones. "I wasn't going to tell you until after this."

"But...how? When?"

Ryan closed his eyes. "The records show he died of a gunshot wound. An unsolved homicide. Fifteen years ago."

"I don't understand." She shoved away from him and sat up, her thoughts blurred and blustery. "That was before my mom told me he came back. She said she told him to go away and never come back." Her forehead crinkled.

"I don't know what to say," he said, sitting beside her and taking her hands in his. "I can't explain it, Sera. He died a long time ago. Maybe you're mixed up about the timing. Do you think your mother didn't even know?"

She shook her head, staring into space. "I don't know." She was sure of the timing. But why would her mother lie about that? Why had she told Sera she'd talked to him, told him not to come back, when she couldn't have? Had she been trying to save face by pretending she was the one who'd sent him away, when she thought he'd abandoned them? It was kind of sad and pathetic, if that's what had happened. But now she would never know.

She'd been alone so long. The whisper of hope that had insinuated itself inside her, that she could have family—a father—had been so faint she hadn't even really known it was there. He'd always been there, a nebulous, distant figure, someone she didn't even want in her life. But in the far outer reaches of her consciousness, he was there.

And now he wasn't.

She took a breath and lifted her head. "Are you sure?"

Ryan gave her a slow nod of his head. "I'm sure."

She sat up. Hollow and empty inside, she wrapped her arms around her middle, tried to control her quivering throat and stinging eyes.

She'd been crazy to think she could have anyone in her life. The emotions she'd experienced last night, the way she'd opened herself up to him, left herself vulnerable, let him dominate her—that had big mistake written all over it in capital letters.

She nodded and swallowed hard. She shook her hair back, drew in a breath, then threw back the covers and bounced out of bed. "Okay then. I guess that settles that. Let's get going. We have a big day ahead of us."

"Sera. Wait." He reached for her arm. "Are you mad at me for telling you that?"

She stared at him. "Of course not," she said stiffly. "It's not your fault."

She pulled loose from his grasp and walked over to her suitcase, pulling out what she planned to wear that day. When she turned, Ryan stood right there behind her, naked and radiating heat...and anger.

"Then what's wrong?" he demanded.

"Nothing's wrong."

"Oh Jesus, don't go getting all mysterious female on me." He shoved a hand through his hair. "Last night—Sera." He stopped. "I love you."

She froze, paralyzed into icy immobility like a stone sculpture. Her breath stuck in her throat and her heart tightened.

"No, you don't." She gave him a wry smile, put some distance between them, clutching her clothes. "Last night we got all wound up about what was going to happen today, and we had really hot sex. I know I felt it pretty intense, but it's not love, Ryan. Don't be ridiculous. We can't fall in love with each other. That would be a huge mistake. We need to get our job done, and then—" She fought to keep her voice steady and light. "And then this case will be over. You'll go back to your life and I'll go back to mine."

He stared at her, eyes blazing, mouth hard. And she turned and walked into the bathroom with her clothes. With the closed door between them, she paused for a moment, head bowed, leaning against the tile wall, dragging gulps of air into her tight lungs through an aching throat. Then she stepped into the shower and let the tears flow, turning her face up, the spray of water washing them away fast enough that she could pretend they didn't exist.

She had to get a grip. She needed to be ready for whatever was going to happen that afternoon. There was no room for messy feelings, about Ryan or about her father. She had to steel her heart against the ache that throbbed in it with every beat, and push away the pain that had shafted through her at seeing the expression on Ryan's face moments ago.

Automatically she shampooed her hair, blew it dry with the hotel blow dryer, applied the usual dark eye makeup that had become like a uniform to her. Then she dressed in tight, black, skinny jeans, boots, and a long-sleeved T-shirt with a rock band logo on it.

She emerged from the bathroom and found Ryan sitting at a laptop computer on the small table in the corner, dressed in his boxers and nothing else. It took every ounce of determination she had to not be distracted by the sight of his nearly naked, muscular body. He glanced up at her, eyes somber, then rose from his chair.

"Have a look," he said. "Carlos emailed me the op plan, final version."

He disappeared into the bathroom and she sank down into the chair, warm from his body, and focused on the computer screen. This was it.

She was going in. Alone. And that was the way she wanted it.

Carrying that much cash around made Ryan and Sera an easy target. A surveillance team was at the bar before them, with a detailed description of Dominick Casas, there to check the place out for anyone who could be a threat. There was always the possibility they'd been set up.

When Sera followed Ryan into the restaurant, they carefully didn't look for the men, but Sera peripherally spotted two of them at the bar, nursing drinks. She surveyed the room herself, the black leather seats of the booths, the light maple wood of the tables and chairs, bronze lamps that weren't needed with the sun streaming in the big front windows. Every nerve ending quivered with tension. She was carrying a hundred thousand dollars. People had been killed for less. Much less. She needed to be hyperaware of any potential threat.

Sera and Ryan took a seat at a table in the back corner of the room, in sight of the surveillance team but not right out in the open.

"Okay?" Ryan murmured. She glanced at him, hardened herself not to melt at the warm reassurance in his eyes.

"Yeah. Fine." Sure she was fine, she was a frickin' basket case of nerves. But she could do this.

They ordered a beer and sat there waiting. Only a minute after two o'clock, Casas strolled into the bar followed, to their surprise, by Zocco.

"Hey, Zee!" Ryan greeted him, as if happy to see a familiar face. "What're you doing here?"

"Dominick wanted me to be in on this," he said, a proud smile stretching his face.

"Have a seat." Ryan nodded to two chairs at the table and Casas and Zocco sat down. A waitress appeared and they ordered beers. Out of the corner of her eye, Sera noticed the two agents who had followed Casas and Zocco into the bar sit down at another table.

"You got the money?" Dominick said as soon as the waitress had left. He seemed tense and Sera didn't like that. She lifted the leather saddlebag she carried. "In here."

"I need to see it."

"Of course." Mid afternoon and the bar was mostly empty, a few tables up front occupied, so when she opened the bag on the floor and showed him what it contained, there was no worry about anyone else seeing it.

Dominick nodded. She could tell he was impressed, even though he was trying to hide it. "Good," he said casually, leaning back in his chair, both hands on his beer bottle. "We can do the deal tonight."

"The lab?" Ryan murmured.

"Yeah, you'll see the lab tonight. You'll get a tour before we do our deal. Just bring the money and we'll take you there and give you the drugs." He looked at Ryan. "You're coming?"

Ryan shook his head with a small smile. "Nah. Sara's going to go. This is her business."

Dominick's eyes widened but he just nodded again. "Okay." He thought a moment. "Okay."

He probably was relieved about that. Sera knew they were likely more relaxed if it was her doing it, less chance she was going to double-cross them, less chance she was a cop. Also, less able to defend herself should *they* decide to double cross *her*.

And yet, the fact that Zocco was there felt reassuring to her. He was a criminal, responsible for who knew how many deaths from these drugs, but his code of loyalty to fellow gang members made her feel like there was less chance they were going to rob her of the cash and run.

Because as far as he knew, they were all going back to Clover City tomorrow.

Unless he knew they weren't. There was always that possibility. Tension tightened her muscles and she forced herself to breathe calmly.

Keep going. Play it out.

She drank some of her beer, even though she didn't want it. The bitterness stung her tongue.

"So, let's meet here again," Dominick said. "Eight o'clock. We'll take Sara to the lab, do the deal and bring her back here. You can wait here." He jerked his head at Ryan.

Ryan nodded, even though Sera and he both knew he had no intention of waiting at the bar.

"Sounds good," he said. He looked around the restaurant idly, then back at Sera. "Want something to eat, babe?"

"Maybe." She picked up the menu as if she could possibly be hungry—not!—and looked it over.

"We gotta go," Dominick said, draining his beer and smacking it down on the table. "Come on, Zee."

Dominick tossed a bill on the table. "Later. Eight o'clock."

"You bet."

233

Sera watched them leave out of the corner of her eye then snapped the menu closed. "I can't eat," she said. Nerves danced a quick step in her stomach.

"Me either."

Two of the agents followed Casas and Zocco out of the bar and would tail them to wherever they were going next. The other two agents remained in the bar with Sera and Ryan.

"Eight o'clock," she huffed out, adrenaline and impatience mingling inside her, making her skin itch and her muscles twitch. "What are we going to do until then?"

"Review the plan."

"We've gone over it a hundred times."

"Now Zocco's here."

"I know." She sighed, met his eyes. "We didn't plan for that."

"I don't know what it means."

"Me either."

"Let's go talk to Carlos about it. We have to get everything in place for tonight."

They met the eyes of one of the agents sitting at the bar who gave them a short nod. He was wearing a wire so he knew it was now safe for them to leave, that Casas and Zocco had driven away, tailed by government agents.

Chapter Twenty-Four

Eight o'clock, same place. Once again a surveillance team was already in the restaurant, now crowded with diners. Another team sat outside in a vehicle, waiting. Sera and Ryan found a seat at the bar since every table was full. The small restaurant hummed with chatter and cutlery clinking, the occasional burst of laughter, smooth jazz music tinkling in the background. Not exactly the DAs usual type of place.

Ryan studied Sera surreptitiously. He hoped she was okay. He'd felt her nerves earlier and tried to send her waves of calm. He longed to hold her hand, touch her and ease her edginess but had a feeling she would not welcome that.

His gut cramped with worry about her and how she was going to do tonight, on top of being sick with the realization that he'd confessed his feelings to her and she'd stomped all over them.

He was a fucking mess of anxiety, love and fear, and he had to get a grip.

When Dominick and Zocco walked into the bar yet again, once more trailed by two agents, he nodded to Sera. He'd tried to argue for her going in with a .38 caliber strapped to her ankle but he'd lost that battle. If they checked her and she was carrying, they'd be done. Same for wearing a wire. She had her phone recording everything, as usual, but the only thing keeping him from losing her was the GPS in her phone and the tiny GPS tracking device planted into her watch just in case she lost the phone somehow. He tried to swallow the fear inside him.

"Ready?" Dominick stopped in front of them.

Sera smiled at him, and stood up, still holding the saddlebag full of money that she hadn't let go of since they'd walked in. The crowded restaurant increased the possibility that something could go wrong, that they could have been set up.

"I'm ready."

"Let's go."

Ryan made to move too, but Zocco put a hand on his shoulder. "You and me are staying here, remember?"

Ryan gave him a hard look. Shit. Zocco was staying with him? That totally screwed up the plan.

He kept his face impassive. Fuck! Now he had to rely on Carlos's team to follow her, to keep her safe. Jesus Christ!

He was experienced enough to know that criminals often changed the plans at the last minute just in case...surely to god they weren't suspicious of him and Sera? But they couldn't be too complacent that just because of their close association with the DAs over the last months that they were trusted.

His stomach rolled over, but he nodded tightly. "Yeah. Sure." He sank down onto the bar stool, and watched grimly as Sera started to follow Casas out of the bar. "Sara. Wait."

She turned and he rose and went over to her. They were still supposed to be a couple. It wasn't that unreasonable that he'd kiss her. He hugged her to him, whispered in her ear, "I'm with you, angel. Got that? You're not alone. And be careful."

She smiled at him and nodded, oh so casual, and it made him grit his teeth.

He returned to the bar stool and sat next to Zocco, who occupied Sera's seat.

There was no goddamn way he could sit there for the next couple of hours and just wait for her. He had to get rid of Zocco, or convince him to come with him or something. Something. But what?

Sera followed Dominick out of the bar, resisting the urge to clutch the bag of money to her chest. She maintained her hypervigilance, her nerves like live wires, knowing it was still possible Dominick had set her up.

Jack London Square was a popular area and many people strolled through the stone-paved streets in the warm evening. She flicked her gaze around constantly, watching for anything unusual, hoping the surveillance agents were tailing them but knowing she couldn't turn around to check.

Dominick led her to a van, where another man waited, leaning against it. On the far side of the vehicle, away from crowds, Dominick nodded to the other fellow. "Blindfold her," he instructed him.

She'd been expecting that, but it was still unpleasant to have her vision obliterated. They tied the scarf around her face tightly and helped her into the van. All the while she kept hold of the bag.

They'd better be following her.

She had no clue where they went, felt the van turn, slow, accelerate, go up a hill, then race down. They apparently pulled onto a freeway because they picked up speed and maintained it for about ten minutes. There was no conversation in the van as they drove.

When they finally slowed, made a couple more turns, and then parked, she assumed they'd arrived. She hated not knowing where she was. Adrenaline pumped through her veins and her heart thudded heavily in her chest.

She wished Ryan was there.

No. God, no, that was senseless. She'd begged him to let her do this, and she could do it. Alone. Like she did everything.

She let them lead her inside a building. The smell was unusual—a chemical sort of smell not unlike nail polish remover. Then they removed the blindfold.

She shook her hair back and blinked, looked around.

"Wow," she said, trying to sound impressed. They stood in a small warehouse type of building, bare brick walls and exposed rafters. Stains and gouges scarred the linoleum floor. A man sat at a counter, another stood at an ancient stove. Equipment, some of it looking like pressure cookers, lined the counter along with bottles of different sizes and shapes and with various contents—most of them unlabeled. She blinked again as she followed Dominick farther into the warehouse.

"This is the lab," he said.

"This is it, huh?" She turned to Dominick. "Only two guys? I thought it would be larger."

"Sometimes there are more guys working. Not tonight."

"Ah."

Dominick frowned. "I thought Jake was going to be here."

"I'm here." A man stepped forward from a small doorway. Sera turned and stared at him.

Ryan could hear Carlos talking through the tiny earpiece he wore. Carlos was in one vehicle trailing the van in which Sera rode with Casas, other vehicles following him.

"They're pulling onto the Eastshore Freeway," he heard Carlos say. Great. The freeway. But where? He hadn't picked up enough to know exactly where they were.

He tapped his fingers on the table. Fuck. He couldn't sit still, couldn't stand this tension zipping around inside him. "Do you know where the lab is, Zee?"

The pair of surveillance agents remained at the end of the bar, sipping drinks, ignoring him.

"Yeah. I been there." Zocco eyed him. "Why?"

Ryan shrugged. "I guess I'm just worried about Sara. She hasn't been doing this that long."

"Whaddya think they're gonna do to her?" Zocco asked. "Don't you trust Dominick?"

"I don't trust anyone," Ryan answered truthfully. Surely Zocco would get that. "Do you trust him?"

Zocco thought about that. "He never did anything to me."

"Take me there. I won't go in. I'll just wait outside and make sure she's okay."

"I don't think so." He shook his head, doubt creasing his brow. "I'd get in shit for doing that."

Yeah. He probably would. Ryan tapped his fingers on the bar.

"Hell," he muttered. "If anything happens to her..."

Zocco was silent, turning his beer in his hands. "I like Sara."

Ryan snorted. "Yeah. Me too." That was an understatement. Christ, he was head over ass in love with her. And despite the way Sera and Zocco had started off, she'd somehow gotten him under her spell too. Ryan rubbed his eyes.

"Dude, you are antsy as hell," Zocco said.

Ryan tried to control the agitation vibrating inside him. He listened to Carlos talk to the others through the earpiece.

"Shit," Ryan heard him say. Ryan's body tensed. "We lost 'em."

Ryan sat up straight, every nerve on high alert. Fuck! He listened to more frantic conversation. Something had gone wrong with the GPS signal.

"Come on, Zee. We're going." He shoved to his feet, fists clenched at his sides. He wasn't going to take any shit from Zocco, they were outta there. Sera was in trouble and Zocco knew how to get to her.

Zocco sighed. "Jesus, Tommy. Get a grip. She's just a chick."

What could he say to that? *Just a chick*? A string of curses ran through his head. Then Zocco heaved another heavy sigh and slid off the stool. "Come on. Let's go."

Exhilaration pumped through him and it was all he could do to not literally push Zocco out of the restaurant.

"Yeah." Zocco kept talking even as Ryan hustled him out. "But we sit outside and wait, and for Chrissake don't tell Dominick we did this. As soon as we see them come out, we're outta there, hightailin' it back here."

Whatever. He knew they wouldn't be coming back here. He flicked a glance at the two agents at the bar as he followed Zocco out. They were shooting him what-the-fuck-are-you-doing looks but he just scowled at them.

"Got wheels, man?" Zocco asked.

"Yeah. Rented a car. C'mon." He led the way to the parking lot where he'd left the rental car, restraining himself from running.

"I gotta drive," Zocco said. "And you have to be blindfolded. You can't know where this place is."

"Fine."

He hoped the agents were on their asses, if he was going to be fucking blindfolded. Zocco whipped off his bandana and tied it over Ryan's eyes, shoved him into the passenger seat and grabbed the keys out of his fingers.

Shit, shit, shit. No way of knowing if the agents had managed to be on their tail. No way of knowing if they'd been able to follow Sera. No way of knowing if the agents sitting outside that lab right now were obvious enough that Zocco would see them when he pulled up.

Where was she?

Sweat broke out on his forehead and his underarms itched.

Then he heard words that made him sag back into the seat with relief. "We got the signal," Carlos said. "Turning right from San Gabriel, onto Tehachapi."

"I'm there," another voice said.

He blew out a long breath.

He wasn't about to tell Zocco never mind now. They were on their way. Whatever. Nerves and adrenaline combined in a potent drug that jacked him up, had his body humming. He was going to catch freaking hell for doing this. This was so not in the op plan. But he had to make sure Sera was okay.

"So, how do you like Oakland?" Zocco was in a mood for conversation. Christ.

"It's okay."

"Where you staying?"

"At the Hilton. Near the airport."

"Yeah. I stayed there once. That time Vince sent me up here to take out that witness."

Ryan went very still. He wanted to rip the blindfold off so he could look at Zocco. "That's the guy Vince wanted the new prospect to get rid of."

"Yeah." Zocco sounded relaxed about it and Ryan felt the vehicle accelerate as if merging through a freeway exit. He gripped the door handle. "He had to go. He was gonna testify against some other guys in an assault trial."

"How come Vince asked you to do it?"

"He knows he can count on me," Zocco bragged. "It was easy. The guy never saw it coming. I took him out right in his own house. Just shot him between the eyes and left. Cops didn't know a thing."

Ryan's brain spun. His recorder was on, as it always was around the DAs. Unfuckingbelievable. The last thing he'd been worried about was getting that murder confession from Zocco, and now he'd just spilled his guts with no prompting whatsoever.

He should have been pumping his fist with excitement, which of course he couldn't, but somehow his anxiety over Sera's safety overrode the triumph he felt at nabbing that last piece of evidence he'd wanted before the operation shut down. Which it was, like...now.

He sucked in a breath. "Wow," he replied. "You don't mess around."

"Nah. Vince knows I'm good. I'm his man."

"Yeah. You are the man."

And he and Vince were both going to prison.

They had to get this over with. Ryan wasn't a religious man, but he supposed what he was doing would be considered prayer, all the way there, as he begged someone to keep Sera safe, to let this all unfold the way it should.

"So you wanted to see the lab," the man said. He stepped forward, and as he moved into the harsh fluorescent light Sera saw his face.

An icy fist of fear grabbed hold of her.

Snake.

Time had not been kind to him over the last fifteen years. A life of drugs and crime would do that to you, but Sera certainly still recognized him, recognized the evil cunning in those small, dark eyes, the cruelty in his thin lips.

This was the man who'd destroyed her mother. And nearly

destroyed her.

How could she not have realized he was still involved in the DA drug operation? Jesus.

"Yes," she said, fighting jittery nerves for casual. "I wanted to see if the lab can really produce enough sugar for me."

"You've been selling a helluva lot of sugar," Snake said. His eyes fastened on her face and she resisted the urge to turn and run as fast as her legs would move, get the hell out of there before he recognized her. Her hair—he'd never make the connection. Would he? She swallowed through a tight, dry throat.

But she had to stay. Had to see this through. Her whole life had been leading up to this moment. Everything she'd done had prepared her for this, led her to this point, to this meeting, to this pinnacle.

"Yes, I have." She smiled confidently. "And I can sell more." She looked at Dominick and lifted a brow. "Who is this?"

"Oh. This is Jake. Jake Rivera. We work together. He's a DA too."

Like she couldn't tell from his jacket and full patch. "I see that." Huh. Jake the Snake. How original. All she'd known was his goddamn nickname—Snake. Shit. No wonder she hadn't realized who he was. But she cursed herself for not knowing. That was inexcusable.

"Did you bring the money?" Jake asked.

She kept going with the pretense. "Right here." She held up the leather satchel. "Where's my angel sugar?"

"Hey, what's the rush?" Dominick asked. "You wanted to see the lab. Let us show you around." The swagger in his step as he led the way toward the equipment made her want to roll her eyes. He was so full of himself.

"Wait." Jake spoke up and her heart stuttered. She turned.

"Did you check her? Make sure she's not wearin' a wire?"

Dominick frowned. "She's one of us, man. Well, almost."

"Check her."

They wouldn't find anything. No weapon. No wire. She was on her own. She endured Dominick patting her down, keeping her face neutral.

"She's clean." Dominick straightened. "Come on, see what we got here."

She frowned and looked around the lab. "I have to say, I'm not all that impressed. This doesn't look like you guys can produce enough sugar here." She deepened the frown. "You better not be screwing me over."

"Fuck, no!" Dominick turned to her. "Look at all the equipment we got here! Just 'cause there's only a couple guys working tonight doesn't mean we can't make all the sugar you need."

His greed was showing.

"It's true," Jake said, following behind them. She wanted to keep her back to him as much as possible. "We have a lot of people selling this shit for us. But not everyone wants to see the lab."

Her skin tingled. She hitched a shoulder. "Well, I did. I'm not getting myself in trouble by promising people something I can't deliver."

"Hmm." Jake walked around her, faced her. Studied her, eyes narrowed. He folded his arms across his chest, his ample belly protruding below. For a long, heart-pounding moment, he said nothing. He tipped his head to one side.

"You look familiar," he said, his forehead creasing.

Chapter Twenty-Five

When they pulled up and stopped, Ryan jerked the bandanna off his face. "Hey," Zocco said.

"I don't have a clue where we are," Ryan assured him, eyes darting around. It was growing dark, which was good and bad. There were a number of cars parked in the lot, any one of them could have been the surveillance team. All the cars appeared empty; he only hoped they had ducked out of sight when another vehicle pulled into the small parking lot.

The old brick building in front of them appeared to be a former warehouse. Ugly and plain, three cement steps led up to an unlabeled steel door with no windows.

"We just gonna wait?" Zocco asked him, hands still resting on the wheel. "I should move to the end of the lot." He put the car in gear again. As they drove slowly past some of the other parked cars, Ryan noted a blinking red light in one. That was it. They'd managed to tail Sera and sat outside waiting now. He could only hope the guys tailing him had not alerted them to his and Zocco's presence.

"I guess."

He actually wasn't sure what he was doing. He tried to time things. According to his watch, which he'd glanced at just as Zocco covered his eyes, it had been about a fifteen minute drive to the warehouse. Sera'd left with Casas about ten minutes before that. He'd been so distracted by Zocco's confession he hadn't heard the radio transmissions, so he wasn't sure exactly what time Sera had arrived at the warehouse. He was guessing she'd been in there ten minutes. The plan gave her half an hour. She had to come out in half an hour, or they raided the place.

He sat there, acid chewing a hole in his gut, and reached for his antacids. None. Dammit.

They waited in the growing darkness. A light over the parking lot came on. Shit.

"What's taking so long?" he finally growled.

"I don't know." Zocco too looked at his watch. "Man, I need a drink."

Ryan rolled his eyes.

They waited another five minutes, and then Ryan couldn't take it anymore. He was going to burst out of his skin. "I'm going in there," he said, reaching for the door handle.

"No, you're not."

He ignored Zocco until he felt something hard jab into his ribs. He turned slowly and looked down. Goddammit. Zocco had a fucking gun pulled on him. Ryan slowly closed the door and sat back in his seat.

Sera shrugged and met Jake's eyes with difficulty. The urge to shift her gaze away from him was almost overpowering.

His frown intensified and she shivered. Kept her face relaxed, her hands on the saddlebag firm so they didn't tremble, but not white-knuckle tight. She cocked a hip. "Can we get on with this? I want my angel sugar." She only had so much time. She had to be out of there before the team raided the place. It'd be too dangerous for her to be caught in the middle.

"This here's Dawg," Dominick said, introducing her to one of the chemists. Dawg's glazed eyes looked like he'd been inhaling too many fumes. "And Reaper." She gave them a tight smile and a nod.

"I swear I know you," Jake said slowly. His brain too was probably fried from drugs and alcohol. He'd never figure out who she was.

"Were you at El Mirage?" she asked. "Maybe you saw me there. With the Clover City DAs." Good idea to remind him of her connection to the DAs.

He shook his head. "Nah. I didn't go this year." His eyes flicked to Dominick. "You sure she's okay?"

Now Dominick was frowning too, as if Jake's response to her was grating on his nerves. "Yeah. We checked her out. Both her and Tommy. They're good. And Vince likes Tommy. Wants him to patch in."

Talking about her as if she wasn't there. Her shoulders tensed up. "He likes me too," Sera added with a tight smile. "Now, where's my sugar?"

Dominick's frown furrowed his brow. "You said you wanted to see the lab. What's the hurry?"

"I've seen it." She nodded toward the two men. The chemical smell was starting to make her temples throb. "I know you can deliver. And Tommy and Zocco are waiting for us."

"The stuff's in your office," Jake told Dominick.

"Okay. Fine." Dominick shot Sera a look. "Let's go get it."

She followed him back out the door and into a narrow hall. Jake followed after.

"Sera."

Heat flashed in her veins at the use of her real name. The two names were so close, though, he could have just been saying Sara. She stopped and glanced at him over her shoulder, lifting one eyebrow.

"You're Sera Manning. Dori's daughter."

Horror paralyzed her, numbed her. Shit.

"What the hell?" Ryan muttered, mind racing, sweat drenching his shirt. Were they busted? Did Zocco know what was going on? "Zee, come on. Sara's been in there for fucking ever. It shouldn't be taking that long."

"We go in there, they're gonna kill us," Zocco said. "You know we can't."

Ryan let out his breath slowly. The big dumbass was doing this to try to protect him. How fucked up was that? Ryan glared at him. "I'll go alone," he said. "You get out of here."

Zocco frowned at him. "You're crazy, man."

"I'll tell them I...I don't know what the hell I'll tell them. If they even care to listen to how I found the place. But I'm going in. Don't stop me, man."

Zocco shook his head, staring at him in amazement. "Your ass, man." He jerked his head, and Ryan opened the car door and got out.

"Leave that way," Ryan said, pointing to the far end of the parking lot. "Security cameras won't see you leave."

Zocco started, as if he hadn't realized there even were security cameras. "Shit!" Ryan closed the door as quietly as he could and watched Zocco drive away in his rental car. There were no security cameras that he could see, but the surveillance team would nab him as he tried to leave the parking lot.

He stood there, fists clenched, aware of the gun tucked into the small of his back. Then he saw movement in one of the cars. He ignored them. They were probably having a major shit fit over his abandoning their plan. He was screwed now, whatever happened.

He walked up to the door. Locked. Of course it was locked. He studied it. Reinforced steel. No window. Several deadbolts. He wasn't going to be able to kick this one in.

He stood there a moment. Bad feelings had made his gut a giant mass of knotted tensions, acid gnawing at his insides to the point of agony.

He ignored the frantic radio transmissions going back and forth between the surveillance cars. So far nobody had stopped him.

The only way in there was with his gun, shooting the locks off. That would certainly announce his arrival to everyone in there. He didn't want to do it, he wanted to get in silently and take them by surprise. There was still a faint possibility that they could save this mission.

The guys had to be almost at the point where they were going in anyway. They'd agreed no longer than half an hour. He looked at his watch again. Seventeen minutes. If his calculations were right. He could only be a couple minutes off. He couldn't wait that long. Something was wrong, he knew it with every fiber of his being.

But how was he going to get in?

"I thought your name was Sara Lambert." Dominick looked between them and scowled.

"No." Jake shook his head and took two steps closer. "I remember you. Dori's daughter. Last time I saw you, you were what...fourteen? Fifteen?"

Her heart lurched to a stop in her chest, then picked up a galloping rhythm.

Then Jake laughed. "The apple doesn't fall far from the tree," he said. "Guess I should've known you'd end up like your mother."

She had to bite her tongue from denying that accusation.

"I thought you were from L.A.?" Dominick said. He scowled at her. "What the fuck?"

She flicked a glance his way. "I am."

"How'd Jake know you then? He's from San Francisco."

She wanted to scream at him. The asshole had pimped her mother, gotten her so hooked on drugs she was ready to sell her own daughter. She'd tried to kill herself to keep that from happening. She fought down the emotions simmering inside her, threatening to boil up out of control. She couldn't lose it. Not know. She was so close.

She could take this slime bucket down. She just had to be careful. Careful. Controlled. She worked on breathing while her mind frantically tried to figure out how to handle this.

If she denied it, he was going to be suspicious. If she admitted it, Dominick was going to wonder what the hell was going on. She was screwed either way.

If she got him away from Dominick, maybe she could make up some story about why the name change. "Could we just get on with the deal?" She held up the saddlebag.

"Dominick, maybe you better call Zocco and tell him this is taking longer than we thought."

"Okay. Yeah." He reached for his cell phone and she started toward the office door. Eyes assessing her, Jake led the way down a narrow hall and into an office, a tiny, dusty room with an old wooden desk, battered file cabinets and a sleek new computer glaringly out of place.

In the office she turned to face him. "Okay. Dori was my mom. Don't tell Dominick."

He waited. "Why not?"

"I changed my name after I got out of jail."

"You did time?"

"Yeah. I moved to L.A. and started over. I didn't want anyone to know."

He frowned. "You don't need to hide shit like that from the DAs."

She lifted her chin.

"Dominick!" Jake yelled.

Dominick appeared in the door. "I can't get holda Zee," he said. He looked at his cell phone. "He's not answering his cell. That's fuckin' weird."

"Did you say you ran a check on her?" Jake jerked his head.

"Yeah. She grew up in L.A. Got fired for embezzlement, but no charges. What? Why?"

Jake shook his head. "Something's not adding up here. You did time? You can't hide shit like that." His brows snapped together. "Unless..."

Her heart froze in her chest and her lungs wouldn't expand. "Unless what?"

"Unless you're a cop."

She laughed. "A cop! You've got to be kidding! Me?"

Silence expanded in the dingy room.

Jake pulled out a gun and leveled it at her. "Sit down."

"What the fuck, Jake!" Dominick stared at him. "What're you doing?"

"She's a cop."

"I'm not a cop!" She sank onto a wooden chair, clutching the saddlebag on her lap. Her body went hot, then icy cold. "Tell him, Dominick." She hoped the tremor in her voice was only noticeable to her. She had to stay in control of her emotions.

Fear jittered over her nerve endings as she waited.

But Dominick just stared at her now. "What's going on?" he demanded. "Are you a narc?"

She looked back and forth between the two DAs. "No!"

"Where's Zocco?" Jake asked.

"At that bar in Jack London Square," Dominick answered. "Waiting with Tommy."

"Go get them."

"But..."

"Go get them. Bring them here. I'll wait here with Sera."

With a last glance at Sera, a look that sent shivers through her, Dominick turned and left.

"This is quite a coincidence, you showing up here like this," Jake said, taking a seat behind his desk but never lowering his gun.

She said nothing. She'd said too much, screwed everything up. Now they were going to get Ryan. Her heart pounded in heavy, sluggish beats.

"Your mom was kinda special to me," he said musingly. "I was sorry when she kicked it."

"You did that to her." She couldn't stop the words that burst from her lips.

He raised a brow. "I did? How'd you figure that?"

"You're the one who got her hooked on meth." She directed an icy stare at him.

"Ah. Is that why you're here? Because you blame me for your mom dying?"

She said nothing.

"You were kind of whacked as a kid, if I remember," he said. "Didn't you OD too?"

"I tried to kill myself," she said through clenched teeth. "To avoid being prostituted. Like my mother."

He snorted. "Your mama liked being a prostitute. She liked being part of the DAs."

Sera pressed her lips together.

"It's true. She loved the parties. The booze, fast bikes and cars, cheap thrills and sex. Mostly she liked the drugs. She had nothing after your old man walked out on her."

She'd had Sera. But Sera said nothing. She knew only too well how women ended up part of a gang, how belonging to a group filled some need they had, how someone alone and abandoned and homeless could confuse sex with love or affection. She sucked in a long, slow breath.

"She was good-lookin' so she was valuable," Jake continued. "I see she passed her looks on to you."

His leer made her skin prickle all over.

"She brought in money. Good money. She made good tips workin' at that topless bar, and then hey, she discovered she could make ten times that by screwing for money."

Sera's heart went icy at his words. She'd known what was going on, but hearing it from this asshole was ripping a hole in her self-control. He was talking about her *mother*. Even though she'd betrayed her daughter in the worst possible way, Dori was still her mother.

"She knew you were gonna be the same," Jake continued with a smirk. "So she was some pissed off when your old man came back for you."

Sera froze. She clutched the bag, the huge sum of money inside forgotten.

"My father?" She didn't want to ask but the words were on her lips before she could stop them. "He came back for me?"

Jake scowled. "Yeah. What a blow up that was. She was pissed beyond belief. He tried to take you away from her. Thought she wasn't looking after you." He laughed. "She wanted him dead. And she knew how to make it happen." He grinned.

"You killed my dad?" She couldn't get air into her lungs.

"Me and Dominick. Yeah."

Ryan stood there, wracked with indecision and yet determination, when to his utter shock the door opened. He had to jump aside to avoid being hit with it.

Casas emerged from the building.

When he saw Ryan standing there, he frowned. "What the hell are you doing here? How did you get here?"

"Never mind that." Ryan grabbed for the door before it could swing shut. "Where's Sara?"

"Inside. With Jake." Dominick's eyes narrowed. "Where's Zocco?"

"He took off."

"Why'd he bring you here?'

"I...uh...convinced him to. I got worried about Sara. Now where is she?"

"In Jake's office."

"Who the hell is Jake?"

"Another DA. Tommy—you ain't a cop, are you?"

What the fuck? "Why the hell would you say something like that?" he demanded. He let Dominick precede him down the narrow hall, peeling paint on the walls and dirty, cracked linoleum on the floor, past an empty room, yanking his gun out as they walked.

The whole op had gone to shit.

He was wearing an earpiece so he could hear what was going on, could hear them frantically trying to figure out what he was doing, but he couldn't communicate with the rest of the team. He was supposed to be sitting in Carlos's vehicle with him, dammit, until Zocco showed up and screwed everything up. Plan B had him sitting patiently waiting in Jack London Square. *Patient my ass.*

Sera stared at Jake.

"He was a useless drunk, took off and left you and your mom with nothing but debt. Apparently he went somewhere and dried out. Got his shit together. He came back to get you."

Every muscle in her body tightened. She blinked. She wanted to hurl the saddlebag she held at his ugly face.

Pain ripped a hole in her and she bowed her head for a moment. Her father. He'd come back for her. He'd cared about her. He'd wanted her.

And her mother had had him killed. Then lied to her about it. How was she ever going to deal with that?

Her eyes stung and her throat throbbed and she had to dig deep for control. She looked up at Jake and eyed him, letting her utter hatred and contempt for him shine through.

"You asshole," she said. "You fucking loser bastard."

And she lifted the saddlebag and did just what she wanted to—she hurled the satchel of money at him with all her strength, hoping her high-school shot-put technique had stayed with her. The blast of his gun deafened her as she propelled herself out of her chair and toward the door, waiting for the pain of the bullet to slam into her. Jake somehow deflected the bag and it flew into the wall and burst open. Money exploded out of it, bills flying everywhere.

Sera closed her eyes briefly against the sight. Shit! If she lost all this money, she was going to be up to her ass in trouble with the suits.

Although that would probably be the least of her problems.

Her hand reached the door knob, hating the fact that her back was now to Jake. Had to get out of there. Had to get out. *Now.*

The door fell open at her touch. Ryan and Dominick stood there.

Chapter Twenty-Six

Sera met Ryan's eyes, a million thought fragments buzzing in her head. The freaked-out panic in his eyes, likely because of the gunshot he'd just heard, made her want to leap into his arms. "I'm okay," she gasped. She took note of the weapon in Ryan's hand, glanced back at Jake, but shit, he still held his gun too.

He and Ryan eyed each other.

"Put the gun down," Ryan said.

Jake didn't move. "How'd you get him here so fast?" he demanded of Dominick.

"He was already here! At the door." Dominick's eyes squinted as he looked at Ryan. "I don't know what he did with Zee."

"Drop the gun," Ryan said again.

Jake didn't move.

Sera glanced at Ryan. Why was he there? She didn't know whether to be relieved she wasn't alone, or pissed off that now he was in danger too. She stepped closer to him. He put an arm out and drew her to him. She expected him to shove her behind him, but he didn't. Warmth expanded inside her. He stood next to her as her equal. Again.

According to the plan, they had about two minutes before the team came charging in, guns drawn. With him and Sera right in the middle. Jesus.

What had happened that had sent everything all to hell? Who was this guy? Questions backed up in Ryan's brain. Adrenaline coursed through his veins. *Get a grip.*

He glanced at Sera. Her eyes were wide, full of fear and…something else. Encouragement. Confidence. Trust. Her absolute faith in him shone out from her eyes like a beacon.

The significance of this was not lost on him. From her it meant so much more than just trusting him to do this. It meant—everything.

He straightened his shoulders, tightened his grip and turned his attention to Jake, who had moved from behind the desk. Ryan narrowed his eyes, his insides burning with determination. "Federal officers," Ryan said, louder. "Drop it. Now."

"Fuck!" Dominick screamed. "You fucking asshole! I can't believe this!"

Jake's face tightened with rage and he took another step closer. "Dominick. You are in deep shit over this."

"*Me?* Kill *him!*" He jerked his head at Ryan. "Kill both of them! They're fucking cops!"

Ryan's eyes connected with Sera's in a charged exchange. He could shoot the guy holding a gun on them. He saw the faintest nod and blink from her. But his hesitation gave Dominick time to lunge toward him and grab his gun arm.

In a split second, Sera dove toward the other man. Ryan fought off Dominick, struggling to maintain hold of the gun. The guy was strong. *Fuck.* As he wrestled with him, out of the corner of his eye he saw Sera wrap an arm around the other guy's throat, pushing his head forward against her forearm with the other arm in a powerful choke hold. She hooked her leg around his and took him crashing to the floor.

Ryan had to file away for later how impressed he was with that as he crashed to the floor with Dominick. Pain sliced through his elbow. He grabbed for the gun, jerked a knee up to the other guy's crotch but missed. Dominick grunted.

They rolled and Ryan's head smacked into the leg of the desk. Silver sparkles danced on a black background in front of his eyes and the gun skittered across the linoleum.

Sera had grabbed the gun from the other dude and lifted it, aimed it.

"Freeze!" she called. *Christ, Sera, no, don't shoot now.* He couldn't see clearly, could barely hear over his own thudding heart and harsh breathing. She'd never get a clear shot at Dominick.

Ryan couldn't reach his goddamn gun. He drew back a fist and aimed it at Dominick's face, driving it with as much power as he could. Bone crunched, blood gushed, and he grabbed a handful of hair, lifted Dominick's head and slammed it down onto the floor. The guy went soft and with a shuddering breath, Ryan knew he'd knocked him out.

He rolled and climbed to his feet, but what he saw had his blood chilling. The asshole Sera had taken out had another gun, for fuck's sake.

"Sera! Behind you!"

Sera turned and saw Jake sitting up with another gun in his hand. Where the hell had that come from?

Commotion erupted outside the office. "Federal officers! Put your hands up!"

Bodies appeared in the door to the office, a swarm of agents and police officers trying to get in.

"What the fuck happened in here?" Carlos demanded, trying to shove his way in.

Jake whipped his body around and aimed the gun at the door just as Ryan lurched to his feet, between Jake and the agents in the doorway.

Sera's heart slammed in her chest. No way was that bastard going to kill Ryan.

She wasn't afraid of dying. She'd died before. She hurled herself toward Jake.

"No!" Ryan shouted. "Sera—" He threw himself at her. They both crashed to the floor, the gunshot reverberating in her brain. His big body heavy on hers, crushing her into the linoleum, she tasted fear, sharp and metallic.

"Ryan!" She shoved at him. Oh sweet Jesus. Blood. Was it hers? She didn't feel anything. In the periphery of her consciousness she was aware of officers taking down Jake, cuffing him. "Ryan."

She managed to wriggle herself out from under him and he collapsed face down on the floor, blood pooling beneath his body.

"Ryan!" Her heart slammed in her chest as she frantically tried to move him, his body so limp and heavy she knew that wasn't a good thing. *Ohgodohgodohgod.*

Blood. Lots of blood. Blood on her. She swallowed her nausea and ignored the throbbing in her head. It didn't matter. He couldn't be dead. But god, so much blood... *Ryan. Ryan.*

Vaguely aware of one of the officers calling for an ambulance, she knelt beside Ryan, panting, heart accelerating, mind racing. She felt for a pulse. Nothing. Shifted her fingers. Still nothing. "Ryan!" She bent lower over his face, pressed to the floor, but couldn't detect any breath. "Ryan! Oh god, Ryan." *Jesus Christ. Jesus. Jesus.* She tore off her shirt and pressed it to the small wound on his back. She had to turn him over. The blood was coming from his front.

He could not be dead. He couldn't. This couldn't be happening.

She loved him.

The pain inside her ripped her heart to shreds. He couldn't die.

"Sera." Carlos spoke to her. She ignored him. He reached to draw her back but she threw his hand off her and leaned over Ryan. "He needs CPR." She heard a voice speak and then Carlos again drew her away and two officers rolled Ryan on the floor, his body lifeless.

"I'll do it," she said, crawling back to him. She started chest compressions like she'd been taught, working mindlessly, repeating the pattern over and over and over.

"Come back, Ryan. Come back. Come on." She was begging but she didn't care. She blinked tears away from her eyes to clear her vision. Adrenaline rushed through her, gave her strength to continue despite the pain throbbing in her temples, the weakness sliding through her body.

"Ryan," she said. "Ryan, listen to me. Come back." Tears streaked down her face, blurred her vision. "I love you, Ryan. Please, come back. You said you were with me, damn you! Ryan." She kept saying his name, her voice thick and choked. "Ryan, I do love you. Please don't leave me." Saying the words aloud sounded so pathetic and needy to her ears, and an image of her as a young girl crying in her bed, *Daddy, please come back, don't leave me, Daddy,* words she'd thought she would never say again, sent a shaft of shocking pain through her.

She leaned into his chest, breathed into his mouth. Over. And over. And over. Until the ambulance arrived and the paramedics took over and took him away.

She sat on the floor. Stared at nothing. Let the police do their job around her, their voices a faint background hum.

"Sera." Carlos spoke to her. She ignored him. Her body pulsed with her sluggish heartbeat. She felt heavy. Wanted to lie down on the floor. Wanted to just rest her head. Wanted to never get up.

He'd left her. He'd promised her he wouldn't. He'd told her she'd never be alone.

And now she knew the truth. She didn't want to be alone anymore. But it was too late. He was gone.

It was the weirdest fucking dream he'd ever had. And the strangest thing about it was, it seemed so familiar.

It was Sera's dream. The one she'd told him about when she'd OD'd. When she'd died.

Shit! Did that mean *he* was dead?

He lifted his head and pried open his eyes. If he'd died, couldn't he have gone somewhere nicer than this crappy office? Then he realized he was looking down on the office, as if from great height. The room was full—uniformed and plain clothes cops. There was Carlos...and Sera. Bent over a body on the floor.

His body.

Jesus Christ.

She was sobbing, leaning on his chest with her hands, talking to him. She had blood on her hands. She didn't like blood. He wanted to tell her to stop, to tell her it was okay. He was okay. He didn't hurt. He felt actually pretty good. Peaceful. Light.

He felt himself being drawn away. Brilliant white light pulled him down a long corridor. He wanted to go. But Sera kept asking him to come back. Telling him she loved him. She loved him.

He'd made her a promise. How could he leave her?

Chapter Twenty-Seven

Sera rushed out of the elevator onto the floor of the ATF field office in the World Trade Center building in downtown L.A. She hated being late, but she'd had things she had to do, then she couldn't find anywhere to park and had ended up jogging three blocks in heels. She could have made it there a lot faster, except for the damn agent, charged with keeping her safe after the raids, trailing along behind her, huffing and puffing.

Now her feet were burning, and her silk blouse clung to her damp skin.

Ah well.

She'd been brought back to L.A. ten days ago, taken to her apartment to get clothes and toiletries, accompanied by her special agent guard—her new best friend, yeah right—then taken to a hotel where she'd have to stay indefinitely. She had no idea when or even *if* she'd ever be able to return to her apartment. Strangely, she found herself worried about Leo. They'd tried to stop her from talking to him, but she'd put up a big fight over that and finally they'd let her go see him for a few minutes. But of course there wasn't much she could really tell him and her heart still hurt, thinking that she might never see him again, thinking about how alone he was. Christ, it was enough to make her choke up.

She yanked open the door to the room where the crisis center had been set up. It was a humming center of activity. When agents had made arrests and executed search warrants at all the Clover City locations planned, they'd discovered other places where drugs or firearms had been stashed that weren't in the warrant. They then called the crisis center where staff immediately began the paperwork necessary to get the warrant so the agents could legally complete the search. Sera had spent the last week there helping identify suspects and giving details about location of weapons when they needed to obtain additional search warrants. Vince, Zocco, Chomp, A.J. and more were now all in jail.

Faces turned to look at her as she walked into the room, male faces mostly, studying her with open appreciation. She ignored them as she strode toward her desk.

Then her eyes returned to one man, tall, wide-shouldered, wearing black pants, a charcoal shirt and silver silk tie. He stood across the room next to a desk, talking to another man she didn't recognize, and looking at some papers in his hand. His dark hair was cut short, with neat sideburns. Holy mother of god.

Ryan.

He was back.

He'd cut off all his beautiful hair.

He lifted his head, did a double take, then stared back at her, amber eyes stretched open so wide she feared his eyeballs might fall out and bounce across the floor. She put a hand to her own hair. The buzz of activity in the room faded into the background as they gazed at each other. Ryan walked slowly across the room toward her, never taking his eyes off her. Seeing him set off a small earthquake inside her.

"Seraphina." Darren Forsythe stepped between them. "Nice of you to join us."

"Seraphina?" Ryan repeated the name, slack-jawed, still gazing at her in stupefaction.

She grimaced at the rarely used name. "Sorry I'm late," she muttered. Her heart pattered a little quickly from the running. Not from seeing Ryan again. No, no. She plucked her damp blouse away from her chest and shoulders with both hands. "I had some things I had to take care of."

She could not drag her eyes away from him. He looked insanely gorgeous. So businesslike. So clean-cut and professional. So...pale and thin. She bit her bottom lip.

"What the hell did you do to your hair?" he demanded.

She blinked at him, then poked his arm. "What did *I* do? What did *you* do?"

He ran a hand over his cropped hair. "I couldn't stand it another day," he muttered.

"Well, neither could I."

He reached out and ran his fingers down a lock of her hair. "You're blonde," he breathed.

"Yeah. So?" Did he have a problem with that? When she'd dyed her hair that near-black color months ago, she'd worried it would stay that way forever. Luckily her hairdresser had worked some magic, and, along with a deep conditioner, she seemed to be back to her normal honey gold color without too much damage.

He stepped closer. "You look so different."

"So do you."

Then her body went soft and she leaned toward him, laid her fingertips gently on his chest. "Oh, Ryan. Are you okay?"

He nodded, the corners of his mouth lifted, and he said, "Yeah. I'm okay."

The sound of a throat clearing had her turning her head.

Darren scowled at them.

Ryan blinked rapidly and shoved one hand in his pocket. He hunched his shoulders, so broad beneath the fine material of his dress shirt, and she longed to reach out and smooth her hands over them.

"My office. Now." Ryan jerked his head.

"I just got here."

"Yeah," Darren said. "She just got here. You two have work to do."

Ryan turned and leveled a look at him. "We need to...debrief."

Darren's mouth opened then closed. "I thought you did that in the hospital," he muttered. "Fine." And he turned his back on them.

Wow. Things must be going well. Or maybe Darren felt guilty that Ryan had almost died.

Nah.

Ryan grabbed Sera's hand and dragged her out of the crisis

center, down the hall, around the corner and into an office.

"I didn't know you had an office," she said as he closed the door. Her pulse skittered and her breathing was shallow.

"I do now."

He turned to face her, and she licked her lips.

"It's so good to see you," she said, voice breathy. They'd talked briefly on the phone a couple of times, but it hadn't been enough and they'd both been aware of the scrutiny they were under. "After they resuscitated you at the hospital and we knew you were going to make it, they wouldn't let me come see you. They're paranoid that someone's going to recognize us. Apparently our lives are in danger. Or something. I've got my new best friend, that Fokker, following me around everywhere I go."

"No need for name calling."

She grinned. "That's his name. Fokker."

He smiled back at her. "Yeah. I have one of those new best friends too. Guess we have to put up with it for a while. And yeah, I'm really okay. I'm sore as hell, and weak as a fucking guppy, but fine." He settled his hands on her hips and drew in a breath.

"Puppy."

"Huh?"

"Weak as a *puppy*."

His lips quirked. "I think a guppy is weaker."

They stood there smiling at each other for a moment.

"It's good to see you too, even though I may get fired over this," he finally said.

"Why would they fire you?" She frowned and trailed her fingers over his short hair again.

His mouth twisted. "Darren hates me because I screwed up a case once before by getting personally involved with someone."

Her hand dropped and she stepped back. She narrowed her eyes at him. "Oh really."

"Not like that." He shook his head, his eyes steady and

reassuring. "She was a young girl, but I wasn't in love with her. She was like a little sister. She was an informant. Her boyfriend was a big dope dealer. She was squealing on him and we were ready to arrest him when she took some bad shit and died." His eyes darkened, and Sera laid a palm on his cheek. "I was so fucking pissed off, when we went to arrest the guy I beat the shit out of him. And the guy got off."

"Oh." Her heart squeezed. "Oh Ryan."

"I swore I'd never get personally involved with anyone while working on a case again. And then you came along and shot that all to hell."

"I'm sorry." A smile tugged at her lips. So that was why Darren rode his ass all the time. That along with the fact that Ryan was everything Darren wasn't—passionate, involved, dynamic. Someone who actually gave a shit, instead of just putting in time.

"You should be." His mouth quirked. "I fought it. But it was—unfightable. Is that a word?"

"Whatever." She folded her arms across her chest. "You're not going to get fired."

"If I do, I don't care. I don't think I can do another undercover op like that one."

"You're not going to be a suit and sit at a desk all day."

"Don't know if I can do that, no. We'll see." He grimaced, then eyed her. "We have a helluva lot to talk about."

She looked like an angel.

It was the first and only word that came to mind when he gazed at her. Her hair glowed like a golden halo around her head, those crystal blue eyes pure and sparkling. She'd been heartbreakingly, gut-wrenchingly gorgeous before, but with her hair and yes, eyebrows, their natural color, her skin glowing, she was...soul-touching.

"Like what? We have work to do."

He grinned. Angelic as she appeared, she was still tough, stubborn and annoying as hell. He moved toward her.

"First, this."

He set his hands on her waist, pulled her against him then wrapped his arms around her, one hand sliding up under the curtain of hair, and kissed her.

Her mouth was soft and sweet, and after one...two...three heartbeats of surprise, she opened for him and kissed him back, hands grabbing at him, body pressing hungrily up against him. Desire sizzled up and down his spine, tightened his balls, surged in his cock.

Their mouths devoured each other in long, starving kisses. "Christ, Sera. It feels like months since I've seen you."

"I know." Her head fell back, and his mouth slid over her throat in hot, opened-mouthed kisses. "More like years. God, Ryan, they wouldn't let me come see you."

He slid one hand down her back to the curve of her ass. She was wearing a skirt, a knee-length skirt that hugged her curves, perfectly respectable and business-like, but he'd never seen her dressed like that and it lit him up. Her silk blouse tied in a bow at her throat, fluttery little sleeves leaving her arms bare.

He pressed his hips into hers, holding her with his hand on her butt, and kissed her mouth again, his tongue sliding inside. She licked him back, and one foot wearing—Jesus—a high-heeled, black pump, curled around his calf.

"Does the door lock?" she panted.

He reached behind him for it, and found the button. Yes! Amazingly, it did. He popped it in and reached back for her.

"Nice skirt," he muttered, inching it up her thighs.

"Thanks." She nipped his chin with her teeth. "I like your tie." Her fingers tugged at it.

"I hate wearing fucking ties."

She choked on a laugh. "Then why are you wearing it?"

"Hell if I know. Seemed like the thing to do now I've put my Coyotes colors away."

Her hands slid down over his chest and worked at the buckle of his belt, then the opening of his pants, while he discovered the tiny thong underwear she wore beneath the skirt that was now bunched around her waist. His fingers trailed over the firm, warm flesh of her cheeks, lingering between them.

Lust roared through him like a speeding motorcycle. He had to have her.

She lifted one leg higher on his hip and he walked her backward until she bumped into a desk. He lifted her by her ass and set her down, stepped between her legs.

She gazed up at him, mouth wet and swollen, eyes gleaming, her hands clutching his shoulders.

"This isn't talking," she said.

"Shut up." His teeth took a tiny bite of her bottom lip. She sucked in a breath.

He covered one breast and squeezed it through the silk blouse and whatever scrap of lingerie she wore beneath it. He longed to see it, but urgent need throbbing in his dick overrode curiosity and he pulled his cock out of his pants.

"Stop."

He gritted his teeth, hand on his throbbing dick.

"Should you be doing this? You could...hurt yourself."

"I'll be careful."

"Okay," she sighed, reaching for him. Her hands on him made his cock twitch hard. She spread her legs wider and he tugged the tiny scrap of lace covering her pussy aside while she guided the head of his cock to her.

"Yes," she hissed, head falling back as he pushed into her.

"Sera," he groaned, one hand on her hips to hold her in place as he thrust forward, afraid he'd send her flying right off the desk. She linked her hands behind his neck and her feet behind his back, and small whimpers and panting breaths were the only sounds in the room as they rocked together.

Christ, she felt incredible, tight and hot and wet, gripping him like a fist, squeezing him, each thrust deeper, each pull out a sweet drag on his sensitive flesh. In only a moment, her breathing accelerated even more and he slipped a hand between them and found her clit, stroking over it while he tried to keep thrusting as deeply as he could. She cried out, burying her face into his shoulder to muffle the noise.

"Sorry," she gasped. Her fingers dug into his neck and he gave one more thrust and then exploded inside her. He too had to swallow the noise that rose up in his throat, and he held himself against her sweet pussy as he pulsed and flooded her with his come.

"Sera. Damn, Sera."

"I'm here." Her fingers relaxed and stroked over his neck. She dragged them through his hair. "Your hair is gone. Your beautiful hair."

"You liked it long?" His chest heaved and he fought for oxygen to form the words.

"I loved it. But..." She too paused for a gulp of air. "I love this look too."

"Okay. Good." He usually didn't give a shit what he looked like, but after months of the undercover biker role he'd found himself dying to get rid of the hair. He wanted, needed, to separate himself from that life. It felt weird, but good.

They rested their foreheads together. Footsteps sounded in the hall outside the office door and they tensed. Their eyes met. But the steps continued past.

They sagged against each other again, still breathing hard, laughing a little.

"God," he muttered, reaching for a tissue on the desk. Cheap, sandpapery ones, not good enough for Sera's soft pussy—or his dick, for that matter—but they'd have to do. "I can't believe we just did that here."

"That was very unprofessional."

"You know it."

Once again their eyes met and they shared a smile.

He helped her clean up, and tossed the tissues into the wastebasket with a grimace. The room reeked of sex. It made him a little hard again, already.

"Okay," he said, helping her slide off the desk and tug her skirt back down. "Now we can talk."

She pressed her lips together as if she was trying not to smile, and tossed her hair back. "Oh sure," she said. "I see where your priorities are."

He nodded, tongue tucked into his cheek. "Damn straight." He zipped up and fastened his belt. Then he reached for her again. Her silk blouse had come untucked and the skirt was a bit rumpled, but who the hell cared? He kissed her once more, long, slow, with lingering tongue, then drew back and smiled at her. "I love you, Sera."

She blinked at him wordlessly.

"C'mon, let's sit." Two chairs sat in front of the desk, and he shoved them together, sat down and tugged her onto his lap. "Sera. That night in the warehouse. When it all went to shit."

She nodded, eyes solemn, her arms around his neck.

"I heard everything you said to me that night," he continued, holding her gaze.

She dipped her chin. He lifted it with his knuckles. "You can't deny it anymore, Sera. I heard you tell me you love me."

He'd been dead. There was no possible way he could have heard her tell him that.

"Sera." His voice was so low she almost couldn't hear him. "It happened to me too."

"What happened?" She clutched on to him for support and stared up at him.

"I..." His teeth worried his bottom lip. "I had that experience. I was outside my body...I saw myself lying there. I saw you."

"Oh." Her mind tried to absorb what he was telling her. "Really?"

"Yes." His eyes dark and serious, he leaned even closer. "I heard what you said to me, Sera. I was floating around, watching you cry and wishing you weren't so sad because I was feeling actually pretty good. I was worried about you, because I know how you get when there's blood. And then...I saw the light. The white light. Fuck, that sounds lame."

"It did happen to you too," she whispered. She touched his face.

"Yeah." He shook his head. "It's fucking with my mind, but I know what I experienced. I couldn't leave, though. I wanted to, but I had to come back. To you. I promised."

Her eyes stung. She laid a hand between her breasts and pressed the ache there.

"Oh hell, I made you cry. Again." He sighed. "And...I came back for a reason. I knew when I came back I had something do to."

"Um...take out the DAs?"

"No. Not that." He shook his head. "I have to look after you. It was like a voice telling me I had to look after you."

"I don't need anyone to look after me."

The words automatically came out of her mouth. Then she looked at him and saw the corners of his mouth lift. She smiled back at him. "Bullshit. You're making that up just to annoy me."

"It's true! I swear it!" He held up a hand, mouth still twitching. "That is now my mission in life."

She *could* look after herself. But she so wanted to let go, to share things, to be looked after by someone, someone she loved and trusted to be there for her. Ryan.

He closed his eyes. "My world is so rocked, in so many ways, by you, Sera."

"I know." She smiled at him, stroked his cheek. "I can't explain it. I only know it happened. You were the only person who ever believed me."

He pressed his lips together, his eyes bright. "I did believe you, Sera."

"I've never needed anyone else."

"I know. I want to be the one."

"You are the one."

Their gazes met and held for a long, shimmering moment.

"You do love me," he said.

"Why did you go there?" she whispered. "To the warehouse. I

couldn't figure that out. You were supposed to sit and wait with Zocco."

"The surveillance team lost you. On the way to the lab." His throat moved as he swallowed. "I couldn't sit there and listen to that and not do anything. Zocco knew where the lab was so I made him take me there. Then they found you. We sat in the parking lot, waiting. When you didn't come out, I was having a heart attack. What happened in there, Sera?" He searched her face.

"That was Snake. My mother's boyfriend. The one she got mixed up with after my dad left."

"Oh Jesus. Jesus Christ. He recognized you?"

She nodded. "I didn't handle it all that well. I denied it, but he and Dominick were both suspicious. I just...didn't expect him to be there. I wasn't prepared for that."

She sighed and leaned into him. "He killed my father, Ryan."

"What!"

She nodded against his chest. "But he told me something really...great too. He told me that my dad came back for me." She lifted her face and smiled through her tears. "He got himself cleaned up and sober and he came back to get me. My mom and Jake didn't want him to take me, though because they...well, you know what they wanted to do. So they killed him." Her voice caught on her last words. "He came back for me, Ryan."

He pressed her face to his chest and they were silent for a long moment. She absorbed the beat of his heart.

"Thank you," she whispered. "For coming in when you did."

She needed him. Needed him with every cell of her body, every cell of her mind, every fragment of her spirit, with a need that should have scared the crap out of her but didn't.

She smiled at him. "I love you," she said, voice strangled. "I love you so much, Ryan. I thought you'd left me too, even after you promised you wouldn't. I've always been alone. That's how I wanted it. But when you died, I knew...I didn't want to be alone anymore."

"I know." He smiled and his eyes were very shiny. Surely to god big, tough federal agent, biker-impersonator Ryan Thomas wasn't getting all mushy on her?

He was.

"I love you too, Sera. God." He bent his head and his fingers twisted around hers again. "I want you with me. Whatever I'm doing."

"I want you with me too. I thought I was okay all on my own. I always have been. I thought I always would be. But since I met you...I don't want to be alone. Without you."

"I'm with you always. Forever. I promise," he whispered. "You'll never be alone again."

Sera wrapped her arms around him and hung on tight. "Neither will you."

About the Author

Kelly Jamieson lives in Winnipeg, Canada and is the author of over twenty romance novels and novellas. Her writing has been described as "emotionally complex", "sweet and satisfying" and "blisteringly sexy". If she can stop herself from reading or writing, she loves to cook. She has shelves of cookbooks that she reads at length. She also enjoys gardening in the summer, and in the winter she likes to read gardening magazines and seed catalogues (there might be a theme here...). She also loves shopping, especially for clothes and shoes. She loves hearing from readers, so please visit her website at www.kellyjamieson.com or contact her at info@kellyjamieson.com.

It's all about the story...

Romance
HORROR

www.samhainpublishing.com

CPSIA information can be obtained at www.ICGtesting.com
Printed in the USA
LVOW06s0146020714

392632LV00004B/285/P

9 781619 213586